CONNED

A BUREAU STORY

KIM FIELDING

Tin Box

— PRESS —

1

S *an Francisco*
November 1928

THE COLD, damp air wafted in, smelling of rotting fish, but Thomas Donne didn't close the window. His back to the murky glass, he laid a cigarette paper on his desk and sifted tobacco onto it. His fingers shook slightly, causing some of the flakes to go astray, but he ignored those, rolling and licking and pinching the cigarette into shape. The lighter flame flickered. Thomas inhaled, closed his eyes on the exhale, and leaned back in his chair to stare at the high ceiling.

One more month's rent on the office, he calculated. Two weeks more than that if he gave up his flat and moved in here. The loo down the hall would suffice for washing up, but he'd have to sleep on the floor. He'd slept on worse.

He heard the footsteps first, weighty and confident, so the heavy knock didn't surprise him. Out of caution—or maybe just habit—he kept one hand on his desk, very near the center drawer.

"Come in."

The man who strode through the outer office and into Thomas's inner sanctum was too big for his expensive gray suit, the waistcoat buttons straining and his neck overflowing the collar. Mid-fifties. Rings on his sausage-like fingers, a florid drinker's face, and when he removed his fedora, thinning hair the color of old wool. He smelled of whiskey.

"Thomas Donne?" he demanded, as if someone else might be sitting in Thomas's office at Thomas's desk.

"Yes. And you are?"

"Where's your girl?"

Thomas lifted his chin. "My girl?"

"Secretary."

"I gave her the year off." Thomas allowed his mouth to stretch into a feral smile.

The man's eyes narrowed. "You're English."

"I was English. Now I am American."

"Huh," the man grunted. "Herbert Townsend." He didn't put out his hand for a shake but instead hung up his hat and overcoat before settling with a loud sigh into the chair across from Thomas.

Something about this man didn't feel quite right, and Thomas wanted to send him away. Wanted, in fact, to retrieve the gin stashed in the desk and drink until he'd forgotten about everything except the taste of juniper berries. But one month—plus two more weeks if he slept on the floor.

"How may I help you, Mr. Townsend?"

"How long have you been in the States?"

"Is that pertinent to our business?"

"Yeah."

Thomas shrugged as if it didn't matter. "I arrived in Boston in 1923. I moved to San Francisco this February."

"Five years." Townsend scrunched up his face thoughtfully. "Were you a copper back in Jolly Olde?"

Instead of answering right away, Thomas rubbed out his cigarette in an already overflowing ashtray. He would have liked to roll another but was afraid his fingers would be unsteady, and he didn't want this man to see it. "I was a member of the London Metropolitan Police."

It was hard to tell from Townsend's expression what he thought of that, but he didn't get out of the chair and walk away. He wore a diamond on his tie, bigger than the ones on his rings; a gold watch gleamed at his wrist.

"It's a strange thing for a man to do," Townsend said at last. "Leave a position in his own country to travel here and become a private dick." He waited a moment as if expecting a response, and when he didn't get one, he pulled out a silver cigarette case, chose a cigarette, and lit it with a gold lighter. He didn't offer a smoke to Thomas, who shoved the ashtray closer to him, spilling the newest butt onto the desk's scarred surface.

If Thomas listened carefully, he could hear the foghorn calling from Alcatraz. Some people said it was a mournful sound, but he liked it. It was a badly needed reminder that, sometimes, someone might care whether others lived or died. On occasion he was tempted to call back to it, but not today.

"What are your credentials?" asked Townsend.

An attempt to distract, although Thomas didn't know why. Townsend wouldn't have come here if he hadn't already learned of Thomas's qualifications—such as they were—and been satisfied with them. So Thomas shrugged again and watched the smoke eddy away from the window as if it feared the fog outside.

Townsend still didn't leave. He smoked his cigarette down to a stub, eyeing Thomas the entire time, and then pressed the stub into the ashes. "I need to find a boy."

"A boy?"

"A young man. He's disappeared and I'm worried about him."

Disappeared could mean a great many things. Thomas hoped he looked sympathetic, but that wasn't a familiar expression for him. "Have you contacted the local police?"

Townsend barked a laugh. "You haven't learned much about your new hometown yet, have you? Not too promising for a snooper. Maybe that's why you can't afford a girl."

Thomas knew better than to let this man get under his skin, with his expensive suit and his diamonds and a demeanor that said he was used to getting his way. Still, Thomas couldn't help but shift angrily in his chair. "I'm a quick study" was all he said.

"Sure," Townsend said dismissively. "I'm not contacting the local police because I *am* the local police. Or near enough. I was Assistant Chief of Police."

"Was?" Thomas had had mixed experiences with the SFPD. A lot of them were good blokes doing their best. Others were little more than thugs, on the take and eager for violence. He didn't know which camp Townsend had belonged to.

"I've retired in order to pursue other career opportunities. Next year I'll be running for mayor."

"And the boy?" prompted Thomas, who already had a hunch where this was going.

"An acquaintance. One of those youths who's taken steps down the wrong path. I've been trying to guide him toward more righteous living, but I'd prefer not to let word of that get out. I like to engage in these small projects outside of public notice."

Sure. And Thomas would go home to discover his one-room flat had transformed into a castle. But it was neither his place nor his desire to judge another man's proclivities. Besides, Townsend's wallet was undoubtedly considerably fatter than Thomas's own.

"And now you can't find this boy?" Thomas asked.

"No. He hasn't been seen at his usual lodging for several days. As I said, I'm concerned."

"And you want me to find him?"

"Discreetly, yes." Townsend reached into his breast pocket and pulled out a bill, which he placed on the desk. One hundred dollars, crisp and new. "This is an advance, for expenses. Bring me his current address within a week, and I'll have two more of these for you."

Three hundred dollars would be enough to keep the wolves at bay for another three months—maybe four if Thomas skipped a few meals. And he wouldn't have to sleep on the office floor. "That's all you want—to know where he's staying?"

"Yes."

"Three hundred is a lot to pay for an address."

"Ah, but I'm paying for more than that, aren't I? I'm paying for silence as well." Townsend's eyes lit with a strange intensity and he leaned forward, his body seeming to increase in size until he hulked like the statue of a mad god. "Today I'm eyeing the mayor's office, but that's not the end of it. Not by a long shot. I'll be governor next, and after that... well, after that the White House."

"You seem pretty certain of a long shot." Thomas kept his voice steady but moved his hand closer to the center drawer.

"But it's not a long shot at all. I have certain methods at my disposal. A little magic, let's say." Townsend's wink was terrifying.

"Magic that might fail if certain rumors about you begin."

Townsend leaned back with a satisfied smile. "You show signs of intelligence. Good. Yes, I'd prefer to keep certain matters out of the public eye. And Mr. Donne, as my star rises, I'll be needing a certain type of man around me—the type who can do his work and keep his trap shut. If you prove to be such a man, well, we may find ourselves in a long and lucrative relationship." He moved his hand slightly, perhaps deliberately making the diamonds flash in the light.

Thomas eyed the money as if he were considering the offer carefully, as if there were a chance he'd send this man away. Nodding almost imperceptibly, he took the bill, folded it in half, and put it in his pocket, fancying he could feel the weight of its promises. A comfortable bed. A hot shower. A cup of good tea instead of the coffee-like swill they served at Bianchi's.

These images were fortifying enough that Thomas trusted his hands to remain steady. He rolled another cigarette and lit it, feeling the drag sharp in his lungs as he inhaled. "What can you tell me about this boy?" He pulled a small notebook and pen from a side drawer, opened the notebook, and prepared to write.

With an expression of smug satisfaction, Townsend settled more deeply into the chair, making it creak in protest. "He calls himself Roy Gage, although I don't know if that's the name his parents gave him. He was staying at the Embarcadero YMCA, but he's moved out."

"Embarcadero."

Townsend's lips quirked into a smirk. "Yes. Of course. You know the area, I presume?"

It was a pointed question. Even if Donne had lived in the city only a few months, Townsend must have known that he'd be familiar with the zone near the ports. It was only a moderate walk downhill from his office. But Townsend clearly meant something more by it. The stretch from the Embarcadero up Lower Market was where men exchanged knowing looks; where the speakeasies admitted everyone, even women in suits or men in dresses; where a boy like Roy Gage could be temporarily employed for a dollar or two.

"Describe him," Thomas said.

"I can do better than that." Townsend reached into his breast pocket again, and for a fraction of a second Thomas was certain he would pull out a revolver, even as Thomas's hand remained on the desk, twitching uselessly.

It was fortunate that Townsend simply produced a photograph. He set it on the desk, oriented so Thomas could see it properly.

Two men stood in front of the arched arcade of the Ferry Building. Perhaps unaware of the camera, they stared into the distance as if waiting for a streetcar. The younger one—Roy Gage, Thomas presumed—looked to be about nineteen or twenty, with a sulky expression. His flat cap sat at a rakish angle and his jacket was too big on his lanky frame. It looked as if he'd borrowed someone else's clothes.

"Who's the other fellow?" Thomas asked.

"His name's Abe France. He employs Roy on occasion."

Thomas's eyebrows rose. "Employs?"

"Mr. France is... a spiritualist and magician. He requires an assistant at times."

Picking up the photo, Thomas took a closer look. It was hard to judge France's age, although he was clearly older than Gage. He was shorter, too, and carried a bit of muscle on his frame. He wore a Homburg and a dark suit that had been carefully tailored to fit. Whereas Gage was pretty, France was handsome, with a strong nose, generous mouth, and square chin. His eyebrows had a natural arch that suggested amusement, but sadness pulled at the corners of his eyes.

"Anything else?" Thomas asked, setting the photo down.

Townsend took the picture and returned it to his pocket with a grunt. "It's been three days since he left the YMCA. I'd like to find him as quickly as possible."

"I'll do what I can."

"I don't want you to talk to him. Might scare him away. Just find out where he's staying."

"Right."

After staring at Thomas for several moments, Townsend grunted and heaved himself to his feet. He flung a business card onto the desk. "Call me at this number when you find him." He retrieved his coat and hat, shot Thomas a final grin, and clomped through the outer office, slamming the door as he left.

2

Mrs. Coakley dabbed at the corner of her eye with a lace handkerchief. "He was so young, you see. Only twenty-two. He was engaged to be married to a lovely girl, and—"

"Please. It is best if you do not tell me details now. The spirits vill speak for themselves."

Nodding, she allowed Abe to lead her to a vacant chair. His parlor was nearly full today, which meant he had fifty dollars in his pocket—forty-five after he gave Rosie Byrne her share. That wasn't bad for an afternoon. He might even make a little more if some of his guests bought occult charms from him. And tonight he had a show at Café de L'Ouest. He was doing all right.

If only his headache would go away.

Pasting a smile on his face, Abe trotted to the front of the nearly darkened room, where a single lamp cast dramatic light and shadows on his face and body, making him seem mysterious. He couldn't discern the faces in his audience very well, but he'd assessed them as they came in.

"Good afternoon, ladies and gentlemen, and velcome." His voice was naturally deep, which served him well, but he had to concentrate to play up his accent. In ordinary life he did the opposite—squashing the remnants of his early childhood in Hungary as much as possible —but Emil had told him to use it when performing. It made him seem exotic, Emil said. So now Abe clipped his consonants, rolled his *r*'s, and changed his *w*'s to *v*'s.

"Ve vill begin in just a few moments. But first I must ensure that nobody here is sensitive to shocks. Some people are quite overcome when they encounter the spirits." This was an exaggeration, but it would get the audience members' hearts beating a bit faster and set up the expectation to be astounded.

As he'd hoped, the audience shifted in their seats. But when nobody said anything, Rosie cleared her throat. "O-overcome?" she stammered.

"Last veek a man fainted. He is qvite all right now, of course."

"I-I...." She sniffed. "I'll chance it, I guess."

His bow wasn't false or ironic; Rosie's acting skills deserved recognition. "Thank you, madam. I vill ask the lady and gentleman sitting nearest her to keep some attention on her, please. I vill be unable to assist her during the séance."

The audience members in question nodded eagerly. Nearly everyone relished the potential role of brave protector.

"Very vell. Now, have I received a sealed qvestion from each of you?" He knew that he had, but it served as a reminder of their own contributions. He waited for them to say yes before pulling the assortment of envelopes from his breast pocket. He set the pile atop the tall table beside him.

He paused, took a few deep breaths, and began his patter. Although he kept the same framework, he changed the details depending on the audience and the particular tricks he intended to perform. This group was dead easy—eager to swallow whatever he fed them—and since his head was pounding, he kept things simple. He spun a tale about the mystical veil that separated the worlds of the living and the dead, and how some people were born with the ability to hear voices from beyond the veil. This gift could be enhanced via certain tools and activities.

The men and women in his parlor listened eagerly. Emil had called them patsies, but Abe had compassion for them. They ached over their losses and were desperate for even the smallest chance to connect with their loved ones. He didn't blame them for that.

When his speech was finished, Abe lifted a metal rod from atop the table. About two feet long, it was nothing more than a length of decorative ironwork to which a metalsmith had attached a cage-like finial. Sometimes Abe told a story about how the rod came from the tomb of an Egyptian pharaoh, but he didn't bother with that today. Instead he walked along the rows of chairs, giving each guest a donut-shaped magnet about the size of two stacked quarters.

"Please rub this magnet upon your temple and over your heart," he instructed. "And vhile you do, you must think of the loved one whom you vish to contact this afternoon." He kept his expression solemn as they obeyed. Then he held the rod in front of each guest and waited as they affixed their magnets to it. Back near his table, he held the rod aloft and chanted quietly in an abbreviated and adapted version of the Haftarah reading from his bar mitzvah. Rabbi Weiss would have been horrified to hear the way Abe was mangling Hebrew, but none of today's audience were likely to recognize the language.

Abe returned the rod to the table and closed his eyes. He put on a pained expression—not difficult at all considering the state of his head—and allowed his upper body to sway. "Ah," he said. "Bárcsak levághatnám a fejem. Bárcsak levághatnám a fejem." None of these people understood Hungarian either. They wouldn't know he was simply complaining about the headache. He continued in English, dropping his voice to a whisper that carried. "I hear them now. I hear... some of them vould like to speak vith you."

He recognized Rosie's gasp and had to hide a smile.

With his eyes still closed, he placed the fingers of both hands on his brow. "Yes. I believe... this vas an older voman. A mother? No, a grandmother. She vas a little plump, with a kind face. She vould like to tell her granddaughter that she still loves her very much. And that of course she forgives her for not visiting more often vhen she vas ill."

Rosie made another noise, this time a muffled sob. The people beside her bent close to give comfort, and while everyone was momentarily distracted, Abe chose one of the envelopes from the table. The small pencil mark on the flap—which he'd made while sliding it into his pocket—informed him that this question had come from Mr. Reed, a stooped man in his sixties. Abe opened the envelope, drew out the slip of paper, and memorized the words upon it. Then pretended to read: "I vish to ask my beloved grandmother if she forgives me for failing her ven she was dying."

Rosie outdid herself with a wail and a showy collapse. As the guests hurried to assist her, Abe, unnoticed, carefully arranged the envelopes so he could see the secret marks he'd made.

Rosie let herself be resettled, and then Abe assured Mr. Reed that, yes, his late wife had been reunited with their daughter in heaven and was now very much at peace. As Mr. Reed sobbed quietly into a handkerchief, Abe opened a second envelope—Mrs. Coakley's—but recited Mr. Reed's question.

It was, all in all, a very simple con. A skeptic would have seen the ruse immediately. But Mr. Reed and Mrs. Coakley and the rest didn't *want* to see the ruse; they wanted very badly to believe that they were indeed communicating with the dead. That desire, combined with Rosie's distractions and Abe's ability for quick memorization, resulted in a successful show.

After the séance was over, most of the guests bought magnets for a dollar apiece. They were identical to the ones he used in the show, except he'd paid to have these covered in bright blue enamel. He instructed the guests to carry them in a pocket or on a chain around their neck to ensure a continued connection with the spirit world.

Everyone filed out, some of them still teary-eyed, all with a more satisfied air than when they'd entered. A few minutes later, Rosie returned and slipped back inside Abe's house. He was waiting for her in the kitchen with a glass of Bacardi in his hand.

"You look like hell, Abe." Rosie took a glass from the cupboard, poured herself a healthy slug from the bottle, and took a big swallow.

"You are always so kind with your compliments."

"And you look like you've been fished out of the Bay and toweled off. Your noodle giving you grief again? That's the third time this month."

Hiding his pleasure that she'd noticed, Abe shrugged. "I drank too much last night."

"I was there, pal. I'd say you drank exactly the same amount as always, which woulda killed anyone but you. That ain't your problem."

He shrugged again and pulled five dollar bills from his pocket. "You were hitting on all eight today, Rosie. Well done." He handed her the payment, which she tucked into her bodice.

"You want me for the show tonight?"

"No. I'll send for Roy or Helen."

"Got it. Don't want to be seen with me."

Abe reached up to stroke one of her gingery curls. "You are the star of my séance. I don't want to risk someone recognizing you the next time you pretend to faint."

"Yeah, I know." Rosie finished her rum, set down the glass, and leaned back against the counter. She stared absently for a few moments, until Abe handed her a cigarette from the case in his pocket and lit it for her. She had long, slender fingers, like a pianist's. He wondered if her dress was new. It was coral pink with a narrow black bow at the collar and a pleated skirt. The dress suited her, although if he said so, she'd complain that her figure was unfashionable: hips too wide, breasts too big.

"I think I know what's wrong with you," she said after a few drags.

"Oh?"

"You need some company."

"You're with me right now." It was good to lapse back into his natural speech, contractions and all.

She shook her head. "That ain't the company I mean, and you know it. And I ain't never gonna be that kind of company for you."

"I'm fine," he insisted. To prove it, he stole her cigarette and took a few puffs before she snatched it back.

"Head on down to Lower Market, Abe. Plenty of company there."

Abe thought about the last time he'd been there, a few months back. He'd found company all right—in the form of a handsome young man who'd tried to lift Abe's wallet. Abe had caught him at it and told him he should find another line of work if he was going to be so clumsy. The man had laughed, kissed him, and slipped away. Abe went home with his bankroll intact and his balls aching. "Plenty of *trouble*, you mean," he said to Rosie.

She tsked, shook her head, and exhaled a stream of smoke. "Take some aspirin at least." Then she stubbed out her cigarette in a glass ashtray and set her empty glass near the sink. "I'll see myself out. Make sure you take that aspirin. And don't overdo it on the rum."

"Thanks for looking out for me, sister."

"Somebody's gotta."

After she was gone, he washed her glass and refilled his own. He spent a long time standing in the kitchen, drinking and smoking, allowing faint memories to float through his head like the spirits he claimed to converse with. Sometimes he massaged his temple, but it didn't help.

He should eat—he'd had nothing but rum today—but his stomach rebelled at the idea of food. If his mother had been near, he might have gone to her and begged for shlishkes, the potato dumplings that had been his favorite when he was a boy. But his mother was in New York City and, considering their history, wouldn't cook for him anyway.

Instead of filling his glass for the third time, Abe put it in the sink and left the kitchen. He didn't look toward the parlor, where the chairs still sat in orderly rows, awaiting the next group of marks. He trudged up the creaky stairs, using the bannister to pull himself along, like an old man. His bed was unmade and the room smelled of stale smoke and night sweats. As he stripped, he was careful to hang his evening suit and white shirt on hangers, to set his white bowtie neatly on the bureau, to make certain his shoes retained their shine. He opened a window and let the moist, salty air creep in.

Naked and goosefleshed, he sprawled on his back on the rumpled bedclothes and closed his eyes. He didn't sleep.

3

Although the YMCA at the Embarcadero had been established a few years earlier for army and navy men on leave in San Francisco, others stayed there too. The modest rooms were clean and cheap, and it was convenient for anyone who arrived by ship or worked along that section of the waterfront. It was also convenient for anyone who wanted easy access to the men along the Embarcadero and Market Street. Thomas knew that much from reputation.

But he also knew the Y personally because he'd been there a few times while investigating cases. It was a good place to search for wayward sons, for instance. And due to the visits by people from around the country and around the world, it was a good place to gather gossip. Thomas had made a point of becoming friendly with Frank Labhard, the blocky man who headed the Y's meager security detail. Well, maybe *friendly* wasn't the right word. *Generous* was a better one.

As soon as Thomas entered the lobby, Labhard's eyes lit up and he sailed over with surprising speed for such a large man. "Donne," he grunted.

Thomas nodded at him as he scanned the area. Not that he

expected Roy Gage to be sitting in one of the chairs and reading the paper, but it paid to be aware of one's surroundings—a habit Thomas maintained even when he wasn't working. Right now the lobby was almost empty, with a bit of late-afternoon light angling through the windows and turning everything golden. "It's quiet."

"That's how I like it. Buncha sailors shipped out this morning. Didn't none of them look like they was happy to be going."

Remembering long, queasy days and nights spent crossing the Atlantic, Donne suppressed a shudder. He'd paid for a third-class stateroom but found the quarters far too claustrophobic, like a slit trench but with clean bedding. He'd spent most of the passage shivering on deck and watching the gray water that stretched to every horizon.

"I have a few questions," Thomas said.

Labhard jerked his big head toward a high table that stood against one wall, and Thomas followed him there. Faded, dusty religious pamphlets were scattered over the tabletop; Labhard rested his elbows on them. "Whatcha want?"

"A boy named Roy Gage."

It was clear that Labhard recognized the name, but he pretended to frown in thought. "Gage."

"Civilian. Twenty or so. Chip on his skinny shoulder."

Labhard snorted like a bear. "Guess that's a good enough description."

"Know where he is?"

"Ain't seen him in a while. Hang on."

As Labhard lumbered over to have a discussion with the man at the reception desk, Thomas wondered how many men had sat in the lobby chairs and where they all were now. Surely some of them must have been English and served during the Great War. Were their dreams untroubled, their waking hours clear and placid? He tried to push those thoughts away by reading a Bible study guide, but the earnest words only made him scowl. Thankfully, Labhard returned.

"Ain't here. He checked out three days ago."

"Do you know where he went?"

"Nah."

"Does he have any friends or associates here who might know?"

"Don't think so. Keeps to himself mostly." Labhard straightened a few of the pamphlets. "I've seen him bring company up to his room, but never the same goose twice." He shrugged his massive shoulders. "I don't care so long as they keep quiet."

And probably so long as somebody passed him a few dollars now and then.

"You don't know why he checked out?"

"Punks like him, they come and they go, mister. Maybe they find someone willing to pay their way somewhere else for a time. Or maybe they get so flat they can't afford to stay here no more. Maybe they even get pinched and trade in our bed for one in the cooler." He rubbed his jaw. "Some of 'em come back."

"Is there anything else you can tell me about Gage?"

For a moment it looked as if Labhard was going to say no. But then he rolled his eyes upward as if performing maths calculations in his head and scrunched up his pale lips. "Yeah. Couple-three times, I seen a guy come looking for him, but they didn't go up to Gage's room. Guy had the desk call Gage down and then they went somewhere."

"Who was this fellow?"

"Don't know him. He's, I dunno, thirty-five? He was dressed in glad rags, like for a big night on the town. Had some kinda foreign accent, but only a little one."

"What kind?"

Labhard stuck a fat finger in one ear and dug around. "I dunno. I hear all kinds in this place but I don't know any of 'em. Like yours."

"London."

"Well, his wasn't like yours."

Thomas wished he'd been able to keep the photograph Townsend had shown him. And when it became clear that Labhard had shared everything he knew, Thomas shook his big paw, transferring a ten-dollar bill in the process. Labhard smoothly tucked the money into his pocket.

"It's a pleasure, Mr. Donne. You come back anytime."

Thomas strode over the pedestrian bridge to the Ferry Building. Along the way he glanced down at the building's base, to the spot where Gage had been photographed. Now he saw a woman with two children, each carrying a suitcase. They all looked tired. A glimpse inside the building showed people hurrying back and forth along the Grand Nave, narrowly avoiding one another and the large potted palms. Donne stopped at a newsstand tucked next to one of the big arches and bought the afternoon edition of the *Call and Post*, then sat down on a bench to read it.

He did this sometimes even when he wasn't on a case. For no reason he could understand, the purposeful movement and meaningless noises of the Ferry Building soothed him. They reminded him that he was in the world, without forcing him to participate. So although today he had a reason to read the paper, he took his time.

Sixty-two nations had signed an agreement in Paris to outlaw war. That made Donne snort. Five girls who'd escaped the California Girls' Training Home and were captured the next day claimed they'd been starved and abused in the institution. Feminists in France were arrested when they tried to storm the presidential palace. Two men in Sacramento shot and killed four people. A rum-running ship had been captured by the Coast Guard and towed into port.

So many people bashing their heads against the cage, again and again, until they couldn't move any longer—as if there were any hope of battering through. As if there were any ending other than pain and death.

Eventually he turned to the theater section and, ignoring the articles, scanned the advertisements. The city offered dozens of diversions every night—and those were just the ones legal enough to advertise.

Ah, there it was, in a notice for Café de L'Ouest. Appearing tonight at eight: *Abe France, Tsar of the Realm of Spirits, presents wonders and mysteries.*

The only wonder was that people paid good money to see that

shite instead of blowing it on something worthwhile, such as booze, strippers, or whores.

Which reminded him: he had money in his pocket.

John's Grill was an easy walk up Market Street to Ellis. Thomas had been in there only once before—tailing the philandering husband of a society woman who was paying his expenses—and he'd had a good meal. Now he entered the, long, low-ceilinged space where wood gleamed everywhere: floors, walls, columns, and a bar with no hooch in sight. They certainly had bottles somewhere, and likely the good stuff, if you handed the waiter an extra dollar or two.

But Thomas didn't bother with that. Not when he could find gin or rum cheaper from the long-coated men who paced the streets of the Mission and the Tenderloin. He splurged on the food, though: a dish of stuffed olives, mock turtle soup, a porterhouse steak with fried potatoes. Thomas was a big man and it took a lot to fill him, but even he couldn't quite finish the cake he ordered for dessert. He lingered over coffee and cigarettes.

Only a few blocks from the Army and Navy Y, Café de l'Ouest was on Spear Street just past Mission. Thomas had never been there, but he'd visited other establishments just like it. Places nice enough to attract a crowd with a little money, but seedy enough to be paying the local beat cops to look the other way. Tables were crowded together, customers openly drinking rum and whiskey as they laughed and talked. Some of the couples were queer; some of the men wore dresses, and some of the dames wore suits. Didn't matter in a joint like this.

Thomas paid a little extra to have a table to himself near the back corner. From there he had a good view of the door and of the curtained stage that ran along the far wall. He remained largely in the shadows, however, so nobody would get a good look at him.

"What kind of coffee you want?" asked the waiter. Not rude, exactly, but he clearly didn't have time to baby his clients.

"Bacardi. Double."

"Got it." Satisfied with their little exercise in make-believe, the waiter hurried off.

Thomas rolled a cigarette and took a closer look around. He recognized a few people from speakeasies and clubs he'd visited, although he didn't know them by name. That skinny person in the silvery beaded dress with the fringes and the fur-collared cape, for instance? Thomas had seen him a month earlier, performing in a drag show. Thomas tried to imagine pulling off a look like that himself and snorted out a cloud of smoke. He was tall and broad-shouldered, with the type of heavy body that might run to fat if he were richer. He had a blocky face with a straight nose and wide chin. He kept his dark blond hair slicked back from his forehead. Although he'd been called handsome now and then, nobody would ever call him pretty.

Only a few sips into his rum, a man appeared on stage with flowery patter about how amazed they were all about to be. Then the house lights dimmed and the curtains drew back.

Thomas recognized the magician at once as the man standing beside Gage in Townsend's photo. The picture hadn't done him justice, however. Without a hat and now resplendent in an evening suit, France was stunning. He had thick, dark curls that looked as if they'd defy taming with Brilliantine. His olive-toned complexion had a rosy tinge over his cheekbones, which might or might not have been makeup. Although he was short—five six, five seven at most—he had enormous presence and moved his tightly muscled body with the lightness and grace of a dancer.

"Good evening," France said. He couldn't have seen much of anything beyond the stage lights, but he smiled and slowly moved his gaze as if personally greeting each member of the audience. "I thank you so much for joining me tonight. Together ve vill engage in a journey beyond anything you have experienced, to fantastic and extraordinary vorlds where the spirits speak to us and anything is possible."

Merely empty patter; Thomas knew that. And whatever that accent was, it sure as hell wasn't French. The magician seemed to glow from within—undoubtedly a clever trick of the lights—and his large dark eyes appeared to absorb everything, as if Thomas might be drawn into them and lost forever.

Dammit. He needed more rum.

France began with a few simple tricks that required nothing more than manual dexterity and marked cards. He claimed, however, that ghosts hid that man's chosen card under the silk kerchief on France's tall table or whispered in his ear which card that pretty girl had chosen. And the audience believed because they were drunk and France was exotic and charming, and because they wanted to believe.

Thomas knew better. There was no such thing as ghosts. He'd seen plenty of dead people—hundreds, if not thousands—but had never once glimpsed a white-sheeted specter floating across a battlefield or hospital. Dead was simply dead, a pile of meat and bones waiting for the worms.

The audience oohed and aahed. They applauded when France seemed to read their minds. They gasped when he levitated of vase full of roses and made it swing across the stage. Even Thomas was entertained, if for no other reasons than sussing out the secrets behind the tricks was an interesting puzzle and France was easy to look at.

Thomas was on his second glass of rum and had very nearly forgotten why he was attending the show to begin with, when France called his assistant from backstage. Ah. There was Roy Gage, gangly and uncomfortable-looking in a suit, his expression serious. He stood beside France and squinted out into the audience.

"My friends," France said, "tonight I have a very special thing to show you. This has been attempted by tvelve magicians before me, but every von of them has failed." He stepped forward and lowered his voice as if sharing a confidence. "Every von of them... has died."

This was what the audience wanted. They remained silent, unmoving, glasses of booze in front of them and cigarettes in hand, their eyes trained firmly on the stage.

France smiled at them. "Vill I be the thirteenth to die? I do not believe so, for I have von protection the others lacked. As you have already seen, I have the spirits to guard me. They vill not let me be harmed."

After executing a tiny bow, France angled slightly toward Gage. "Raunak, if you please?"

Before Thomas could snort at the name that suited Gage so poorly, Gage reached into his pocket and pulled out a gun.

Without thinking, Thomas reached into his own pocket and barely stopped himself from drawing his weapon. *It's just a bloody show*, he reminded himself. *Nothing but a trick*. Still, he kept his right hand over the pocket as he took a close look at what Gage held. It was a small gun with a metal-and-wood barrel. A single-shot weapon, and an old one. A derringer of some kind, but Thomas couldn't tell the make since Gage's hand covered much of it.

France took the gun and cradled it in his palm. "Friends, I first read of this demonstration in an ancient tome from my own country. It was a test, you see, for men to prove their faith and bravery before setting to var with the Ottomans. Early on, this test vas done with arrows shot by the most skilled marksmen or perhaps blades thrown vith precise aim. It vas only later that my predecessors used veapons such as this." He stroked the gun's barrel with two fingers, a gesture so erotic that Thomas shifted in his seat.

"You see, vonderful ladies and gentlemen, a deadly missile is aimed at the man to be tested. If it strikes him, he vill surely die. And how can it not strike him? For it is launched at close range vith perfect accuracy. The only thing that vill save him is intervention from... beyond."

France then went into a long tale about several people—no doubt imaginary—who had been killed by this particular trick over the centuries. It was just storytelling, nothing else, but he was damned good at it. The audience hung breathless on his every word, tracking him as he moved gracefully across the stage. Even Gage appeared entranced, and he must have heard this plenty of times already. The show itself was only mediocre, but Thomas figured that everyone who'd seen it would go home thinking they'd been grandly entertained—if not by the illusions, then by the man himself.

Eventually France paused and straightened his shoulders. "It is time. Let us hope my spirit acquaintances are compassionate tonight." He handed the gun back to Gage, pulled a bullet from a pocket, and held it high. "Ve shall need a volunteer to mark the bullet and load it into the veapon. Please, only those of you who are vell acquainted with guns such as this."

At once, a dozen or so hands shot into the air, all but one belonging to men. The sole woman, a stout matron in her sixties, had a flinty look in her eyes.

"Raunak, you may choose."

Gage hopped down from the stage and took time at his task, wandering among the tables with a thoughtful expression. In the end he chose the woman, which made the audience cheer. He watched as she slowly loaded the gun. Then he took it from her and led her by the arm to the stage, helping her up the steps.

France bowed to her. "Madame, you have experience vith veapons such as these?"

She lifted her chin and spoke loudly and clearly. "I was born in Colorado, before it was even a state and when you never knew who might try to steal from your ranch. My papa taught me to use a shotgun before I knew how to read and write. I've been a dead shot with a pistol since I was ten. I carried a pearl-handled derringer until my husband begged me to stop. He was afraid the police would come after me." As the audience laughed, she shot a glare in the general direction of where she'd been seated, presumably aiming at her spouse.

For his part, France seemed delighted. He bowed to her again. "Then I am most honored that you are villing to assist me tonight. In a few moments, Raunak vill return the gun to you. He vill show you vhere to stand, and then I shall ask you to shoot me. Please aim directly for my head."

"What if I kill you?"

"Then that is entirely my own fault for not sufficiently pleasing the spirits. You vill not be held legally accountable."

"All right then."

He nodded. "Please, just give me a short time to summon the spirits from beyond."

A peaceful expression settled over France's face as he closed his eyes and went very still. As a move undoubtedly intended to heighten the tension, it worked; the audience thrummed with expectation. Thomas wondered what excited them so: the prospect of a wondrous spectacle or the prospect of a bloody death. Maybe they'd settle for either.

Just when the crowd might have grown restless, France opened his eyes. He wasn't smiling now; instead, a tiny frown of concentration creased his brow. "I hope that is enough," he said quietly, as if to himself.

He walked toward the back of the stage, placing himself at a slight angle. That way the audience would have a better view of the woman when she faced him and, presumably, a stray bullet wouldn't kill anyone in the audience. "Raunak, kindly show madam vhere to stand."

Gage did as ordered, placing her very precisely. Then he trotted to a brightly painted cabinet where France had stored some of his props and returned, holding a thick pane of glass.

"Madam, Raunak vill hold the glass in front of you. Its breakage vill demonstrate that the gun has truly fired."

There was a bit more fussing, a few more instructions, and finally the woman raised the derringer. She had an admirably steady hand. Gage, standing as far from her as possible, used one hand to hold the glass less than a foot from the muzzle. France closed his eyes and mouthed something that might have been a prayer.

"Shoot, please," he said.

The sounds of the gunshot and shattering glass blasted Thomas so hard that he jerked back in his chair. For a second or two, he heard the screams of falling shells, the deep thuds of blasts, the shrieks of wounded men. He smelled gunpowder and blood and felt mud caking his body.

Then everything cleared and he was back in a San Francisco club

—and France had collapsed onto the stage. In the echoing silence, nobody breathed.

Abandoning the woman, Gage raced to his fallen employer and knelt beside him. He set one hand on France's shoulder... and then scrambled backward when France leapt to his feet. The crowd gasped. France swept to the front of the stage, pulled a copper shot glass from his trouser pocket, and spat into it. The sound of metal on metal was unmistakable.

Smiling triumphantly, he fished the bullet out of the receptacle and held it high. "Friends, I am overjoyed to report that the spirits are vith me tonight!"

The applause was almost as deafening as the gunshot, although it didn't trigger Thomas's unpleasant memories. France bowed, shook the woman's hand—giving her the bullet as a souvenir—and asked the audience to thank her. Gage took the gun from her and led her back to her seat. She held her head high, clearly enjoying the attention.

Apart from more clapping and bowing, that was the end of the show. The curtains closed with France and Gage still onstage. Some people began to file out. Thomas hurriedly paid his tab, gathered his coat and hat, and joined the outflow.

He'd cased the club before the show, so he knew that the only exits were the big double doors in front and a smaller door that opened off the side onto an alley. The alley dead-ended, so the only way to leave it—short of climbing brick walls—was to go out onto Spear Street. So that's where Thomas waited, in the shadows of a doorway across the street.

He waited for over an hour, although it felt longer. He wanted to smoke, but since the glow would have given him away, he instead turned up his collar against the night chill and sulked.

By the time the kid finally emerged from the alley, most of the magic crowd had gone, replaced by patrons who simply wanted to drink. At first Thomas thought France was with Gage, but as the streetlight hit them, he got a better look and saw it was a different bloke. Taller than France and heavier, with far less grace in his movements.

Thomas followed the pair up Spear to Market and tailed them up Market all the way to Eddy and Mason, only a block from John's Grill. But Gage and his friend didn't go in, and they surprised Thomas when they didn't continue into the Tenderloin. He'd thought they might be going to a speakeasy or show, or maybe to cheap rooms.

Instead they entered the Ambassador Hotel, an imposing red-brick building. Rooms there would set a fellow back upwards of a dollar-fifty a night. Big spending compared to the Army and Navy Y.

A minute or two after Gage and his companion went inside, Thomas followed. He was just in time to see one of the lifts stop on the fourth floor. After that, a little persuasion and ten dollars convinced the desk clerk to spill. Gage was registered, he'd shown up three days earlier, and he was staying in room 412.

Conveniently, there was a payphone in the lobby, and Thomas gave the operator the number from Townsend's business card. Townsend himself picked up on the third ring.

"Yes?"

"Found your boy. Ambassador Hotel, room 412. He's there right now."

"Excellent! Most excellent. Well done, Mr. Donne. I'm happy my confidence in you was well-placed. I'll have the remainder of your fee brought to your office in the morning."

"After ten."

Townsend chuckled. "Very well. Enjoy your evening, Mr. Donne."

After Thomas hung up, he thought about the dollars still in his pocket and the blind pigs only a short stroll away. Plus he had no need to wake up early. Lovely.

That had been easy as pie.

4

The show had gone well despite Abe's aching head. It had been a good crowd, eager and responsive, and Ray had done his part well. The woman volunteer had been a happy accident; Abe couldn't have wished for a better person to pull the trigger. Maybe he should track her down and invite her to participate in his next several shows. The idea made him smile, even as he collapsed wearily into the back of a taxi.

Most of his show patter was nonsense, but the bullet catch was a legitimately dangerous trick. Several people had been injured or killed performing it, including the magician Chung Ling Soo, who had died ten years earlier in London. Emil had advised Abe not to do this illusion.

Abe liked the bullet catch nonetheless. For one thing, it always pleased the crowd. Even if the rest of the show was mediocre, this trick finished it literally with a bang, leaving the audience satisfied. More importantly, though, seeing the gun aimed at his face made Abe's heart gallop. Ironically, in that moment of near death he felt most alive. Besides, he'd always thought it would be a good way to permanently exit life. People would remember him. He might even become a part of future magicians' patter.

After a successful show, and especially after the bullet catch, Abe didn't usually go home right away. He'd head to a speakeasy or stroll Market Street, and soon he'd exchange looks with some handsome fellow. They'd retire to the fellow's house or Abe's or a nearby hotel room or, if the need was urgent enough, a back room or hidden alley. Those exchanges also made Abe feel alive, at least for a time.

Tonight, though, his head still pounded damnably. Abe had sent Roy off a bit early—accompanied by an acquaintance of Roy's—and had finished packing up the props himself. Now he sat in the taxi, eyes closed, as it bumped its way to the Richmond District.

Emil had also disapproved of Abe's neighborhood. It was too far out, he said, and not grand enough to make a good impression. But Abe had bought a house on Twelfth Avenue near Clement because he could afford it and because the languages and accents of his Jewish and European neighbors made him feel at home. He could even find some of his favorite childhood foods at the nearby markets and restaurants. People made their way to him for séances, and the streetcar was only a block away.

Although Abe was usually content with where he lived, tonight the drive felt endless, the hills steeper, the roads especially uneven. He intermittently massaged his scalp or rubbed his temples until the taxi halted. His house, which he generally found comfortable, seemed cold and forbidding tonight. All the windows were dark, the doorway hidden in shadows. It was as if nobody had lived there for years.

Abe paid the driver and got out of the car, but he staggered with his first step and fell back against the vehicle.

"You all right?" asked the driver through his open window.

"Sorry. A little dizzy."

"You want my advice, lay off the rotgut. That stuff'll do you in."

Abe stood upright but kept a hand on the car to steady himself. "I'm not drunk."

"Then you need a doctor."

"I think I just need some sleep."

His front steps proved a small challenge, and he used the railing to pull himself up. He fumbled his key, dropped it, and nearly toppled when he bent to retrieve it. By then the taxi had rumbled away, which was perhaps just as well. He didn't want more advice.

Finally inside the house, he made his way to the stairs, shedding his clothing onto the floor as he progressed: hat just inside the door, overcoat past it, suit coat in the hallway. He leaned against a wall to unlace his shoes, which he kicked off hard enough that one left a mark on the opposite wall. He'd address that another time. Getting up the stairs took so much effort that he nearly gave up, and when he made it to the second floor, he had to run to the bathroom and vomit into the toilet. He was beginning to wish the woman had shot him after all.

Eventually he reached his bedroom and got the rest of his clothing off, leaving it in a disgraceful heap on the floor. He doused the lights. For the second time that day, he climbed into bed naked and waited for sleep to take away the pain.

5

———————

Although Thomas's head still buzzed with rum, when he reached home he took a bottle of gin from the cupboard and poured a glassful. The Jefferson Hotel wasn't the worst in the city, although it was a long way from the best. Three dollars a week meant Thomas had to walk up four flights of stairs, but he had his own toilet, shower, and sink. The main room had a table with two chairs, an armchair, a bureau, and a bed that folded into the wall. A kitchen would have been nice, but the flat kept him warm and dry, which was good enough. He didn't mind the noises that drifted up from the street, and the neighbors minded their own business, as did he.

He sat for a while near the open window, drinking, rolling cigarettes, and smoking, exhaling gray puffs that dissipated in the late-night darkness. As he watched, the jazz club across the street closed, and musicians and employees spilled onto the street, laughing loudly. His eyes followed as they disappeared down the block.

If he let his mind go, it might wander into enemy territory, where mortar shells crashed and men screamed, where blood turned dirt to stinking mud. So instead he thought about Townsend, and Roy Gage, and options for spending the remainder of the fee. He could move from the Jefferson to somewhere nicer, or hire a girl for his front office. He could buy some new suits. Or a lot of rum.

Or he could keep it somewhere safe to ward off the wolves a bit longer.

The sky was still dark when he pulled down his bed, but dawn wasn't far away.

~

THOMAS EXPECTED a messenger to arrive in his office shortly past ten, but none did. By eleven, he took out the card with Townsend's number and set it on the desk but didn't reach for the phone. He figured Townsend for the type who paid his debts. There was no good reason for the man to have promised him three hundred dollars if he didn't intend to pay; they both knew Thomas would have accepted the case for far less.

Just before noon, his patience was rewarded by heavy footsteps in the hall. Not a messenger but Townsend himself, who strode inside and hung his hat and coat on the rack.

"Doing your own errands?" Thomas asked.

"I don't always trust other people to perform satisfactorily." Townsend pulled out a plain white envelope and set it on the desk before taking a seat. "Go ahead and count it."

"I will."

It was two hundred, exactly as promised. Thomas tucked the crisp bills away. He rolled a cigarette and lit it, Townsend's gaze sharp upon him, and leaned back in his chair as if nothing in the world ever troubled him. "You want me to follow more boys home? I could give you a group discount."

"What if I offer you something even more remunerative?"

"Such as?"

Townsend gave the type of smile a fellow might show after landing a particularly big fish, and he paused to light a cigar. "It shouldn't be much trouble—just a little more than tracking Roy down."

"I'll be the judge of how much trouble it is."

"Fair enough." Townsend gave an amicable nod. "Fair enough. All I want you to do, Mr. Donne, is bring Roy here to your office so I can meet with him."

Thomas stubbed out his cigarette. "Bring him here. Simple as that, is it?"

"You may need to employ your powers of persuasion. I take it, Mr. Donne, that you can be quite persuasive when necessary?"

It wasn't that Thomas was above strong-arming now and then. He was a big man who knew how to use a weapon, and he'd employed those advantages more than once. They were, in fact, a good part of the reason he'd chosen this particular career. But he wasn't keen on dragging boys somewhere against their will—not unless they deserved it, anyway.

"What will you do with him once he's here?"

"Nothing, nothing at all. I told you already that he has strayed. I hope to lead him back onto the proper path."

"You intend to preach at him?"

Townsend laughed long and hard, which set his jowls and belly shaking. "My good man, I leave the preaching to those who believe in God and other fairy tales. I believe in hard work, hard currency, and a sprinkle of magic." He grinned for a moment longer and then his gaze hardened, his pale blue eyes going flat and opaque. "Five hundred."

"What?"

"Bring him here today, give me a call when he gets here, keep him here until I arrive—and I'll pay you another five."

It was a ridiculous amount, but Thomas didn't bother pointing that out. Townsend already knew. "You have deep pockets."

"Roy Gage is important to me, my boy. I am always willing to pay well for things that matter."

Rents paid on apartment and office for over a year. Cupboards and bottles filled. Enough to silence the screaming? No, never enough for that. But enough.

"All right."

"Very good!" Townsend stood, scooting back his chair with a squeal on the wooden floor. He shook Thomas's hand, then gathered his coat and hat in one hand while keeping his cigar between the fingers of the other. "Call me when he's here," he reminded.

"Yeah. I got that."

Looking smug, Townsend sailed away.

THOMAS CONSIDERED STOPPING for lunch but decided against it. Better to get this business over with and the additional pay in his pocket. Then he could eat wherever and whatever he liked. He wished Townsend had made this request last night—the Ambassador Hotel was only a few blocks from the Jefferson but was a considerably longer walk from Thomas's office. On the other hand, Townsend was certainly paying well enough to make the journey worth it.

The desk clerk at the Ambassador was busy with an elderly couple and didn't seem to notice when Thomas entered. The lobby was otherwise deserted, potted ferns gathering dust in the corners and the lingering smell of coffee wafting in from next door. He strode purposefully to the elevators, and a car arrived right away.

A housekeeper greeted him in the upstairs hallway, apparently unaware or uncaring that he wasn't a registered guest. She was carrying a tall stack of folded towels. Thomas waited for her to enter Room 402 before he knocked on 412. Nobody answered.

After a pause, Thomas pounded harder. "Gage? Mr. France sent me with a message." A fabrication, of course, but more likely to gain a positive response than mentioning Townsend.

Still no reply. Could be that Gage was a heavy sleeper or wasn't in the mood for callers. Or he could be out. Well, if that was the case, Thomas wasn't going to wait in the hallway. He tried the knob, but the door was locked.

After a quick glance up and down the corridor, Thomas threw his considerable weight against the flimsy door, which immediately flew open. Thomas stumbled into the room, and what he saw made him draw his gun. The place was a disaster: mattress pulled off the bed springs and standing on its side, nearly blocking the door; bedding and clothing in heaps on the floor; all the dresser drawers open; even the curtains torn from their hooks. With his pistol at the ready, Thomas crept around the mattress... and froze.

"Aw, fuck," he growled as he lowered his gun.

Roy Gage lay naked on the carpet, neck gaping in a grisly smile, his open eyes fixed sightlessly on the ceiling.

Thomas's first instinct was to run and pretend he'd never been here. But the housekeeper had seen him; perhaps the desk clerk too. And Townsend—fuck him for setting Thomas up! Calling the cops would do no good, not when Townsend was so recently one of their own.

It took all of Thomas's will not to kick the walls in a fit of rage. He was angriest at himself, at his stupidity for falling into Townsend's trap. All it took was a few hundred bucks dangled in front of him, and Thomas had fallen as easily as a naïve child.

And there was a boy dead on the floor. Not an innocent boy by any means, but a young one who likely hadn't deserved to bleed out on a carpet in a San Francisco hotel.

Thomas caught his reflection in the mirror—his face a hard mask of rage—and had to look away. Which is when he noticed the telephone on a little stand beside the bed, behind Gage's pale corpse. Since no other course of action seemed open, and delaying wasn't going to help anything, Thomas walked carefully around the body. He winced when his shoes squelched in the blood-soaked carpet.

He managed to keep his voice steady for the operator, but not when Townsend came on the line. "You son of a bitch!"

Townsend paused before responding. "Mr. Donne? Is that you?"

"What the hell are you up to? If you think I'm taking the fall for this, you're sadly mistaken. I promise I won't go down without a fight."

"Mr. Donne, whatever are you so worked up about?"

Thomas ground his teeth, hard. "Murder, you bloody bastard. And blaming someone else for it."

An even longer silence fell, and when Townsend spoke again his tone was urgent. "Are you trying to tell me Gage is dead?"

"You know bloody well he's dead."

"Where? At his hotel? Are you there now?"

"Look here, Townsend. I won't—"

"Mr. Donne! Listen carefully if you wish to stay out of prison."

Although Thomas snorted in disbelief, he didn't say anything more, and after a moment Townsend cleared his throat. "Is anyone there with you? Is anyone else aware Gage is dead?"

"No. Not that I know of."

"Very well. Stay where you are. Don't let anyone else into the room. I'm going to send a man to you. Detective Munroe. He's a friend, you understand?"

"I don't want your friends," Thomas spat.

"Perhaps not, but you need this one. Do whatever he tells you. Then call me when you return to your office and we'll have another talk."

"Our last talk put me in a room with a dead boy."

"I know, and I'm sorry." Townsend's sorrow was patently false. "But I'll put things right."

"You'll bring Roy Gage back to life?"

Townsend huffed into the phone. "Wait for Detective Munroe." Then he hung up.

Even though Thomas didn't want to obey, he didn't leave the room. He stepped back around the corpse, however, and used his handkerchief to wipe the soles of his shoes clean. He pushed the door closed as well, although it would no longer latch. He waited. Ray Gage made poor company.

Thomas didn't want to disturb the scene any more than he already had, and he was out of tobacco. With nothing more to occupy his mind—except the looming probability of going to jail—his thoughts turned to corpses. He'd seen a great many of them. Hundreds at least. They'd long ago lost their shock value, and now he stared at Gage's sad, twisted remains with cold objectivity. Thomas had never been a religious man, but it had always been clear to him that when a person died, something fundamental left their body. A life force, a soul... he didn't know. He'd seen with his own eyes the moment that thing departed; he'd sometimes been holding a man in his arms when it happened. The carcass that remained was heavier without the spirit.

He wondered if Gage had family to mourn him. The *real* end came when there was nobody to remember the departed—of that Thomas was certain.

His fingers had begun to twitch, and he'd almost decided to leave when a single soft rap sounded on the door, which swung open from the contact. The man who stepped inside was young for a detective, with a thin build and shiny black hair, his gaze as sharp as a blade. He pushed the door closed behind him.

"Mr. Donne?"

"You have a cigarette? I could use one."

Munroe raised his eyebrows but pulled a case from his pocket and handed Thomas a cigarette before taking one himself. They lit and inhaled almost in unison.

"Hell of a mess here, Donne."

"Murders usually are."

"You've seen a lot of them?"

Thomas shrugged. "My fair share."

"I'm told you have a valid private detective's license."

That wasn't a question and didn't seem worthy of a response. After waiting a few moments, Munroe sighed and gestured with his cigarette. "Were you the one who tossed the place?"

"No."

"All right. What have you touched?"

"The door. I'm the one who busted it, incidentally. It was locked when I arrived. I touched the telephone. And I stepped in the bloody part of the carpet. That's it."

Munroe seemed to chew that over for a while as his gaze slowly scanned the room. Thomas reckoned that the detective missed very few details. "Well," Munroe finally said, "I do appreciate that. It'll make my job easier."

"Your job? What exactly *is* your job?"

Flashing a quick grin, Munroe stepped around the upended mattress and whistled when he saw the body. "A mess for sure," he said, shaking his head, although he didn't seem any more shaken up over Gage's death than Thomas was. He turned to look at Thomas. "My job is to pinch the bad guys. You know that."

"And who's the bad guy here?"

The grin returned. "I don't know. But I've been told very specifically that it ain't you."

Relief made Thomas want to slump, but he kept his posture straight. For all he knew, Munroe was lying—or Townsend had something worse in mind for him than an accusation of murder. "I'll leave you to your detecting then."

"Hang on. I got a couple questions first. Anyone see you come here?"

Thomas put his right hand in his coat pocket and felt the weight of the pistol. "The housekeeper. The desk clerk may have seen me walk toward the lift."

"All right then. Good. You have any idea who knocked off this punk?"

"Not really." That was only a partial lie. Thomas had two or three leads, but nothing close to solid.

"Right. And you were calling on him because…?"

"I was hired to bring him to meet with someone."

"Who?"

Thomas smiled humorlessly. "I don't reveal my clients' identities." Not even when that client was the same man who'd sent Munroe here. Thomas didn't know what Townsend had told the detective and had no desire to twist any lies loose.

"Look at that—an honorable man. I don't meet too many of those."

"Maybe you should choose a different line of work, detective."

Munroe laughed hard at that, slapping his thigh with his hat. "I like you, Mr. Donne."

"Am I free to leave?"

"As free as any man ever is." Munroe waited until Thomas had the door open before tossing out one last comment. "Be seeing you around, pal."

As soon as Thomas reentered the lobby, the smell of grilling meat from the cafeteria next door reminded him he'd missed lunch. He walked quickly in the direction of his office but stopped two blocks before arriving and entered Bianchi's Grill. It was past the mealtime rush, so finding an open table was no problem.

"Cheese sandwich?" The waitress knew Thomas had been scraping by lately.

He gave her a genuine smile. "Two ham-and-egg sandwiches today, Bertha. With french fries. And a vanilla milkshake. Coffee too."

"Well, look at that. All of a sudden you have the bees. What'd you do, rob a bank?"

"A bit like that."

She swept away with a laugh, the strawberry-honey scent of her perfume momentarily masking the stronger aroma of hamburgers on the grill.

Thomas took his time over lunch, enjoying every bite. He even ate an extra-large slice of apple pie a la mode. It was a ridiculously big meal, but he was a big man. Besides, right now he was alive and free, with money in his pocket. Who knew what the future would bring?

He was almost whistling as he returned to the office. Until he unlocked the outer door and found Townsend waiting, seated behind the dusty receptionist's desk.

Thomas yanked the gun from his pocket and pointed it at Townsend.

"It shouldn't take so long to walk from the Tenderloin." Townsend puffed on a cigar, apparently unperturbed to have a Smith & Wesson aimed at his face.

"What are you doing here?"

"Waiting for you. I would have poured myself a drink, but you seem to be out." Townsend clucked his tongue. "I can get you some more if you like. Good stuff."

"How'd you get in?"

"I'm good with locks. Now, if you don't mind, we've some business to conduct and then I must get going. I'm a busy man."

Thomas didn't lower the gun.

Townsend balanced the cigar on the edge of an ashtray and, moving slowly and carefully, slipped a hand inside his suit coat. Although Thomas tightened his grip slightly, he didn't pull the trigger. He let his hand drop to his side when Townsend produced another white envelope.

"Five hundred, as promised." Townsend set the envelope on the desk and gave it a little pat.

"I didn't bring him to you."

"No. Although it appears you did your best to fulfill your end of our agreement. Ah, the poor boy."

Thomas had seen people evince more genuine sorrow over a dead mouse. "So you're paying me anyway."

"I'm a man of my word, Mr. Donne."

An honorable man. Thomas found that prospect as unlikely as had Detective Munroe. But he couldn't walk away from five hundred dollars. He returned the handgun to his pocket, grabbed the envelope, and ripped it open. Five hundred-dollar bills, each as crisp as if they'd just rolled off the press. Tossing the empty envelope onto the desk, he tucked the money away. "Our business is over."

"Our *old* business, yes. But now it appears as if we have new."

Suddenly weary of games, of wondering what unpleasant news might blindside him next, of seeing Townsend's self-assured florid face, Thomas threw himself into one of the chairs lined up against the wall. "Exactly what is it you want from me?"

"Nothing beyond what anyone might want from a private detective. I want you to find the person who killed Roy Gage."

"It wasn't you?"

Townsend didn't bother to appear offended. "It was not. Had I wanted him dead, I'd have done a neater job of it."

"Right. You're not a *sloppy* killer." Thomas stretched out his legs and leaned back. The chair creaked under him. "Why do you care who did it?"

"I told you. The boy was a sort of protégé of mine, and—"

"Cut it. That story's as dead as Gage. Tell me the truth."

Townsend sucked on his lips and stubbed out the cigar. He had big hands, long and wide and meaty. A laborer's hands, except his nails were clean and neatly trimmed. His rings shone as if the stones contained flames. "It's self-interest," he said. "Gage and I were... linked, even if tenuously. I need to make sure his murder is unconnected to any threats against me."

Thomas wasn't sure whether he believed this, although it was more credible than Townsend as an angelic savior. But even if it was the truth, it didn't explain everything. "You have ties to the police department. Munroe said he'd look into it. Why isn't that enough?"

"More information is always better." Townsend narrowed his eyes shrewdly. "And you know as well as I that even those who are connected to us cannot always be fully trusted. Also, the priorities of the police department might be different from my own."

"So you want...?"

Now Townsend leaned forward. "Find me the murderer, Mr. Donne. His name and his location. That is all. I will pay you generously for this."

"How generously?"

"Ten thousand dollars."

Ten grand. Thomas could buy a house and one of those new Model A cars and still have money left over. He could take a true holiday for the first time since... a very long time. The wolves would be banished for years.

He stood suddenly and strode to the window, staring out with his back to Townsend. Not much of a view from here. Only the gray building across the street, where a pigeon stared back from a window ledge. He couldn't hear the foghorn, but perhaps the wind was carrying the sound in another direction. The fog itself wasn't heavy today, at least not in this part of the city, and he missed it. He liked its blurring grayness.

Thomas swung around and looked at Townsend. "I'll do it for fifteen."

6

"You look better today." Rosie stood in Abe's kitchen. Today she wore a simple yellow drop-waist dress, and her short reddish hair was styled in waves with a little curl near one ear. "Did you take aspirin like I told you?"

"Yes," he lied. In truth, he'd simply woken up midmorning to find the headache gone. Which was fortunate because he had two séances scheduled for today. The first had gone well, and now he and Rosie were seated at his little table, finishing off some sandwiches before guests arrived for the second.

"I read the paper this morning. They had a review of your show last night."

"Was it a good one?" Feigning nonchalance, Abe repositioned a slice of bread. He was never brave enough to read his reviews.

"Yeah. They said you were mesmerizing and captivating."

He breathed a relieved sigh. "I'm happy to hear that."

Rosie made a humming noise and dabbed at her mouth with a napkin. She wasn't much past twenty but her path had been a difficult one, giving her a wisdom and gravitas unusual for her age. She liked to mother Abe now and then, even though he was twice her age and her employer to boot. He didn't much mind, although now he sensed disapproval.

"What's wrong?" he asked.

"I couldn't do it—stand there and let someone shoot a gun at me. I'd run away."

"Ah, but it's a trick, remember? Like our spirits."

She shook her head. "Sometimes it's not so much of a trick though, is it? And even with tricks, things go wrong."

"You've withstood much scarier things than a little stage illusion, Rosie. I bet you could face an entire pride of lions without so much as a waver."

"Oh, you!" She laughed and waved away his comment, then finished the last bite of her sandwich and pushed the plate aside.

Together they cleared the table, washed the dishes, and put them away. He thought she was through with the subject, but she paused as she was buttoning her coat. "It's death, you know. Just one little twitch of a finger and bam! It's all over. All the things you always wanted and now you're never gonna get them, so those things are dead too. I couldn't do it."

"Well, luckily you don't have to." He pasted on a smile and handed over her cloche. The smile became genuine as he watched her fuss to arrange it just so on her head. He handed her the little beaded purse she'd bought the previous week—straight from Paris, she'd told him breathlessly while showing it off. Rosie took a pair of white gloves from the purse and pulled them on.

"One hour," he reminded her before opening the back door.

She winked at him. "On the dot."

By the time Rosie returned for the séance—through the front door, pretending they'd never met—several of the other guests had arrived. She stood with them at the long table at the back of the parlor, sipping watered wine and chatting quietly. She had a true talent for getting strangers to divulge their secrets and their feelings. Later she'd subtly indicate the most skeptical of them as well as the most gullible.

Abe had already set up the chairs and props and now sat in a throne-like seat in the corner, trying to look otherworldly and mysterious even though his collar made his neck itch. He stood whenever the doorbell rang and greeted each newcomer with a deep bow and thick accent. He kissed the women's hands and shook the men's, automatically noting which of them blushed or lingered a bit over the contact. It was easier to deceive people who were too distracted by attraction to notice a sleight of hand.

But Abe wasn't prepared for one of the final guests to arrive: a tall, muscular man with a brutally handsome face and eyes the oddest shade of pale gray, as if they'd captured the city fog. Abe felt them pierce right through him. When they shook hands, Abe was the one to feel his cheeks heat. "Velcome," he said, hoping to distract from his blush with a flourish of his hand. "I am Abe France, at your service."

"Thomas Donne."

Abe recognized the deep voice with an English accent. Donne had called just an hour earlier to ask whether he might join the afternoon séance. It was unusual for people to make appointments on such short notice, but since Abe had room, he'd allowed it. Besides, every dollar counted.

Speaking of which, Donne was holding out a green bill. "You said five, correct?"

"I did." Abe palmed the money, intending to tuck it away later. That had been another of Emil's many suggestions. Making the payments disappear set the mood much better than prosaically shoving them into a pocket or wallet. "I hope you vill find the fee vorthvhile."

Donne grunted and followed him down the narrow hall. Abe found it disconcerting to feel that solid gaze on his back. Although the scrutiny tensed his muscles, it hardened his cock as well, so he was grateful to duck behind a curtained cabinet when they reached the parlor. "Please help yourself to a refreshment," he said, waving toward the table at the back. "Ve shall begin shortly."

After giving Abe a knowing look, Donne followed the instructions. Abe watched his movements: a solid sureness, as if he feared nothing and expected the world to bend to his will. When he reached the table, he hung his coat and hat on the rack and took a glass of watered wine but didn't drink it. He didn't mingle with the other guests either, although he examined them closely as he stood near the corner.

What does he want? Abe had no time to find out. The doorbell rang as the last guests arrived, and then it was time to begin.

"Vill you please take your seats?"

Everyone scurried to obey except Donne, who finally drained his glass in one long swallow and then chose a chair in the back. He didn't shift around, although he probably wasn't comfortable. The scrutiny of those gray eyes remained both unsettling and exciting.

Never mind that. It was time to work.

"Velcome." Abe spread his arms open.

Years ago, Emil had spent weeks coaching Abe on his opening patter, refusing to teach a single illusion until he was satisfied. "What you say at the beginning is essential. You either hook them or you lose them, so your words must cast a spell."

After considerable practice, Abe had learned that the best way to engage his séance audience was to be as truthful as possible. So today, as usual, he spoke about the veil between the worlds of the living and the dead and the urge to pierce that veil. "Some of the living vish to see beyond, to have a glimpse of vhat lies beyond. But this is very dangerous. The power of the other side is greedy and jealous, and vonce it seizes us, it may not let go. It vill be as if you are standing on the edge of a great chasm—you feel quite safe, but vhen the edge begins to crumble, you find yourself stepping forvard instead of avay."

Some members of the audience shuddered and others nodded. Good. They were on the hook already. Donne remained unmoving and expressionless.

After a brief pause, Abe continued. "But it is not only the living who might vish to breach the veil. Sometimes the dead vish this as vell. It may be because they are angry at having moved on, or frustrated they didn't achieve vhat they hoped in life. Perhaps they blame others for their death. Or perhaps they have a final message they vish to convey." He sighed deeply. "And a few feel the bonds of love so deeply that they continue to reach out, to clutch at those whom they've lost. These efforts are always clumsy—the dead have no place here—and may even endanger the living. The dead become the force that tempts us to step into the abyss."

An older woman began to cry, sobbing quietly into a handkerchief. That wasn't unusual. The younger women beside her silently offered help, but the older one declined. Maybe she wanted to cry. It wasn't often people had the chance to express grief outside of cemeteries and the confines of their homes.

"Some of us," Abe said, "vere born vith the ability to help others safely pierce the veil, but only for a few moments. I am one of those who vas granted this gift. I suspect this is because I had a tvin brother who died shortly before birth. My connection to him—in that indistinct time between not-life and life—forever tied me to the other vorld. I can touch it more safely than most, and I can assist the dead who vish to send a message. But friends, still this is not completely safe, you understand? Ve must tread vith care."

He had them all now. Except for Donne. This didn't exactly worry Abe, because he knew how to handle a disbeliever. In fact, Abe's methods could withstand almost any scrutiny, and responding to someone like Donne usually helped convince everyone else even more. That was why Rosie would play skeptic when the audience seemed to waver. No need for that with Donne there, though.

Abe looked calmly out at the room. "Is each of you prepared for this journey today?"

They nodded and murmured, and Donne shot him a sharp, crooked smile.

No two of Abe's séances were the same. The variety kept him fresh and also meant a person could attend more than once without becoming bored or jaded. Today he began with a talking board, a plank of varnished wood painted with letters and a few simple words.

After placing the board on top of his high table, Abe invited the crying woman to come forward. Then he handed her a wheeled planchette made of thin ivory. He'd had this set custom-made, preferring it to the Ouija boards that were mass-produced as parlor games.

"Mrs. Teche, kindly place the planchette on the board and rest two fingers of your right hand upon it." As she obeyed, he stepped back, demonstrating that he wasn't controlling anything. "Now, please form a clear picture in your head of the deceased loved one vith whom you'd like to speak. Yes, very good. And formulate three or four qvestions. Make sure they can be answered quite simply—conversing across the veil is difficult."

Her brow furrowed in concentration, and then a determined expression settled over her features. "I'm ready." Her voice was thin but firm.

"Excellent. Pose your first question, please."

"Alice? This is your sister speaking. Oh, I miss you so." Mrs. Teche sniffed but held her ground. "My grandson Philip is grown now and keeps telling me to invest my money in the stock market. He says we can become wealthy this way. Should I listen to him?"

She waited.

This wasn't the most spectacular thing to do in a séance; nobody else in the audience could see the board. But it was quick and easy and nearly always worked. It didn't even require trickery; the person's unconscious mind would make the fingers move the planchette without the person being aware of it. And if nothing happened, it was simple: the spirits weren't in the mood to communicate that way.

Something did happen, however, as it usually did. The planchette rolled slowly across the plank until it stopped atop the word No.

Abe read the result aloud for the sake of the audience. "It appears as if you should save your money, Mrs. Teche. Have you another question for dear Alice?"

She had several, and the audience listened raptly as the board answered them. Donne, however, watched Abe instead, his head slightly cocked and his brows creased. His lips twitched every time their gazes caught.

After Mrs. Teche was back in her seat—still sniffing, but looking satisfied—Abe chose a middle-aged man who wanted to speak to his dead father, with whom he'd had a falling-out in his youth.

Then Abe moved on to another séance staple, the talking slate. There were a variety of methods to accomplish this particular illusion, some of which required help from a hidden accomplice. Lacking that today, Abe used a combination of sleight of hand and intuition about his guests, along with chalk-written messages that were vague enough to suit nearly anyone. Except for Donne, everyone else was fully hooked, and it took little effort to impress them.

Abe was confused by Donne's silence. Now and then someone was willing to pay good money to sit in a séance and carry on loudly about what hokum it all was. Abe was accustomed to handling those people. But Donne didn't seem interested in disruption; he sat in the back where nobody but Abe could see his disbelieving smirk. It was frustrating and distracting not to know his intentions.

When Abe was done with the slates, he would ordinarily have turned to the third and final act of the séance. It involved darkening the room, asking the audience to concentrate on their loved ones beyond the veil, and then operating a series of trap doors and curtains via hidden controls. Masks and gauzy drapery covered in luminescent paint would make flickering appearances. One key here was for his accomplice to have the first sighting. Rosie would gasp or scream before Abe had yet showed a prop, making everyone else eager for their own glimpses. The other key was to do this illusion after the guests had lost any lingering doubts.

It was a wonderful illusion, one that would send his guests away feeling as if their money had been well spent. But today one guest continued to have doubts, and Abe's curiosity was too strong to resist. He decided to postpone the finale.

"Friends, I vill now move among you and see if I receive any messages from beyond."

Rosie lifted her eyebrows, clearly surprised he was going to do a cold reading. He generally did that only during séances where he'd given the guests a brief refreshment break and Rosie had the opportunity to slip him notes about the people she'd spoken with at the beginning. It certainly hadn't been part of today's plan.

Nonetheless, Abe moved among the chairs with his head atilt, as if he were listening for a faint sound. He stopped in front of Rosie and closed his eyes. "Ah. I'm hearing a voice.... A woman. Mary? No. Margaret."

Rosie gasped and clutched her chest. "My sister Meg?" she asked tremulously. "She passed five years ago from rheumatic fever."

In fact, Rosie had two sisters—neither named Margaret and both quite alive—who she didn't especially get along with and spoke to only infrequently. But she wobbled her chin convincingly as Abe nodded. "Yes. She says she misses you. She remembers the... the necklace you gave her for her birthday. It vas such a lovely gift, she says."

Tears started to leak from Rosie's eyes. Crying convincingly on cue was one of her many strengths. "She loved that little thing. We buried her in it."

"She vants you to know that she's very happy vhere she is now. She knows your life vill be long, but someday you shall see her again."

"Th-thank you, Mr. France. Tell her I love her too."

"She knows."

Abe moved down the row to a man in his fifties, a Mr. Van Goethem. He was dressed moderately well but not richly, and his weathered face and battered hands suggested he'd once labored outdoors. He had an accent—Dutch or Belgian; Abe wasn't certain—but it wasn't strong, so he'd been in the United States for a long time. These observations and a general knowledge of human beings allowed Abe to make some safe guesses.

"I am hearing a woman again. She is.... I see the letter A?"

"Anna?" Mr. Van Goethem seemed confused.

"I am not sure. I believe the A is not at the beginning of her name."

Mr. Van Goethem let out a noisy sigh. "Johanna. My mother."

Perfect. Abe had chosen A simply because it was common in feminine names; after that, he could get the guest to lead him on the right path. "Yes, your mother. She says.... Oh." He frowned deeply as if distressed.

"What? What does she say? Mama, I—"

Abe held up a hand to silence him. "It's.... Oh, I see." He bent so as to put his eyes on level with Mr. Van Goethem's and lowered his voice as if to tell a secret. He knew his words would carry nonetheless. "She says she forgives you, sir. She knows you are a good man at heart. She is proud of you."

Mr. Van Goethem didn't cry, but he clamped his lips together and his throat worked. He gave a jerky nod.

This had been nothing but a guess. In Abe's experience, nearly everyone had disappointed a parent at one point or another.

At last, heart pounding, Abe moved to the back row and came to a halt in front of Donne. Standing this close, he could see a bit of pale stubble on those broad cheeks and stubborn chin. Donne's eyes were more fog-like than ever: opaque and chilling. The type of eyes a man could get lost in. He sat straight-backed but not tense, heavy muscles relaxed beneath his cheap suit and good shirt. But his hands—yes. They hung over the armrests and moved with the hint of a tremor.

Interesting.

Without truly intending to, knowing it might even be dangerous, Abe reached out and settled a palm on Donne's shoulder. Although Donne flinched slightly, he didn't strike out or move away. His jaw tightened, though, and his eyes narrowed.

The war, Abe thought. Yes. Donne was the right age for it, and his accent thick enough to suggest he'd come of age in England instead of the United States. Besides, there was something about the set of his body and the creases around his eyes. "I hear... a man," Abe began.

And then he did.

As clear as if the person stood next to him, a voice spoke in Abe's ear. It sounded young and sad and thin. *Tommy. Oh, my darling Tommy, what have they done to you?*

Abe unwillingly echoed a phrase, the words tearing his throat. "My darling Tommy."

Donne leapt to his feet, jerking back so violently that he toppled the chair. One hand went into his coat pocket, and Abe was certain he was about to be shot. The idea didn't frighten him, mostly because he was too deeply awash in the spirit's sorrow. "Don't hurt him, Tommy." From his own mouth, but it wasn't his accent or his voice. "Please don't."

The spirit... the man had been in his early twenties, perhaps. A pointed chin and sharp nose, thin mobile eyebrows, a wide mouth always a moment away from a cheeky grin. Ears that stuck out a little. Abe *knew* this although he couldn't see the spirit. Just as he knew the spirit's name. "Albert," he said in his own voice.

Donne jerked again but held his ground. He was breathing hard.

Abe's knees felt weak, his head swam, and Albert whispered in his head: tiny snippets and phrases that Abe couldn't quite catch. Reaching out for a chair back to support himself, he became aware of the wide eyes and gaping mouths of his guests.

With considerable effort, he gathered his wits, giving Donne a quick apologetic glance before striding to the front of the room. "I am sorry, friends. Today the spirits have qvite exhausted me. I hope you have found some of the answers you sought."

The guests seemed pleased as they gathered their coats and hats and filed toward the hallway and the door. They thanked Abe as they shook his hand. Soon only two others remained: Rosie, looking about as if perhaps she'd mislaid a glove, and Donne, towering and jut-jawed in the back of the room.

"I need to talk to you," Donne growled.

Abe simply nodded. He took Rosie gently by the arm and led her down the hall, surreptitiously offering her five dollars at the door. She took it but paused with her hand on the knob. "Are you all right?" she whispered.

"I'm fine."

"That was—"

"I'll explain another time, sweetheart."

She scrunched her mouth together. "But that big fella, he don't look too safe."

"Nothing worthwhile ever is. I'll see you tomorrow, Rosie." He gave her a gentle push out the door and locked it behind her. Then he turned and walked back to face Donne.

7
____

Thomas was accustomed to anger, but it usually sat cold, heavy, and permanent—like an iceberg in his chest. Now, though, his anger was searing-hot and wickedly sharp. The fear and uncertainty were new, although the anguish wasn't. He'd thought it buried deeply inside, but here it was again, as fresh as the day it first hit him.

He stood in France's parlor and resisted the urge to draw his gun.

Most of the séance had been innocuous. Quite literally parlor tricks. Well-executed, yes, but the gullible marks had done most of the magic themselves, eagerly swallowing whatever tripe France fed them.

But the end....

France returned to the room alone, his face pale and eyes bleak. He didn't seem frightened of Thomas, which was a surprise. But he looked exhausted. "Do you want a drink? Not that stuff"—he waved at the glasses of watered wine—"but a real drink."

The offer calmed Thomas. "All right."

"Follow me."

France led him to a small kitchen. Nothing mystical about it; the white cabinets and bright curtains were almost shockingly homey. "Have a seat."

The wooden table was small and round, its top scarred from years of use. Thomas sat with his back to the corner and watched as France filled two glasses with clear liquid from a bottle. Before bringing the drinks over, France removed his evening coat and hung it on a hook, then rolled up his shirtsleeves to reveal wiry forearms. He set the glasses on the table and took the other seat.

"L'chaim." He lifted his glass, took a healthy slug, and laughed.

"Why is that funny?"

"It means *to life*. Ironic, yeah?"

Frowning, Thomas tried a swallow. The stuff was stronger than he expected, hot and smooth on his throat. "What is it?"

"Slivovitz. Plum brandy."

Thomas nodded and drank some more. France silently drained his own glass, fetched the bottle, and refilled them both.

"What happened to your accent?" Thomas asked, although that was the least relevant question at the moment. But the heavy Eastern European tones had disappeared, replaced with American ones.

"I put it away, along with my other props."

"You're good at it."

France chuckled. "I spent my first six years in Budapest. When we got to New York, my parents insisted we all talk in English instead of Hungarian or Yiddish, but they never stopped sounding like foreigners. I can pick it up again whenever I need to."

Budapest. And he was Jewish too. "What's your real name?"

"Abraham Ferencz. My parents called me Avi. Nowadays people mostly call me Abe. You can call me whatever the hell you want to." He squinted one eye. "And you're Tommy Donne from England."

"Thomas," he snapped, ignoring the fresh kick to his gut. "How did you know that?" He'd given only his last name when he phoned to reserve a spot at the séance. "And how did you know about—" He gritted his teeth and glared at his glass.

"About Albert?" France—no, Abe, apparently—finished the sentence gently.

"Yes."

After remaining silent for a moment, Abe nodded to himself. "Tell you what. You got questions, I got questions. You answer mine and I answer yours."

"What do you want to know?"

"Well, I guess we can start with why the hell you've come here. I don't think you had any intention of talking to dead people."

Dammit. In the thick of everything else, Thomas had almost forgotten his original goals. "I came to talk *about* dead people. One in particular. I'm a private dick." He removed a card from his pocket and slid it across the table.

Abe didn't touch it but bent down to read it. "Thomas Donne, Private Investigator. All right, Thomas. What are you investigating?"

"A murder."

"Who was murdered?"

"Roy Gage." Thomas watched Abe's reaction very closely.

The blood drained from Abe's face and his eyes widened. Then he dropped his head and muttered something in another language. Yiddish, Thomas thought. Abe's eyes were shiny when he straightened again and polished off his second glass. He might be a consummate actor—he was a skilled performer, after all—but Thomas didn't believe this was a put-on. Until this moment, Abe hadn't known the kid was dead.

"What happened?" Abe's voice sounded rough.

"That's what I'm trying to figure out."

"And that's why you came here—to investigate me."

"He worked for you."

"Sometimes, yeah." Abe filled his glass for the third time. "He was — I saw him last night. I had a stage show and he assisted me."

"I know." Thomas opted not to reveal that he'd been there. No reason to give away more information than needed. "Do you know who killed him?"

Abe pressed his lips together and shook his head slowly. "Could be.... He had a rough time of it growing up. He is—he *was*—smart, really smart. Could have made something of himself if life hadn't fucked him. But his father killed Roy's mother when Roy was nine. The old man's doing life in San Quentin, and Roy was mostly on his own. Boys like that end up hardened. They have to be, to survive."

Thomas wouldn't argue with that; he'd seen plenty of those hard boys on both sides of the Atlantic. But none of this was useful information. "So?"

"So he had his fingers in a lot of things he shouldn't have." Abe huffed a laugh that was almost a sob. "I first hired him years ago, after he tried to pick my pocket. Nimble hands are helpful for a magician's assistant."

"Did you fuck him?"

Instead of anger, Abe responded with a grin. "No. I like men, not boys."

I like men. Those three words rocked Thomas like a blow. He wasn't surprised that Abe was queer, but Thomas had never met anyone who admitted this so baldly. He'd experienced veiled euphemisms and meaningful looks, but never a man stating his preference so openly and plainly without a hint of shame. Abe stared knowingly at Thomas, as if he were dead certain that Thomas felt the same.

But he knows about Albert, doesn't he?

Thomas pushed away that intrusive thought. He'd suss out that trickery soon enough, after he'd discovered any information pertinent to the murder.

"Did he do any other work for you?"

"When he was younger he'd run errands for me sometimes—anything to earn a nickel or two. Lately, though, he rarely works for me at all. Enough money in his pocket from other sources. Honestly, I think he mostly stayed because he enjoyed being on stage. He could have made a fine magician if he'd had the patience for it." Abe sighed, emptied his glass, and poured again.

He must have been at least a little drunk by now, yet his large eyes remained clear, amber in the bright light of the kitchen. Everything about the man was warm, it seemed: his gemstone eyes, his olive-toned skin, his coffee-colored hair that showed no gray. Thomas wondered if he also felt hot to the touch.

No. That was not the point of this visit at all.

Thomas wanted a cigarette very badly but didn't take out his tobacco; he knew his fingers would shake. But then Abe rose, crossed to his evening coat, and as if he'd read Thomas's mind, returned with a gold cigarette case and a silver-and-enamel lighter. He lit two cigarettes and handed one to Thomas before sitting down again.

"Who else did Gage work for?" Thomas asked.

"I don't know. I didn't want to get mixed up in any of that."

"You think you're too good for that? You con people for a living."

Again, Abe smiled instead of becoming angry. "I do. But you've seen it yourself—they *want* to be fooled. Some of them leave lighter in their hearts after speaking with the dead. The rest were at least entertained."

"They're *not* speaking with the dead," Thomas growled.

"That doesn't matter. They think they have. And I've harmed no one." Abe leaned forward. "But now it's my turn to ask a question. Who hired you?"

Thomas didn't answer.

Abe tapped his cigarette into a chipped ceramic ashtray and looked thoughtful. "Roy has no family members who'd care, poor boy. So was it those *gonefs*—the villains he worked for?"

Thomas couldn't have answered that question honestly if he'd wanted to. He wasn't sure whether Townsend was a villain and didn't know if he'd employed Gage. Both were quite possible. "Can't tell you," he said.

"You can't say who hired you; I don't know who hired Roy. It doesn't sound as if we have anything to offer each other." Definitely a tease there, or a challenge of some sort.

"Who did Gage leave with last night?"

"After my show, you mean? That was Leo Zook."

"You know him."

"We've met." Abe shrugged. "He goes home with Roy sometimes.

Maybe he pays Roy—I don't know. But he's not a criminal. He sells jewelry at Gump's."

Thomas waved away Abe's easy assumption. Someone with a straight job during the day could just as easily be a crook at night; Thomas had seen that plenty of times. In fact, it was often the well-respected businessmen who were the biggest scoundrels of all.

"All right." Thomas helped himself to another cigarette and the lighter but didn't take any more slivovitz. "Is there anything else you can tell me about who might have killed Gage?"

"No. I'm sorry. But I hope you find him. Roy was no angel, but he didn't deserve this."

Thomas could poke a little longer, but he doubted it would get him anywhere. Abe sat there, burning like the devil himself but unsinged, downing plum brandy as if it were water. Drawing Thomas in as if he'd hooked him on a line.

"How do you know about Albert?" Thomas's voice almost caught on the name.

Abe slumped in his chair, suddenly ten years older. He reached for his glass and considered it a moment before refilling it. By now the bottle was almost empty. "The guests at my séances, they believe my lies because they want to. You won't believe my truth because you don't want to." He tapped his chest with two fingers. "Belief is here, my friend. Not here." He tapped his head.

"I believe facts."

"Facts! *Der oylem iz a goylem.* My father used to say that. Do you know what it means?"

"No."

"*People are idiots.* He was wrong, though. It's the world that's stupid. We just try to make the best of it that we can."

Thomas finished off his slivovitz, grabbed the bottle, and poured the rest into his glass. "I'm not here to talk in riddles."

"Fine. Here's how I know about Albert." His face drained of expression. "Most of my spiel is utter nonsense. But the part about the veil? That's mostly true. The dead pass on, move away. I don't know where they go. Heaven? Hell? I have no clue. Some of them don't progress, though. They remain near the border for reasons of their own. Sometimes they're strong enough to reach across on their own—those are ghosts, but they're rare. Others, though, they need to find something on this side to latch on to, or more often, some*one*. And some of us are easier for them to reach."

"Because of your dead twin." Thomas blew a long plume of smoke.

"I never had a twin."

"Then why?"

Abe raised his palms. "*Ver vaist?* Why was my cousin Sara born with a clubfoot?"

"So you see ghosts."

"I told you, ghosts are something different. I hear spirits speaking from the other side. And once in a while, one of those spirits crosses over—crosses *into* me, you understand? Shares my body like two men squeezing into a single coat." He shuddered.

Thomas raised an eyebrow. This was, of course, the rubbish that made Abe a nice little living, that brought people to his cozy house at five dollars a head. A good enough scam that it wouldn't eat too much at his conscience. "How do you know about Albert?" he growled.

The planes of Abe's face toughened and his eyes went hard, like fire turned suddenly to ice. He stood slowly and paced the short length of the kitchen. When he turned back to face Thomas, that full upper lip was lifted in a sneer. "His name was Albert Dixon but you called him Birdie—with a *d*, not a *t*—because he talked a lot and you said he twittered like a bird. You met in 1916, not long before the Battle of the Somme, when you were transferred to his division. The moment he first laid eyes on you, he decided to seduce you."

Thomas's rushing heartbeat threatened to drown out Abe's quiet voice. He lurched out of his chair and across the kitchen. By the time he reached Abe, the familiar weight of his Smith & Wesson was heavy in his hand.

Abe didn't back away, didn't flinch. Didn't appear surprised or frightened. In fact, warmth returned to his eyes and the corners of his mouth lifted into a sorrowful smile. "He loved you, Tommy. Even when the fever took him and his lungs filled, he was thinking of you."

Roaring, Thomas rushed forward, driving Abe back and pinning him against the wall. He held him there with the bulk of his body, the gun trapped between them. "Shut up!" he shouted into Abe's face.

Abe reached up with both hands, laced his fingers into Thomas's hair, and pulled his head closer. And he kissed him.

Scorching hot, strong but soft, and tasting of sweet plums. A kiss to get lost in and be both grateful and chastened for having been led astray. A sorcerer's kiss, a sublime trickery, an inferno that consumed intellect and wisdom and self-restraint. The gun was still there, but so was Abe's cock, hard through the fabric of his trousers. Thomas pushed against it with his own.

Somehow Abe escaped from beneath him—but that was no miracle; he was a magician, after all. Instead of moving away, he grasped Thomas's shoulders and shoved him back against the cabinet. Gently took the gun from Thomas's slack hand and set it on the counter. Dropped to his knees and unfastened Thomas's fly.

Thomas had thought Abe's mouth was hot when they kissed, but that was nothing compared to the molten slickness that enveloped him. He braced himself on his hands and closed his eyes, aroused almost as much by the obscene licking and sucking noises as he was by the friction. The sight of Abe's bobbing head would have been too much. Abe proved as agile with his mouth as with his hands, and when Thomas gave a few inquiring thrusts, Abe moaned around him and pulled Thomas's hips forward, encouraging him to go deeper.

Thomas spilled with a guttural cry.

As he was replacing his clothing with shaking hands, Abe gathered Thomas's coat and hat and handed them over. His reddened lips were a little swollen, and hectic color had appeared on his cheeks. His hair stood in frantic curls. But his expression was serene.

"Don't forget your gun," he said, waving toward the counter.

"I could have shot you."

"Sometimes I like to catch the bullet."

8

Abe didn't have dinner that night. He tidied up the parlor: putting away the slates, washing the wine glasses, and straightening the chairs. When he cleaned up the kitchen, he drank the last few drops of slivovitz from Donne's glass. And then he went upstairs, stripped naked, and sat in front of an open window in his dark bedroom.

Although the street was quiet, he could hear the clatter of streetcars over on California. Lights glowed in the windows of the houses opposite. He liked to imagine he could smell the ocean, even though it was many blocks away.

"Are you still there, Birdie?" he whispered. Nobody answered. No surprise, since he hadn't felt the spirit's presence since the séance ended. But the sensation lingered within him, just as the taste of Donne lingered on his lips.

Quite suddenly he wondered about Roy Gage's spirit. He hoped the death had been quick and he'd moved on effortlessly.

Who was Donne working for, and what did his employer want? No use wasting thoughts on those questions; Abe was a magician, not a detective.

Tomorrow was Saturday, and he hadn't scheduled any séances.

Perhaps he'd go for a swim at the Sutro Baths and then take himself out for a nice dinner. Or maybe he'd do a bit of shopping, followed by a visit to his former mentor, whom he hadn't seen in months. Emil was in his late seventies and had looked somewhat drawn the last time they'd met, as if he'd been battling an illness.

For now, though, Abe sat at the window and stared out into the night.

9

Thomas took dinner at Bianchi's. Bertha had long since gone home, replaced by a surly relative of Bianchi's who sometimes liked to pretend he didn't understand English. Afterward, Thomas stopped to buy some tobacco and cigarette papers and then restlessly strolled the streets.

He seriously considered contacting Detective Munroe to ask for help in tracking down Leo Zook. He decided against it, however, on the principle that he didn't want to have to share his fee.

Somehow he ended up at the Embarcadero, leaning against a rail and looking down at the dark water. He'd been a good swimmer as a lad but hadn't tried it since the war. The bay would be cold, saturating his clothing at once and dragging him down. He'd die with his lungs full of fluid, just as Birdie had, although Birdie had met his end on dry ground.

A memory came to him of a rest camp in Flanders. He and Birdie had managed to get their four days there together. It had been lovely to get clean and dry, to eat decent food, and to simply relax over card games. When the other soldiers had become involved in a football game, Thomas and Birdie had snuck off to a tent. If anyone had found them, Birdie had a ready-made story about needing his feet tended to. Nobody would have believed the tale, but they might have pretended to. In any case, Birdie and Thomas weren't discovered, and they spent almost an hour passionately trying to forget about the war.

Birdie's laugh had been delightfully ridiculous, and he liked to make fun of Thomas's posh accent. Sometimes they planned for a future neither of them expected to have, wherein they'd return to England and share a London flat. Birdie would work as a plumber and Thomas would be a policeman, and if anyone asked, they'd simply be mates splitting expenses.

"I might have loved you too," Thomas whispered at the water. Let the Pacific make of that what it may.

SATURDAY MORNINGS WERE quiet in Thomas's neighborhood, most of the people sleeping off the night before. He didn't like the quiet, which echoed with the phantom sounds of shelling. Today he ended up at the waterfront, watching the fishing boats come and go. He ate breakfast at a standup joint near the cannery. Even at this time of year, he thought he caught the faint scent of peaches mixed in with fish and brine and damp.

He could have afforded a taxi, but he took streetcars to Post Street instead, arriving shortly after Gump's unlocked its doors. He'd been in the upscale department store before, mainly out of curiosity; the wares were much too expensive for his budget. On display were items imported from Asia and Europe to grace San Francisco's finest homes: bright silks, gleaming crystal and jade, shining porcelains, polished bronzes.

While pretending to browse the whimsical Limoges boxes, Thomas scoped out the jewelry counters. There was no sign of the man he'd seen with Gage two nights before. The sales clerk—a thin man with a mustache perched above a permanently sneered lip—eyed Thomas distrustfully for several minutes before marching stiffly over. "May I help you?" Judging by his expression, he'd prefer to help Thomas to the door.

Thomas stepped closer, towering over the clerk. "I need to speak with Leo Zook."

"Mr. Zook is not here. However, I'd be happy to help you make a selection."

Like hell he would. Thomas produced a business card and held it out. "I need his home address then."

The clerk's face scrunched up even more tightly as he took the card between two fingers and read it. "I shall have to get my manager."

"Go ahead."

Holding the card as if it were something scraped out of the gutter, the clerk strutted away. Thomas inspected the closest jewelry case while he waited. Pretty things, nice and sparkly, but he could never fathom why people spent so much money on such baubles. His mother used to wear large, gaudy pieces on her ears and around her neck, and she'd worry aloud that the servants might steal them, although none of them ever had. Townsend seemed to like big diamonds too.

The unhappy clerk returned, accompanied by an older man with a rounded body and a soft face that resembled over-risen dough. "I'm Mr. Yarbury," he said in a squeaky little voice. Thomas's handshake met Yarbury's clammy palm. "How may I help you, Mr. Donne?"

"Where's Zook?"

"I don't know, I don't know. He didn't show up for work yesterday or today, and that's not at all like him. He's usually so reliable."

Thomas swore under his breath. "Where does he live?"

"Has he been kidnapped, do you think? Or robbed?" Yarbury's jowls wobbled with agitation. "Sometimes he conveys new acquisitions to the store—we're always getting exotic new finds from the ships, you see—but he wasn't doing that this week. A robber might not know that, though."

The clerk, who'd remained several feet away, pretended to polish a glass case that was already perfectly clean. His mustache wriggled like a tiny snake.

"I don't know what happened to Zook," Thomas said as evenly as he could. "If you give me his address, I might find out."

"Of course, of course." But Yarbury didn't walk away. He frowned instead. "Now, three weeks ago, that would have been a better time for a robbery. A gentleman arrived from China with the most exquisite piece! It was a tiny gold box inset with sapphires and carved jade. Simply breathtaking! Our buyer negotiated the sale, but Mr. Zook was the one who—"

"His address."

Yarbury sniffed and nodded before waddling off and disappearing behind a door. He returned a few minutes later, clutching a piece of paper. "Here you are, Mr. Donne. I sincerely hope that—"

Thomas snatched the paper. "Thank you for your help, Mr. Yarbury." He shot a sneer at the clerk before leaving.

Zook's apartment was on Mason and California, only a half-dozen blocks away. Thomas hurried up Stockton, taking the stairs at the tunnel two at a time, and didn't even slow for the steep slope between Bush and Pine. His destination was kitty-corner from the Fairmont, a pink building with wrought-iron balconies. The entrance on California had beautiful columns and an elaborate awning, and of course the lobby was posh too: crystal chandeliers, marble floors and walls, tasteful statues and frescoes. Thomas hadn't been aware that Gump's paid its employees so handsomely.

"Yes?" asked the antique gentleman at the reception desk.

Weary of dealing with barriers, Thomas simply handed him a business card. "Here to see Mr. Zook."

Apparently unsurprised, the man gestured toward the lift.

The flat was only one floor up—evidently Gump's wasn't flush enough to pay for a penthouse—with the door at the end of a rose-scented hallway. Nobody answered when Thomas knocked, or when he knocked again. When he tried the knob, it turned easily.

Zook—what was left of him, at any rate—was slumped on his parlor floor. There were no knife wounds this time, but his tongue protruded amid a swollen face. Thomas didn't bother looking to see whether the ligature remained around Zook's neck. Instead he sighed, walked to the telephone, and called Munroe.

"It's very convenient of you, Mr. Donne, to keep bringing the bodies to my attention. Saves me half my job." Munroe grinned at him over Zook's corpse.

"Maybe you should give me half your salary then."

"Oh, I suspect you're being well compensated already."

Thanks to the cool weather, the reek of decomposition hadn't yet set in, but Thomas thought he could sense the beginning of sickly sweetness. He walked to the window for a few breaths of clean air and had to pull hard to open it. When he turned back, Munroe was kneeling beside the body.

"Zook was a big fellow," Munroe said.

Thomas grunted.

"Woulda taken a strong man to strangle him."

"Yes."

"You look pretty strong."

"If I'd killed him, do you think I'd ring you and invite you over? Besides, he's been dead at least a day, and I just got here."

Munroe stood, dusted off his knees, and lit a cigarette. "Maybe you killed him yesterday, had an attack of conscience, and came back."

"I don't have a conscience."

That made Munroe bark with laughter. "All right then. Why don't you tell me how you ended up in this Joe's company?"

"I'm looking into Gage's death. Zook went to the Ambassador with him the night Gage was murdered. Took me until now to track Zook down."

"Okay." Munroe rubbed the back of his neck. He had dark circles under his eyes, as if he hadn't slept well, and he hadn't shaved today either. Carefully avoiding Zook, he moved around the room, eyeing the pretty little knickknacks on the shelves but not touching anything. It took several minutes for him to complete the circuit, and then he left to look around the kitchen, the bathroom, and the bedroom. "Nice place," he said when he returned.

"Yeah."

"So what do you figure? Same hatchet man for both? And if so, which one did he knock off first?"

"I don't know."

"Hmm." Munroe was a restless man, or perhaps he needed to move to stay awake and alert. He paced the room a few times before pausing near Thomas. "Surely you must know something, Mr. Donne."

"I know Gage and Zook are dead."

"Very astute. I can see why Mr. Townsend would want to pay you the big bucks."

Thomas straightened his hat. "I'm going."

"What if I collar you?"

"If you're going to arrest me, go ahead and do it instead of threatening. I'm in no mood to play games."

Munroe looked almost disappointed, but he took a step back. "Nah. You're too heavy to drag down to the station, and I already got him to deal with." He hooked a thumb in Zook's direction. "But how about if we share information? It'll make both of our jobs easier. If you're worried about getting paid, you can take the credit when we catch the bastard."

"I work alone."

"Suit yourself. Now scram. I gotta come up with a story about how I discovered our pal Zook."

It was a relief to be back out on the street, looking down Nob Hill toward the Embarcadero. He could walk to his office from here, but what would be the point? He wouldn't find any answers there. He spun to the west instead, toward the only real lead he had. With a feeling of heavy inevitability—and an unwanted thrill of excitement—he trudged across to the Fairmont, where a taxi had just dropped off a woman in furs.

Thomas slid into the back seat. "Twelfth Avenue, between Clement and California."

10

———

Roy Gage was haunting Abe. Not literally—Abe didn't hear his spirit and certainly hadn't seen his ghost. As far as Abe was aware, poor Roy was far on the other side of the veil, safely away from the tedious affairs of the living.

But the thought of Roy had been lingering in Abe's head since he woke up, and nothing would shake it. Abe had tried reading but couldn't concentrate on the printed words. Then he'd attempted to practice card tricks, but his usually adept hands felt awkward and stupid. Twice he even dropped some cards, a failure he hadn't experienced since his earliest training. He went to the grocers and had a conversation there with Mrs. Osinova about whether talkies were a fad or were here to stay, and if it would be worth taking a trip to Yosemite Park to stay at the Ahwahnee Hotel, and whether pelmeni were better made with lamb or beef. As usual, this meant his simple little shopping trip took nearly an hour, but today he found his mind wandering, so that he mostly just nodded as Mrs. Osinova talked.

It was only that Roy was so young. Yes, he'd experienced a lot of life in his few years, and he'd made choices that put him in danger. More than once he'd refused Abe's offers to help him lead a safer life. Not that Abe's existence was necessarily all that appealing, but at least nobody came after him. And when Abe faced death with bullet-catching, he did so willingly. Roy, he was certain, had not wanted to die.

After putting away the groceries, Abe wandered the neighborhood until he found himself in Golden Gate Park. Because it was a Saturday with fairly pleasant weather, quite a few people were enjoying the grounds. He strolled past the de Young Museum, the Conservatory of Flowers, and the Children's Playground, where boys and girls rode donkeys under the trees.

But Roy Gage came with him, dogging every step.

In a desperate effort to rid himself of morbid thoughts, Abe considered Thomas Donne instead. A handsome man, a hard man, and a puzzling one indeed. A dangerous man. But he'd been loved very much by Birdie Dixon, who'd first noticed Tommy when they, along with many other soldiers, were bathing naked in a river in France. Tommy had been magnificent even then—tall, blond, and muscular—and when Birdie caught Tommy's gaze lingering on Birdie's bare arse, he'd determined to make Tommy his.

Was it the war in general that had toughened Donne, or was it specifically Birdie's gasping death? And why did it matter to Abe?

He walked to the Japanese Garden and sat under the wooden roof of the tea house, where a pretty woman in a kimono brought him a steaming pot and poured fragrant liquid into his cup. He would have preferred liquor, but he'd have to leave the park for that, and for now he wanted to stay. The tea was hot enough to burn his tongue.

It would have been easy to blame yesterday's actions on Birdie's influence. After all, the spirit had squatted inside Abe's body, sharing its memories and emotions. But it had been only Abraham Ferencz on his knees, feeling Donne's pulse against his tongue, tasting the musky saltiness of his skin. Swallowing Donne's essence. And late last night when Abe had finally gone to bed, *he* was the one—all by himself—thinking about Donne while stroking himself to completion.

Maybe it was the gun that did it. The knowledge that when he reached for Donne, the man could shoot him. Might shoot him. And when Donne didn't, there was the thrilling rush of knowing he'd caught the bullet once again.

Maybe.

Abe wandered the park for a long time after finishing his tea, so it was nearly dark and he was footsore by the time he returned home. He'd bought the makings for dinner from Mrs. Osinova, and now he started heating the borscht, the cabbage rolls, and the sauce. He'd purchased a loaf of brown bread as well and was about to slice off a piece when the doorbell rang. He set down the knife and walked to the front door.

"Mr. Donne." Abe pretended his heart wasn't pounding.

"I need to talk to you."

"More questions for me, yet you refuse to answer mine? That's hardly fair."

Donne pushed past him into the house and Abe locked the door.

"You might as well join me for dinner," Abe said when Donne hesitated in the hallway. "I suppose I have enough for two."

"This isn't a social call."

"Would you rather just sit and watch me eat? Because I'm not going to let my meal get cold."

Although Donne glowered, he hung his coat and hat on hooks in the hall and followed Abe into the kitchen. He sniffed the air. "What's that?"

"Russian. Now sit."

To Abe's considerable surprise, Donne obeyed, taking the same chair he'd occupied the previous day. He rolled a cigarette while Abe finished preparing dinner. Neither of them said anything, but it was pleasant to have company while doing these small, familiar tasks, just as it was pleasing to set the table for two instead of one.

"I'm out of slivovitz," Abe said as he placed a bottle on the table. "I hope this will do instead."

Donne eyed the label. "Egri Bikavér? What's that?"

"Bull's blood." Seeing Donne's reaction, Abe laughed. "It's only a name. It's red wine. According to legend, the Ottomans had laid siege to Eger Castle. When they saw the soldiers in the castle drinking this, the Ottomans thought they were drinking bull's blood, and that the blood would make them too strong to conquer. So the Ottomans fled."

"Can't blame them." Donne uncorked the bottle and poured them each a generous glass. But he didn't touch his until Abe had brought over the food and sat down opposite him.

Abe lifted his glass. "Egészségedre!"

"I can't say that."

"Cheers, then."

Donne snorted softly, but the corners of his mouth twitched. "Cheers."

There was no interrogation over dinner. Not much talk at all, in fact, but the dual clink of cutlery and slurping of soup was conversation enough. Donne silently accepted seconds when Abe offered them.

"I haven't had a home-cooked meal in ages," Donne said thoughtfully as he gazed at the ruby liquid in his glass.

"It's not exactly home-cooked. It's all from the grocer's. I just heated it."

"Do you know how to cook?"

"I do." Although it wasn't usually worth the bother for only himself.

"I never learned. Unless you count camp cooking, but nobody wants to eat that swill. I don't have a kitchen anyway." It was a very personal admission, although Donne didn't seem to realize that. He simply twirled the glass stem between his broad finger and thumb.

"Why did you decide to move to the States?"

"Home didn't feel like home. Never had, really, but it got worse. If I was going to be a stranger anyway, might as well do it... somewhere strange."

Abe nodded thoughtfully. New York hadn't fit him well either, even though he'd arrived when young. Since the meal had evidently put Donne into a mellow mood, Abe pushed further. "Why San Francisco?"

"I fancy the weather."

Now that Abe's hands were idle, he was tempted to reach across the table and touch Donne. He stood instead, gathered their dishes, and carried them to the sink. Since the wine was gone, he returned with fresh glasses and a bottle of Cutty Sark.

"You'd keep a team of revenuers busy," Donne observed, breaking the seal.

"Are you going to turn me in, detective?"

"I'll let it pass." He poured two heathy doses and slid one across the table. Abe caught it neatly, which made Donne chuckle. "You have good hands."

"A necessity of my employment. I enjoy practicing my dexterity." Abe threw in a leer for good measure, but Donne chose to ignore it. All right. Apparently they were going to pretend that, just the previous evening and in this very room, Donne's cock hadn't been in Abe's mouth.

Donne took a long look around the kitchen. "Do you do all your drinking in here?"

"I do a lot in speakeasies and restaurants."

"No, I mean when you're home. You don't take guests into your parlor?"

Abe had no idea where this conversation was going, but he was willing to play along. "We can go into the parlor if you like, but you've been in there already. It's not any more comfortable than the kitchen."

"Dining room?"

"I use it as an office and to store my props. That leaves a WC down here and two bedrooms and another WC upstairs, in case you're wondering. We can drink here or in bed."

Again, Donne ignored the invitation. "It's unusual not to have a place to entertain visitors. The non-paying sort." He swirled the amber liquid in his glass—possibly because he was fidgety, or maybe to hide the tremor in his hand.

"I don't. Entertain, I mean. If I'm going to meet someone, we go out."

"Why?"

Abe leaned back with a grin. "My father trained as a psychoanalyst under Dr. Freud, and you're sounding a lot like him."

As Abe expected, Donne snorted, drank some scotch, and stopped his questioning about Abe's social habits. But his eyes remained full of questions; perhaps that was as necessary to his vocation as manual skill was to Abe's. "Why did you become a magician? And don't tell me it's because of the bloody veil." He waved a hand dismissively.

"It wasn't. It was my father's influence, actually. After we immigrated, he couldn't psychoanalyze anymore. He was a streetcar conductor instead. But he used to hypnotize people—mostly for fun—and he'd lecture me about the hidden actions of the mind. He and my mother hoped this would steer me toward a career as a physician. I preferred the stage." His father had died bitter with disappointment, and Abe's mother had never forgiven him.

"And the séances?"

"A natural extension, and an easy way to earn money." And then, because Donne was still silently denying the truth, Abe leaned toward him. "The veil is real, though. But I very rarely encounter spirits during my séances."

The fog in Donne's eyes hardened to ice. "You're not fooling me."

"And you're not fooling yourself. Isn't that why you returned—because you know I spoke with Birdie?"

"I returned because I'm trying to solve two murders!" His voice grew loud and his usually pale complexion reddened.

"Two?"

"Zook's dead."

Abe jerked backward in his chair. When he had the breath to speak again, he croaked, "Did you kill him? And Roy?"

"I've killed a lot of men, but not those two."

Abe believed him. "Then who did?"

"That's what I'm trying to find out." Donne's voice had dropped from an angry roar to its more usual rumble. "And right now, you're my best lead."

"I'm sorry to hear that, because I don't know anything."

Abe drained his scotch in one long swallow. He felt it burn, but the sensation had long ago stopped bothering him. He imagined it was akin to being a fire-eater, except unlike them, he was left with a pleasant buzz in his brain—a buzz that tended to keep the spirits away.

Donne had been watching him. "You know something," he finally said. "You knew Zook."

"I've spoken with him briefly after a few of my shows. That's all."

"Who knew him first—you or Gage?"

Time for a refill. Abe spoke as he poured. "Roy, and I don't know how they met. Roy knew a lot of men, and he was especially inclined toward men with money. He was good at sniffing them out."

"Zook was pretty flush for a department store clerk."

Abe spread his arms wide, not quite sloshing the liquor out of his glass. "I don't know about that either. Maybe he inherited a fortune. Maybe he was on the take with a gang. Maybe he could make dollar bills appear out of thin air."

"That'd be more your line of work, wouldn't it?"

"I can do an illusion to that effect," Abe replied, grinning. "But I have to provide the dollars up front." It was one of his least favorite acts, because although it impressed the audience, they ended up pocketing the money.

"What did Gage tell you about Zook?"

"Nothing, as far as I can recall. Look. Roy brought Zook to a few shows—four or five, I think—and Zook would sit in the front and stare at Roy as if he were the sun itself. Then Zook would wait around after the show while Roy and I packed up, and we'd chat about nothing much for a minute or two before they left."

Frowning, Donne tapped his fingers on the table. Abe wanted to know what those fingers would feel like on his skin, digging into his flesh hard enough to leave bruises or stroking slowly and gently, making him beg for more. He already suspected what Donne's fingers would taste like, but what if Donne dipped them in scotch and told Abe to suck them clean? What if Abe bit them at the same time that

Donne bit Abe's shoulder, and they both called out so loudly the neighbors heard?

"Did Gage bring other men to your shows?"

Abe laughed. "Sometimes. He was a pretty boy with a lot of suitors. But if you think one of them was jealous enough to commit murder, I doubt it. Anyone who knew Roy knew who he was and what he was after. He never tried to hide it."

In fact, Abe had envied that a little. As a man who lied for a living—or at the very least, stretched the truth beyond recognition—he'd long wondered what it would be like to be open with others, to tell them precisely who he was and what he wanted. At this point, he wouldn't even know how.

A thought occurred to Abe. Maybe belatedly, but he was no detective. "Are you sure the same person killed both of them?"

"It would be an awfully big coincidence otherwise."

"But this can be a dangerous city."

Donne shook his head. "The killer knew Gage, likely knew Zook as well."

"How can you tell?"

"They let him into their flats. He got close enough to stab Gage and strangle Zook. And Gage was naked. Most people put on clothes around strangers."

"Most do," Abe agreed sadly. Poor Roy, expecting a friend or lover and getting a blade instead.

"Stabbing and strangling, those are personal ways to kill someone—not cold and distant like a bullet. Of course, they're quieter than a gun too. Our murderer might simply have wanted to avoid disturbing the neighbors."

"*Our* murderer?"

Looking smug, Donne raised his glass in an ironic toast and took a slug. He didn't wince when he swallowed.

Abe stood, walked to the sink, and began washing dishes. He could see Donne out of the corner of his eye, watching him the way Abe's mother's cat used to watch the pigeons on the window ledge. Abe didn't exactly mind, although he didn't know whether Donne was hungry for information or hungry for him. Maybe it didn't matter.

The water ran and the dishes and pots clanked. Donne rolled a cigarette and smoked it. The little kitchen felt warm and shut in, but Abe had never minded enclosed spaces. He'd once seen Harry Houdini escape from a locked milk-can and twice saw him perform his Water Torture act. Abe had even toyed with the idea of doing escape acts himself, but his early efforts were unsuccessful, mostly because he'd settle comfortably into the straightjacket or chains and lose the will to get out.

He didn't want to get out now, either.

Abe had just put the last of the dishes into the cupboard when Donne stood and came up behind him, looming so close that his breaths tickled the back of Abe's neck. "How do you know about Birdie?" Donne whispered. Maybe he'd drawn his gun. Abe didn't turn around to see.

"I don't have all his memories, you know. Only the ones he shared with me yesterday. But I can tell you things only he and you knew. The first time the two of you made love, you were so clumsy that he thought you were a virgin. He laughed when you told him about some of the boys at school, and Birdie said it was lucky you'd finally found a man instead."

Donne didn't say anything, but his breathing grew faster and louder.

Abe closed his eyes. Sorting through a spirit's recollections was difficult. He didn't experience them as he did his own; they were more akin to a motion picture. No—a play, because they were three-dimensional and in color, with full sound, and with scent and taste and feel. He even knew what emotions the person had experienced. But these borrowed memories lacked the substance and context of his own.

"You and Birdie were in a trench, I don't know where. Everything was damp and brown and smelling like shit, and the war had been going on for a thousand years and was never going to end. But the two of you were playing cards, and Birdie was trying to make you laugh. He loved your laugh, you know. Maybe because it was rare. But your hands were shaking badly, and you'd hardly slept for days. You kept waking up with nightmares. So he told a long joke about the devil digging latrines, and then you did start to laugh. But you didn't stop. Couldn't stop. He had to slap you to quiet you, and by then he was crying."

It hurt Abe to feel the recycled anguish of the dead. He clutched the edge of the countertop and wished his whisky glass were closer. Even with his eyes shut, he saw a younger version of Donne in a helmet and muddy battledress, eyes filled not with fog or ice but with a terrible emptiness. Mouth drawn back into a corpse-like grimace.

"Birdie," whispered Donne—the real Donne, standing in Abe's kitchen with the weight of years and sorrows heavy on his broad shoulders.

Still facing away, Abe nodded. "I could reach for him now and bring him forward." Although it was an honest offer, he couldn't suppress a shudder.

"No. Let him rest."

Abe slumped with relief. "That's not up to me. But I don't have to invite him here now."

Donne moved away, leaving Abe's back feeling barren and exposed. But instead of returning to the table or leaving the kitchen, he stood against the wall, at the very same spot he'd pushed Abe into the previous day. He ran a hand through his hair, loosening it from its Brilliantine fetters. "Ghosts," he said.

"No. Spirits. I've explained the difference."

"But you said ghosts exist as well."

"They do." Abe approached him carefully. "And other... beings too. It's a complicated world. I've seen glimpses of things, heard stories. And I wonder what else lies right next to us but hidden from most people's sight."

"Things," Donne echoed.

Abe chuckled, remembering a story he'd heard a few years earlier from a retired magician. "Did you know about the Sasquatch riots?"

"The *what*?"

"In Oregon, twelve or thirteen years ago."

"I was in France then."

"Of course." Abe patted Donne's arm, and Donne didn't push him away. "They're giant hairy creatures who mostly keep to themselves in the forest. I guess a few of them decided to fight back after their home was cleared and turned to farmland."

Donne reached up, and for a moment Abe thought he was going to hit him. Instead he was shocked when Donne cradled his cheek with a wide palm. "Spirits… invade you. Doesn't that make you angry?"

Abe wanted very badly to lean into the caress. To fall into it. But then he'd be lost, and Thomas had asked him a question. "My people tell stories about two types of spirits. There are dybbuks, which are evil. When they possess a person, they make him do all kinds of terrible things. But an ibbur is the soul of a righteous man that joins a living person—always with the person's permission—in order to do a mitzvah, a good deed. You understand?"

"Yeah."

The hand was still there, warm against Abe's skin, strong even in its relaxed state. Abe's cock began to fill, and he realized he was licking his lips. "Harboring an ibbur isn't enjoyable, but neither is visiting the dentist, and I do that when necessary. Maybe it's a little like being a soldier agreeing to something difficult and dangerous in order to achieve a greater good."

"Dangerous?"

"There's a risk the spirit won't return to the other side. They become more powerful as they remain here. They can stay stuck to the host. I met someone like that once." A woman on the Lower East Side had claimed she'd come to America from Ireland sixty years earlier, although she didn't look a day past thirty. Other people had called her insane, but Abe had seen the truth in her tale, the two consciousnesses, not quite overlapping, gazing through a single pair of eyes. She told him she had been different since the ibbur began, being neither her original self nor the spirit but an entirely new entity, and one who fit poorly into the world. Abe had been much younger then, and the woman had terrified him by her very existence.

"What about the dybbuk?" Thomas asked.

Abe would have trembled were it not for Thomas's touch. "If I were the type of man who prayed, I'd pray very hard to never again encounter a dybbuk."

"But Birdie...?"

"Was a righteous man," Abe said with a smile. Meaning it.

For a moment, Thomas's hard face softened and his eyes shone bright as the sky on a sunny day. He dragged his fingertips tenderly along Abe's jawline before letting his arm fall to his side. His gaze became foggy again. "I'm not righteous."

"Nor am I." Abe smiled wickedly. "But then, you already knew that."

If Thomas's eyes were fog, his mouth was smoke: a mix of peaty scotch and tobacco. His arms caged Abe, holding him close and proving that Thomas was as hard as Abe was. But although Thomas was bigger and stronger, Abe felt powerful indeed as he worked a hand between them and squeezed Thomas's erection, causing Thomas to moan into his ear. It was a beautiful sound.

Abe squeezed again and would have kept at it, simply for the lovely noises Thomas made, but Thomas grabbed his wrist.

"You mentioned bedrooms," he panted.

11

Abe truly was a sorcerer—there was no other explanation for it. With seemingly no effort he could make Thomas forget his job, forget his past, forget safety and rationality. Thomas couldn't fight this spell and didn't want to.

Bloody hell, wasn't a man entitled to a bit of magic now and then?

He followed Abe up a narrow staircase to a short hallway. Out of long habit, he made a quick assessment of the premises. One room looked out onto a garden and was almost empty except for a few dusty boxes. Next to that was a washroom with black-and-white tile and a clawfoot tub. A plant trailed leafy stems from a pot on the windowsill. They passed built-in cupboards and drawers in the hallway, perhaps holding towels and extra bedding. He followed Abe into the second bedroom.

It overlooked Twelfth Avenue, and the window stood slightly open despite the night chill, curtains stirring in the breeze. An oriental rug covered most of the wooden floor. There wasn't much furniture—a bed, a dresser, a chair, a pair of nightstands—all made of dark wood without elaborate carving or other decoration. In fact, the entire room was plain. No pictures on the white walls, no knick-knacks cluttering the dresser or the fireplace mantel. If it weren't for the handsome blue-and-white blanket on the bed and the little stack of books on the nightstand, the room would have rivaled a bare hotel chamber.

"I saved all the fussiness for my parlor, where my guests can see it," Abe explained, matter-of-fact and unembarrassed. "I prefer simplicity where I sleep."

"Interesting, considering you're a complicated man."

"Am I?"

"You're a confidence man in fancy clothing. With props."

"So maybe you'd rather see me naked, without the props."

When Thomas arrived tonight, Abe had been dressed casually in a yellow-and-gray-striped shirt with the sleeves rolled up, without a coat or tie. Now he began to unbutton the shirt slowly, with a teasing glint in his eyes.

"Doesn't mean you won't lie to me."

Abe palmed his own crotch, his erection obvious. "*This* doesn't lie."

"Maybe not. But did you bring me up here because you want to fuck me, or because Birdie does?"

"Did you come up here because you wanted to fuck me or Birdie?"

Thomas tightened his jaw. "Does it matter?"

"I guess so, considering Birdie's not here right now."

It was funny, really. At first Thomas hadn't believed that Abe could harbor Birdie's spirit, and now he wondered if Abe might. He saw nothing of his dead lover in Abe's face, however, and when Abe shrugged out of his shirt and pulled off his undershirt, he didn't resemble Birdie at all. Where Birdie had been skinny and pale and nearly hairless, Abe was sleekly muscled and dark, with thick curls on his chest and a line of hair on his lower belly. Birdie had been as clear and straightforward as a glass of cool water on a hot summer day, but Abe was the ocean, changing and fathomless.

Abe removed his shoes and socks and unfastened his trousers. Clearly enjoying Thomas's visual appraisal, he stepped out of the last of his clothing and stood with his legs slightly spread and hands on his hips. "You see? Nothing left but me."

He was even more beautiful naked, with a trim waist and slightly plump arse. His cock stood proudly.

Still fully dressed, Thomas strode forward and grabbed Abe for a bruising kiss. There was something delightfully wicked about all that bare flesh pressed against his own wool and cotton. Perhaps Abe felt so too, because he returned the kiss with equal vigor, groaning when Thomas gnawed lightly at his lower lip.

Abe was entirely wanton and unashamed. A magician must be accustomed to carnality, seeing as he had to control and manipulate his own body in many ways. And Abe in particular, knowing well the thin line between life and death, might be eager to experience joys of the flesh. Thomas had long since tended to place a barrier between his mind and his body, and he envied Abe.

But no need for envy now, when Abe was rutting against him.

Thomas used his greater bulk to drive Abe back all the way to the wall, and when Abe tried to unbutton his shirt, Thomas grabbed his wrists and held them over Abe's head.

Some men might have struggled against that, but Abe didn't. In fact, his muscles visibly relaxed and his mouth sagged open. His pupils widened so much that they nearly eclipsed the amber of his irises. It was obviously not fear or panic that quickened his breaths. "Thomas," he begged. Not *Tommy* and not *Donne*.

"Get onto the bed. On your back."

Abe licked his lips and smiled when Thomas released him. He didn't hurry across the room, but sauntered, possibly with an extra sway to his hips. When he reached the bed, he yanked the blanket off and onto the floor and lay back on the sheets, exactly as Thomas had told him. Well, not exactly. Because Thomas hadn't said anything about what to do with his hands, but Abe grinned and rested his wrists against the rails of the headboard.

"Are you sure there's no dybbuk in you?" Thomas asked.

Abe's expression turned earnest. "There's no sin in this. Not if we both truly want it. And I know I do." Now the grin crept back. "But you're just standing there, so maybe you—"

Thomas rushed over and jumped on him, making Abe *oof* and the bedsprings protest. But Abe didn't complain. He kept his hands in place and pushed up hard with his hips. "I'd want this even if it was a sin," Thomas said. "I'm not a righteous man, remember?"

"Good."

Just for the hell of it, Thomas thrust against him a few times, and when Abe threw his head back, Thomas latched his teeth onto the juncture of Abe's neck and shoulder. Salty and so very sweet.

It took considerable effort for Thomas to regain his feet. He shrugged out of his coat—the gun in his pocket thudding softly against the floor—and then unknotted his necktie. When he reached down to tie Abe's right wrist to the headboard, Abe's cock jerked against his belly.

Abe waved his still free left hand. "I keep my neckties in the closet."

"No need." Thomas used one of Abe's socks instead.

Now Abe was the very embodiment of debauchery, his legs spread, the reddened head of his cock glistening. Color bloomed in his cheeks, his hair had erupted into soft curls, and his nipples were tight brown peaks.

Thomas slowly removed his dress shirt, undershirt, shoes, and socks, but kept his trousers on for the time being. He so rarely had the opportunity to take his time.

He sat on the mattress and slowly trailed fingers across Abe's cheeks, down his neck and sternum, over the points of his hips. Abe raised his arse, clearly inviting Thomas to stroke his groin, but Thomas palmed the inside of this thighs instead and then the solid line of his shins.

"Do you play this game often?" he asked as he twisted a nipple between finger and thumb.

"No."

"Why not?"

"I don't trust most men enough."

That made Thomas blink. "You shouldn't trust me."

"But I do. I think you're the type who does exactly what he says he will. If you say you're going to find a killer, you do. If you say you're going to do the killing, well, you do that too."

"So you understand that I will kill—that I *have*—when it suits me?"

Abe smiled. "I do. But I think that right now death isn't want you want from me."

"La petite morte, perhaps."

"A joke from you, and in French, no less." Abe's chuckle turned to a moan as Thomas bent and trapped the abused nipple between his teeth. He soothed the sharpness with a press of his tongue.

Thomas decided at that point that he had better uses for his mouth than talking. His lips and tongue explored Abe's body, sometimes aided by strategic pets with his hand. Abe's mouth remained free, and he panted, begged, and swore in at least three languages. He writhed quite prettily too.

At last Thomas couldn't take any more of his own torture. His balls ached and his nerves sang with need. He stripped out of his remaining clothes and stood for a moment, letting Abe admire him.

"*Káprázatos.*"

Based on Abe's husky voice and lustful look, Thomas took it as a compliment.

Following Abe's lascivious example, Thomas stroked himself slowly, ostentatiously. It wasn't an act he generally did with an audience. In fact, he couldn't recall the last time he'd fully undressed before fucking someone. Yet it was lovely to watch Abe's reaction: rapid breathing, wide eyes, and twitches of his as yet untouched cock. Abe had barely responded to Thomas's usual shows of power—his brute force and his Smith & Wesson—but now he seemed prepared to surrender completely.

"You could escape from those bonds if you wanted to, couldn't you?" Thomas's voice came out low and ragged.

Abe grinned in return. "There's Vaseline in the bathroom. In the medicine cabinet."

It took Thomas only a minute or so to fetch the tube, yet he half expected to return and find Abe gone. But no, Abe waited for him, legs spread even wider and knees bent, his soles resting on the mattress.

Thomas knelt between Abe's knees and wanted to plunge right in. But he found it so satisfying to just look at the body, spread out and waiting, with unfeigned eagerness in his partner's eyes. Whatever lies and half-truths Abe had told him, he'd been honest about this at least.

Abe chuckled softly. "You could put that in me, you know. I wish you would."

Thomas was unaware that he'd been tugging on himself, but he now realized that he was very close to reaching his peak. He moved his hand away quickly.

Abe didn't seem to want or need much preparation, but Thomas took it slowly nonetheless, marveling that the heat inside Abe's body didn't scorch his fingers. Ah, but if that heat was already so remarkable, how would it feel engulfing his cock?

With that thought, Thomas urged the bent knees toward Abe's chest and sank inside.

"Oh, God," Abe keened, his eyes rolling up in his head.

Thomas agreed but couldn't manage words—just grunts and desperate whimpers as he burned, as the furnace inside Abe turned him to raging flames.

Perhaps it happened very fast, or it might have taken hours; he couldn't tell. It was very much like the heat of battle, when time became a living thing with a will of its own, stretching and contracting like a python. But there were no shells exploding now. Just the sounds of panting, and flesh against flesh, and the periodic lovely music of Abe's multilingual curses.

An exquisite bomb exploded, and Thomas was turned to ash. But it was a joyous demise, knowing he'd soon rise from it like a phoenix newly hatched.

Oversensitive now, he withdrew from Abe's body, bringing a

whimper of protest. Thomas quickly countered the lack with two fingers, pressing just so, as he took Abe's cock into his mouth.

It didn't surprise him at all when Abe rapidly climaxed with a triumphant shout.

But then Thomas did a strange thing indeed. Normally he would have wiped himself perfunctorily clean, perhaps using a pillow or a discarded sock. Then he would have put on his clothing, straightened his hair, marched downstairs for his hat and overcoat, and left.

Instead he lay on the mattress beside Abe and, after retrieving the blanket off the floor, spread it over them. He untied Abe's left hand, but when he reached for the other, Abe laughed and waved it, demonstrating that he'd freed it himself.

"I don't have the energy to leave yet," Thomas informed him, expecting Abe to kick him out of the bed.

"Whatever you're going home to, is it better than this?"

"No." Thomas's mattress was thinner, the radiators inconsistent, the neighborhood noisier.

"Then you might as well stay."

"What do you want from me?"

"I've had as much from you as I can manage tonight, thanks." Abe sat up slightly so he could turn off the bedside light. That left the room in darkness, although the streetlamps provided a bit of illumination through the uncurtained window.

"It's too early to sleep."

"Call it a nap then." Abe yawned. "Call it whatever you want."

It must have been another of his enchantments: Thomas's eyelids grew so heavy he had to close them. Even under the blanket, the room felt a little chilly, and he found himself moving closer to Abe for warmth. Abe scooted over as well, until they were cuddled together like a pair of newlyweds and not two near strangers. Thomas found his muscles relaxing and his thoughts dissipating like fog on a sunny afternoon.

He woke up much later, possibly hours later, lying on his side and wrapped around Abe's smooth, warm back. His arm was trapped and had gone to sleep, but he didn't try to move it.

"You're a noisy thinker." Abe sounded sleepy and a little grouchy.

"This isn't right."

"Because we're both men?"

"Because we are who we are."

"Well, tonight we can be men who sleep comfortably with other men."

He made it sound so easy. But it wasn't. "Even if one of us is a killer?" Thomas asked.

"Nobody's killing anyone tonight. Or... you know, whoever offed Roy and Zook, how do we know he won't come for me next?" Abe didn't sound especially alarmed at the idea, just thoughtful.

"Why would he?"

"No idea. But I knew both of them and saw them both the night Roy was murdered. So I guess it's possible."

Thomas huffed impatiently. "If you know something more, now would be a good time to tell me."

"I don't. But I'd feel safer if you stayed the whole night, detective."

That was the biggest load of horseshit Thomas had ever heard, but—tingling arm aside—he was too comfortable to protest. It was almost too much to even think of leaving the warm bed, putting on clothes, traveling across the city, and trudging upstairs to his gloomy flat. "I won't stay past morning, though."

"Right. You have a killer to track down. I'm going to help you, though."

"What?"

Abe rolled over to face him. "I feel kind of responsible. Roy was my assistant—I watched that kid grow up. And the two of them were at my show. Besides, if the killer does have a reason to bump me off, I'd rather find him first."

"You're not a detective."

"But I'm good at figuring people out."

"Abe—"

"I've made up my mind about this. So unless you're going to shoot me, you're stuck with me."

Thomas wasn't as dismayed as he should have been. "I expect locking you up somewhere would do me no good."

"Nope," Abe replied smugly. Then he turned back around and settled more firmly against Thomas, pressing his arse into Thomas's groin.

"I'm not up for another round. Too old for twice in one night."

"How old are you?"

Thomas had stopped keeping track and had to calculate in his head. "Thirty-six."

Abe scoffed. "I'm ten years older than you. If I can fuck again, so can you."

As if on cue—or maybe it was the firm pressure of Abe's arse—Thomas's cock began to stir. But he was still distracted. "You don't look forty-six."

"Forty-seven in December, in fact. And it's the ibburs I have to thank."

"How so?"

"Remember that Irish woman I told you about? Being possessed makes people age more slowly. I'm not sure why—something to do with life forces or the veil or... I don't know. I've only spent a short time with spirits in me, so it hasn't affected me as much as it did her."

Thomas stroked Abe's flank. "It's a rather nice side effect. One many would envy."

Abe stopped rocking his hips and grabbed Thomas's wrist very hard. "Is it worth it, though? Would you take in the spirits of the dead —have them inside you, sharing their memories and emotions—if it meant you'd look younger?"

"No," Thomas said with a shudder.

"What I do, some people call it a gift, and maybe it is. But it's a curse too. Don't forget that."

Then Abe wiggled around again and kissed him. As it turned out, Thomas *was* capable of a second round.

And when they were done, he slept deeply.

12

Abe never conducted séances on Sundays. He could have made some money doing it, because that was the only day off for some working people. But spiritualism on the sabbath made certain religious leaders uneasy, and they didn't seem to care that Sundays weren't Abe's sabbath. They'd made a little fuss in the past, and to avoid a repeat of that unpleasantness, he took the day off to read and develop new techniques. Or to stroll the Embarcadero in search of company.

Of course, on this Sunday he already had company in the form of a big, blond English private dick who was currently staring at him over a plate of scrambled eggs. Thomas looked a little rumpled in the previous day's clothing, but he smelled of Abe's soap, which was oddly gratifying.

"You're not my wife," Thomas announced. He waved to indicate the entire kitchen, as if that somehow proved his point.

"Agreed. As we both know, I'm not properly equipped for that position."

"You don't have to make me breakfast."

"No, I don't. But I'm hungry, and it'd be damned rude if I didn't give you some food too."

Thomas scowled, but he also scooped up a forkful of eggs and popped it into his mouth. He followed it with a bite of toast and a swallow of coffee. "I'd rather have tea," he grumbled.

"We are in America, so you have coffee."

"Why did you move to the States?"

It was a non sequitur, but Abe didn't mind. "I was six. I didn't have much choice in the matter."

"Why did your parents move?"

"Oy." That was a story Abe had heard many times, mostly in conjunction with a lecture about how he ought to be a more grateful son and pursue a more appropriate career path. "Life isn't always peaceful for Jews. It wasn't that bad in Hungary at the time, but there were pogroms in Russia, and my parents feared the sentiment would spread. And in the Austro-Hungarian Empire, everyone was supposed to be a good citizen of the empire and forsake their own traditions. Also, there was the likelihood I'd be conscripted into the army when I grew older."

Thomas's hand shook and he spilled some coffee. He set the mug down. "You never served."

"I was thirty-five when conscription began here, so I don't know if I'd have been called up. But my mentor, Emil Magnus, used to be a physician. He wrote me a medical exemption."

"You lied to escape service."

Abe picked up his fork and looked Thomas squarely in the eyes. "I see spirits of the dead. Sometimes I'm possessed by them. Can you imagine what would happen in a war zone?" The horror in Thomas's expression suggested that, indeed, he could. Good. Abe had revealed his ability to very few people, and it was important that those people understood what a burden it was. "I avoid hospitals for the same reason."

Thomas frowned. "You're implying that spirits remain near where they've died, but Birdie died in France."

"No, it's not like that. They're not bound the same way we are. I think they can go anywhere. But where they tend to go—or at least where I can sense them—is near something or someone important to them."

"Birdie had no interest in San Francisco."

Was Thomas really this thick? Surely not—he'd make a terrible detective otherwise. He was simply blind when it came to matters close to him, as so many people were. "He had interest in you," Abe said softly.

"You said he loved me."

"He still does. It's.... I don't think it's the same, but—"

"You're telling me that love survives death." Thomas's lip was lifted in scorn.

"Why not? Other emotions do. And love is so central to who we are."

"How can you love if you don't have a body?"

Ah. Abe affected his father's thick accent and the tone he used when attempting to plumb the depths of someone's consciousness. "You are confusing love with lust, young man."

"Same thing."

"I don't think even you believe that," Abe said in his own voice. "There's nothing wrong with lust, but love exists on its own. When I was young, I had a close friend, Benjamin Ginsburg. He loved me as much as I loved him, but for him, it was like I was his brother. He wasn't queer. I, on the other hand, definitely did not think of him as a brother." He hadn't meant to mention Ben—he'd never told *anyone* about him—but it slipped out. A way to make his point.

And he'd probably given away even more than he intended, because Thomas nodded astutely. "That's why you moved to California."

Yes, Abe had been right—Thomas was no fool, except when it came to himself.

"Partly." Abe passed the plate with the good brown bread from last night's dinner, sliced and toasted. Thomas took two slices and they ate in silence. The newspaper lay on the table, still folded, and Abe skimmed the headlines. "Election's coming up. Who will you vote for?"

"Nobody."

"You're not a citizen?"

"I am, but I won't vote. It doesn't matter anyway. Politicians—every one of them is a bigger scam artist than you."

Abe laughed. "Likely. But I'll vote for Hoover anyway."

"You don't like Catholics?"

"Ah, so you are paying attention to the election. I don't care if someone's Catholic—they're all goyim anyway. And I do like that Smith opposes Prohibition. But he's tied to Tammany Hall, and Hoover's a steady man. A solid businessman. You know, 'a chicken for every pot.'"

As Abe expected, Thomas snorted dismissively. "That's claptrap."

"Maybe. But poverty—real poverty—isn't claptrap. I've seen babies dead in their mothers' arms. A hundred and twenty-five women and girls killed at the Triangle factory." Although he hadn't wanted to visit the site of the fire, he'd been drawn there nonetheless. He'd encountered the spirits of some of the dead, including a sixteen-year-old girl named Tillie, who'd leapt from the ninth floor. Her spirit begged him to tell her sister about the stash of money hidden under a floorboard in their apartment. When Abe tracked down the sister and told her, she'd broken down and sobbed in his arms.

Thomas stopped arguing and finished his breakfast. When his plate was empty, he carried it to the sink and then disappeared into the hallway.

"There's no point trying to leave without me," Abe called. "I'll find you."

"How?"

Birdie would lead him—but maybe Thomas was already figuring that out. In any case, Thomas waited for him to clear his own dishes; washing up could wait for later. Abe joined him in the hallway to don his overcoat and hat.

They took the streetcar rather than a taxi, and Thomas didn't say a single word as they rattled along. He leapt off so suddenly in the Tenderloin that Abe almost missed the stop and then had to hurry to keep up with Thomas's longer legs.

"It's a dump," Thomas said when they reached his apartment. He hung up his hat, overcoat, and suit coat and immediately began to strip off the rest in an entirely businesslike manner, very different from the previous night.

Abe looked around, which didn't take long; there was very little to see. While the walls and outside windowpanes were grimy, everything else was clean and neat: the floor swept, the bed folded into the wall, the surfaces in the tiny bathroom gleaming. "I've lived in much worse," he said mildly, which was true. When he was a child, his family had shared a single room in a tenement, the lavatory down the hall used by the entire floor. They'd considered themselves lucky not to have an outhouse.

"So've I." Thomas was naked now, his magnificence even more marked in these modest surroundings. He hung his suit in the closet, stuffed his shirt and underclothes into a laundry bag, and went into the bathroom without closing the door. He turned on the shower, which sounded barely more than a trickle.

"You could have showered at my house," Abe pointed out, but Thomas didn't reply.

Once he was dried and dressed, they took another streetcar, this time disembarking in North Beach. They entered a building on Montgomery just off Columbus. The ground floor housed a plumbing supply store, but Thomas took them upstairs, where there was a closed door on each side of the hallway. One door was unmarked but the other read *Thomas Donne, Private Detective*. Thomas let them in.

"This is nicer than your apartment," Abe said.

"Gotta make a good impression on clients. You know that."

The outer office had an unused air to it. The inner sanctum, however…. Thomas obviously spent a lot of time there. It smelled of him, in a pleasant way—cigarettes and Brilliantine, aftershave and rum. A large shelf was stuffed with books, a file cabinet lurked in a corner, and three chairs and a small table took up a good bit of space. But the star of the room was the massive desk, scarred yet sturdy, as if it had successfully made it through a war or two.

Having removed his overcoat, hat, and suit coat, Thomas propped open a window before collapsing into his high-backed leather chair. He immediately began to roll a cigarette.

Abe perched on the corner of the desk. "Where do you keep the booze?"

"This isn't a speakeasy."

But after glowering for a moment, Thomas reached into a desk drawer and produced a bottle of Bacardi. He brought out a pair of glasses and poured, filling Abe's especially full. Then he watched with something akin to admiration as Abe gulped his and held out the glass for more.

"Never seen anyone handle his liquor like you," Thomas said, refilling.

Abe gave a mock toast, not admitting out loud that he handled liquor a hell of a lot better than he handled sobriety. "All right, detective. How do we find this killer?"

Thomas grumbled something that sounded like "*We* don't," then took a pen and black-covered notebook out of the center drawer, opened the book to a page near the middle, and looked at Abe.

"Name everyone Gage knew."

ALTHOUGH ABE COULDN'T BEGIN to list everyone who had been acquainted with Roy, he tried his best. Boys that Roy had lurked with on street corners when he was younger. Men he'd taken to bed.

"What about other people he'd worked for?"

Abe shook his head. "He didn't tell me about them. And I didn't ask."

Thomas didn't look pleased, and Abe didn't blame him. It wasn't a promising list. "What about your other employees?"

"I have two other assistants, but they rarely work together."

"Names? Addresses?"

"Do we have to drag them into this?"

Thomas stared until Abe gave in.

They walked down to the Embarcadero and dug up a few of Ray's acquaintances, but most of them hadn't even realized he was dead. Then they stopped for lunch—they went Dutch—before hitting the streets again. They got nowhere.

"I'd never have the patience for this line of work." Abe leaned against a building and watched smoke rise from Thomas's cigarette.

"Then go home."

Abe grinned at him, although he suspected it wasn't seen. Thomas was staring at the streetcars in front of the Ferry Building. He finally said, "What if we went to his room?"

"You think somebody might have seen something?"

"No. But maybe his spirit's there. He can tell you himself who did it."

"Unlikely."

Thomas insisted, however, and since they were closer to the YMCA, Abe figured they might as well go there first. Roy's spirit was just as likely to be there as at the Ambassador. But when Abe roamed the halls, all he encountered was a sailor who'd died five years earlier and wasn't ready to accept the need to move on.

"There's nothing for you here," Abe told him patiently; he'd had this same conversation with other spirits. Thomas looked on, brow furrowed.

"I was only nineteen," lamented the spirit.

"I know. But you're never going to get a day older than that. Stop torturing yourself over what you can't have."

"I miss my family."

"And I'm sure they miss you. But kid, everyone's time on this side is limited. Sooner or later they'll join you." That was a promise Abe couldn't back up with facts, but he *thought* it was true. He hoped so.

"I'm lonely."

"That's because you're insisting on sticking where you don't belong. Let go. Then you won't be lonely anymore."

Abe couldn't see spirits any more than he could see electricity, but he imagined that this one was biting its spectral lip as it considered. Poor kid. Hanging around this place for so long, and his only hope for company was Abe, who didn't have time or energy to comfort all the spirits who came his way.

"I have to go," Abe said. "And so do you."

"I'm scared."

"If there was anything in the beyond to be scared of, it would've already got you. You'll be fine."

After a brief pause, the spirit disappeared. There was no way to tell whether it had taken Abe's advice or merely moved somewhere else for the time being. Abe slumped against the wall and looked at Thomas. "I need a drink."

"You look like hell."

"Like I said, I need a drink."

They found a speakeasy only two blocks away, and Abe had four shots of rye while Thomas nursed one and watched him. Abe was starting on his fifth when Thomas finally spoke, gesturing at Abe's glass. "Explain."

Abe didn't want to. But Thomas was a fucking detective who'd gnaw and tug until he got the answers he sought. "Getting close to the veil like that, it...." Drained him. Tore him. Pulled him so firmly that one day he'd give in. "It hurts." He lifted the glass. "This helps. And don't give me your damned pity, because I don't want it. Probably don't deserve it."

Thomas simply shook his head.

They went to the Ambassador after that, which was blessedly free of any spirits, including Roy's. Then they stopped by Helen's apartment, nearby. She didn't answer the door. Probably off enjoying a late Sunday afternoon with her girlfriend.

"Rosie lives close to your apartment," Abe said. "But I don't know if she's home."

"We can try."

They walked together, a tiny island of silence among the bustle of the street. When they paused before crossing a street, Thomas turned his head slightly. "Is it always like that for you? How can you stand it?"

Not pity, Abe thought, but an honest question. "Booze. And I usually keep myself pretty closed off—like putting in earplugs, you know? That helps."

"But you opened yourself up to look for Gage."

"I said I'd help you."

Rosie lived two stories above a jazz club, and her building was in better shape than Thomas's. It even had an elevator. When Abe knocked on her door, she answered right away, wrapped in a pink bathrobe and with her hair a bit mussed, as if she'd just woken from a nap. Her eyes widened when she caught sight of Thomas.

"Sorry to disturb you, sweetheart," Abe said. "Detective Donne here wants to ask you a few questions."

Now she looked alarmed. "Detective?"

"Private eye. Rosie, Roy's dead."

She covered her mouth with her hand. She'd carried a bit of a torch for Roy at first—she and Helen both, with his good looks—and knowing he wasn't interested in dames hadn't made much of a difference. Fortunately for everyone, the women's interest had cooled, and the three of them had become friends of a sort. "What happened?" she asked.

"Murdered. Donne's trying to figure out by who."

Nodding mutely, she stepped back to let them in.

Abe had been to Rosie's place three or four times before, but only briefly, stopping by to pick her up before a show. She had two rooms plus a bathroom, and she'd made efforts to make her apartment homelike. Knickknacks were scattered here and there, and a few bright pillows decorated the shabby furniture. She'd hung magazine photos on the wall: a few glamorous Hollywood stars and some exotic travel locales.

She sat heavily on her unmade bed and waved Abe and Thomas toward chairs. "I probably have something to drink," she said vaguely. She wasn't crying, but her eyes looked misty.

"Don't worry about it, sister," Thomas said. He wasn't gentle about it yet somehow implied sympathy. He pulled his pen and black notebook from his pocket. "Do you know who might have done it?"

"No, I...." She squared her shoulders. "I don't know. Was it a robbery?"

"Maybe."

Thomas hadn't mentioned that possibility to Abe. Before Abe could comment on it, though, Thomas pushed on. "What makes you ask?"

"He had some money lately. I don't know where from. Roy is—was—like that. He'd get some dough and live high for a little while until he was broke again. I used to tell him he should put some away." She looked down at her clasped hands. "I guess that doesn't matter anymore."

"Who else knew he was flush?"

"Everyone, probably. He liked to brag. Show off, you know?"

"These people he'd show off to, mostly friends of his? Would any of them murder him for his money?"

Her bleak expression answered for her. Roy had been acquainted with some rough men, some of them maybe desperate enough to kill over very little. He thought he was tougher than they were.

Thomas had a few more questions, but Rosie didn't have much in the way of answers, and soon he gave up. "Thanks for your time," he said, standing up.

As Abe and Rosie stood, she asked him, "You want me there at one tomorrow?"

"I don't know. Maybe I should cancel tomorrow's séance." His experiences over the past few days had left him feeling exhausted, and he could afford to take a few days off. Besides, he wanted to stick close to Thomas.

Rosie set a hand on Abe's arm. "It's really nice of you to pay for a detective. I bet the cops don't care at all that Roy's dead. They'll never do anything about it."

"I'm not paying."

Her brow furrowed. "Then who is?"

Abe looked at Thomas, who merely stood there like a monolith in a cheap suit. "He won't tell me," Abe admitted.

That only added to her confusion. She cocked her head and

squinted. "Then what are you doing with him, Abe? Why are you—" Her eyes widened and then her lips pressed tight together. She was a very perceptive woman. "Abe."

"It's— Don't worry, sweetheart. I do want Roy's killer caught. And I'm hoping he's not after me. You be careful too, you hear? Don't trust anyone."

Her smile was brittle. "I never do."

Rosie walked them to the door. She gave Thomas a curt nod when he said good-bye and caught Abe's arm before he could follow Thomas down the hallway. "You're the one who needs to be careful. That man is dangerous."

"All men are dangerous, sweetheart."

13

B ack on the street, Thomas looked at his new shadow. "Go home. We're not getting anywhere."

"You're not giving up this easily, are you?"

"I need to think."

Abe gave him an already-familiar grin, one that said he knew he was irresistible. "You might as well think during dinner."

Thomas should have made him leave. Abe wasn't his partner and shouldn't be tagging along. Only... it was nice to have company with meals. Fine. Abe could scram after they ate.

Thomas flagged down a taxi and Abe scrambled in beside him, eager as a puppy. It wasn't a long trip, not much over a mile, but Thomas was footsore and not in the mood to scale hills. The car let them off just a couple of blocks from his office.

"Italian." Abe sounded pleased as he followed Thomas inside.

Although Thomas liked the food at Fior's, he couldn't often afford to eat there. Still, the owner, Marianetti, had a seemingly perfect memory of every customer who stepped foot in his restaurant. He greeted Thomas like a long-lost friend. "Mr. Donne! It's been so long since we've seen you."

"You have a table free?"

"For you? Of course!"

They checked their hats and coats and followed him to a spot in the back, where the dim lighting lent a cozy ambience. "You want to start with some red coffee?" Marianetti asked with a wink. "Or maybe you brought your own drinks."

"Red coffee, sure. And if you could find some grappa?"

"I might." Marianetti handed them menus and bustled away.

They made the owner a very happy man that night. Abe drank several cups of red coffee—wine—and most of a bottle of grappa, and Thomas ordered enough food to fill even his stomach: oysters, prosciutto with fruit, bread-and-cheese soup, ravioli, and osso buco. Abe ate his share, too, and did most of the talking. He had stories about New York City and San Francisco, and even a tale about a coffeehouse his father would take him to in Budapest when Abe was very young. "He'd give me paper and pencils and tell me to practice my letters, but mostly I drew pictures."

"You were an artist?"

"I was never any good at it. But I liked being there with my father. The cakes were good too. Have you ever had Dobos torte?"

"No."

"It seemed like it had a hundred layers." Abe switched from dreamy to thoughtful. "I wonder if there's someplace in San Francisco to get it."

"Not here at Fior's."

That grin again. "I'll be satisfied with the poached pears."

Nothing in their conversation was important, and it certainly wasn't going to help solve the case, but Thomas was happy to stretch things out. Sitting with Abe among a sea of other diners, all of them eating and talking, he felt for once as if he wasn't alone. As if maybe somehow, somewhere, there might be a place for him.

And pigs would fly.

Thomas and Abe sat quietly after the meal, relaxing with cigarettes and strong coffee. Out of habit, Thomas scanned the room, and every time he brought his attention back to his own table, Abe was staring at him. "Why a private detective?" Abe finally asked.

"It pays the bills."

"I've seen your apartment. You could do better working the docks."

"It's none of your business why I do it."

"Nope, it ain't," Abe said cheerfully. "But I think you're gonna tell me anyway."

"Why would I do that?"

"'Cause nobody's ever asked you before and it's nice that someone cares enough to wonder."

The bastard's words hit Thomas like a bullet, making his hands shake and ears roar. He almost got up and stormed out of the place. Let Abe pay the damn bill. But he knew that if he stepped outside, the open air would press down on him and steal his breath, and the ground would pitch and roll under his feet.

"I was a copper before the war, and then again after. A bobby. Decided to go out on my own when I came to the States. Less trouble that way." He scowled at Abe, who was squinting at him. "What?"

"I'm trying to picture you in the black uniform and the tall helmet with the shiny star on it."

"I prefer a suit."

"Sure. But you'd look good in the uniform, I bet. Imposing."

That wasn't even worth a response. Thomas knew that Abe was needling him. Goading him. Hoping he would respond by dragging him to his office and fucking the insolence out of him. Which wasn't an unattractive scenario, except Thomas knew that no amount of sex would make Abe less audacious.

"Why'd you become a policeman in the first place? And don't tell me it was because it paid the bills."

"Who says I put that much thought into it? If a job comes when you need one, you take it."

Abe looked as if he was going to say something but stopped. He toyed with his empty coffee cup, stained red from the wine. When he spoke, he kept his gaze fixed on the table. "Birdie told me a few things about you."

Thomas swore under his breath. "I'm none of your business. I'm not—"

"I didn't ask him; he just shared. Things he wanted me to know, although I don't know why. So don't be angry at me, and there's no use being angry at him either. He's dead."

Punching the bastard would make Marianetti angry, but Thomas clenched his hands into fists anyway. If Abe noticed, which he likely did, he apparently didn't care. "You came from a rich family. Nannies, public school, holidays abroad. Policeman is an unusual career choice for someone like that. And you were only a private in the army. Why?"

"Ask bloody Birdie," Thomas growled.

"He's not here right now, and I can't face more spirits today."

Damn this magician and his smug face! "I walked away from my family when I was seventeen. My father would have disowned me at any rate."

"Because?"

"We agreed on nothing. I got into fights at school and drank when I was home. I wasn't interested in marrying any of his friends' daughters. And when my older brother confronted me about my behavior, I beat him so badly he ended up in hospital."

Abe grunted and sat back in his chair, as if he'd known this all along.

Although Abe offered to pay for their dinners, Thomas refused. Abe had provided dinner the night before and breakfast this morning, and Thomas still had money from Townsend in his pocket. By the time they got out onto the street, the fog had gathered, muffling the sounds of streetcars and tires.

"I'm going to my flat now, and you're going to your nice little house."

To Thomas's surprise, Abe nodded. "All right. I could use some rest."

"Don't let anyone in, not even if you know them. Especially if you know them."

Abe's eyes danced with amusement, flickering flames in the night's chill. "I can defend myself."

"What happened to Gage and Zook wasn't stage artifice."

"You were there at my last show, weren't you?"

"So?"

Abe stepped closer and lowered his voice. "That trick where I catch the bullet? I wasn't lying when I said others have died doing that."

"Well, you won't catch a real bullet from a real killer. Or dodge his knife."

"Maybe not."

"Do you *want* to die?"

Abe paused as if he were truly considering the answer. "Not especially. But I know death, and there are things in life that scare me more."

"Like what?"

Instead of answering, Abe tipped his hat and walked away.

MOST LIKELY DUE to all the excellent meals he'd had lately, Thomas slept heavily. When the quiet click of his door woke him, he shot out of bed and dove for his gun. Fortunately he recognized the intruder before pulling the trigger.

"You pick locks as well."

"Of course I do," said Abe. "It's one of the first things I learned."

Thomas returned the gun to his bedside table and shambled to the bathroom, where he took a long piss and scrubbed his face at the sink. He returned to the main room to find Abe sitting on the edge of the bed. The clock read 8:17. He couldn't recall the last time he'd slept so late.

"Why are you here?" Thomas wanted a shower, but it was

Monday morning and he wanted answers even more. He began to pull on fresh clothing.

"So I can go with you."

"Go where?"

"You tell me."

"You're so bloody infuriating! Just because we fucked doesn't mean you can attach yourself to me like a limpet on a rock."

Abe fell back on the mattress and deliberately bounced a few times as if testing the springiness. "No. But we can do it again if you want. I'm game."

"I've work to do."

Now Abe popped back up, expression serious. "You have a plan. You came up with it last night over dinner—I could see it in your eyes—but I don't know what it is. So now you're going to tell me and I'm going to help you."

Thomas was beginning to wonder if mind reading was one of Abe's talents. It made Thomas uneasy that Abe was so clearly wise to him, especially when Thomas was still unsure how to distinguish Abe's lies from his truths. But he also didn't want to waste time in arguments he'd lose.

He finished buttoning his shirt and fastened his trousers, and then he rolled and lit a cigarette. "You've already been drinking, haven't you?"

"But I'm not drunk."

Thomas pulled a chair close to the bed, as if he were a guest in his own home, and lowered himself into it with a sigh. "I've been going about this case backwards."

"How so?"

"Chasing dead ends about who Gage knew, that's messy. Better if I start by knowing the killer's motive, and then I can narrow it down from there."

"Interesting." Abe stood and walked the few steps to the open window. He turned his back to it and leaned against the casing, lower lip caught between his teeth. "I thought you said the motive was robbery."

"No, your Rosie said that. I simply didn't rule it out. Gage's room was thoroughly tossed when I found him. Someone was searching for something. But Zook's place was untouched, so I'm thinking maybe he got offed because he was a witness."

"But Zook wasn't murdered at Roy's place."

Thomas watched smoke rise lazily from the end of his cigarette. "I think the killer showed up at Roy's place while Zook was there. And Roy lets him in because he knows the fellow. They both send Zook packing. Then...." He made a slicing motion across his throat. "Roy dies. Maybe they argued first, I don't know. The killer ransacks the room in search of whatever. Maybe finds it. But then he realizes that Zook can place him at the scene of the crime, so he goes after him too." It was helpful to think out loud like this; he'd never tried it before.

"How does the killer know where Zook lives?"

"Don't know. Maybe they're acquainted. Maybe Gage told him at some point. Or... Zook's got a phone, so maybe the killer got his address from the operator. Or rang Zook himself and asked." Still too many unknowns, but it was a step in the right direction.

"So it's not necessarily a robbery per se. Roy might have had something the killer wanted. Some of Zook's jewelry?"

"Perhaps. I think I know how to find out."

Abe straightened up and stepped away from the window. "How?"

"We're going to my office. I need to make a call."

"IF YOU HADN'T TRACKED Roy, he'd be alive now." Abe sat on the edge of Thomas's desk, glaring at him.

"I don't know that."

"Because it's just a coincidence that you tell this Townsend fellow where Roy is and within hours Roy's dead."

"Unlikely. But if I hadn't done it, another detective would. Besides, how was I to know this would be the result?" Thomas pushed away a pang of conscience as he said that. He'd known from the start that

Townsend's story about mentoring the boy was nonsense, and although he hadn't expected murder as the outcome, he'd suspected that Gage wasn't going to be nurtured in Townsend's bosom.

"Did Townsend kill them?" Abe asked.

"If he did, I don't understand why he'd pay me good money to investigate."

"To deflect suspicion?"

Thomas shrugged. "Could be."

"So, what? You're going to wave your gun at him until he confesses?"

"It's often a productive technique."

"Not with me." Abe huffed and launched himself off the desk and toward the bookshelf as if an old edition of the *California Penal Code* fascinated him. He trailed a finger along the wood as if checking for dust. Thomas knew him well enough by now; the set of Abe's shoulders showed he was having trouble getting out something he wanted to say. And since there was very little he had trouble saying, this was probably important.

"I can help with Townsend." Abe kept his back to Thomas as he spoke.

"You've a gun to point at him as well?"

"The only gun I own is the one I use in my show, and I keep it locked up tight."

Thomas wondered whether it operated like a real gun, shooting real bullets that would actually kill someone. But that was immaterial now, and anyway, Abe might not tell him. "How can you help?"

"Spirits are... powerful. I've told you that." Still averting his gaze from Thomas, Abe returned to the open window and stared through it, perhaps watching the pigeons on the window ledges across the street or the fog tendrils melting away to blue sky. "If a spirit possesses me, I become powerful too."

"You don't age properly."

"That's part of it, yes. With Birdie's help I could... persuade Townsend to give us some information."

"Persuade?" Thomas's heart beat slowly and steadily.

"It's not pleasant, and it doesn't always work. I've seen it done three times. Done it once myself." He shuddered. "It's one reason I moved here—to get away from the people in New York who would have... have used me as a tool."

"Because you have too pure a soul to get mixed up with that lot."

Still facing away, Abe made a sound that might or might not have been a laugh. "Nothing pure about me. But they were using dybbuks, and that...." Another shudder, this one more violent. "I came here out of self-preservation."

"And yet you're willing to do this with Townsend."

Abe looked over his shoulder. "Birdie is not a dybbuk. An ibbur's still rough, but it's not nearly as bad."

"If you're willing and it'll get me some answers, I'm all for it." Better than wearing away the soles of his shoes and getting nowhere. And also better than pointing a gun, although he'd keep his handy nonetheless.

After a moment, Abe wandered to the other window, which had an identical view but was closed. He twisted the lock and tried to lift the sash, which had evidently been painted shut. After a short period of tugging and grunting, it broke free and he slid the window open, leaning out so far that Thomas was faintly worried he'd fall. Despite that concern, Thomas admired the curve of Abe's arse under the taut fabric of his trousers. Perhaps that was Abe's intent.

"You do realize," Abe said after ducking back inside, "he's not going to pay you anymore after today."

"That had occurred to me."

"Then why go through with this?"

"Because if I don't, it's unlikely I'll solve the case."

Abe shrugged. "So just walk away."

"I told him I'd find the murderer, and I will."

"Even if nobody pays for your work?" When Thomas didn't answer, Abe prowled closer, his gaze sharp. "A mensch."

"What?"

"You're a genuine mensch. I didn't think I'd ever meet one."

Uncomfortable with the scrutiny, Thomas busied himself with tobacco and paper. "I don't know what that means."

Abe smiled enigmatically and returned to the bookcase and the penal code.

"Section 286," Thomas said as he lit his cigarette.

"What's that?"

"The crime against nature."

Abe laughed. "Do you plan to bring me down to the police station for that, detective?"

Thomas's response was waylaid by heavy footsteps in the hallway. A moment later the outer door opened and Townsend sailed through from the outer office. "Mr. Donne, I don't— Oh." He stopped in his tracks and raised his eyebrows at Abe. "I wasn't aware you had company."

Still holding his cigarette, Thomas stood and crossed to the center of the room. "Herbert Townsend, meet Abe France."

"The magician!" Townsend appeared more surprised than alarmed as he shook Abe's hand. "I've heard you're quite talented."

Abe had a relaxed smile. "Thank you, sir. I'd be honored if you'd attend one of my shows. Just let me know when you'll be coming and I'll reserve the best seat in the house."

"Ah. I'd be delighted."

It was an odd little dance: neither man trusting the other, yet each pretending an effortless bonhomie. A showman and a politician at their finest. Thomas could never enact that charade so well.

"Have a seat," he said.

Townsend hung his coat and hat and sat down. Abe took the chair beside him, and Thomas planted himself behind his desk, pulling a bottle of Bacardi and three glasses from the drawer. Although Abe shook his head before Thomas poured, Townsend seemed eager for his portion. "I don't know that I can abide a teetotaler," he said jovially, nudging at Abe's empty glass with one fat finger.

"I'm no supporter of the temperance movement. But I do avoid liquor before I work."

A masterful lie, Thomas thought, especially because it was the literal truth: alcohol would inhibit Abe's spiritual abilities, and he was planning to use those abilities soon. But Townsend no doubt assumed Abe was simply referring to a preference for remaining sober before performing a show or séance.

In any case, Townsend seemed satisfied with Abe's explanation. He took a careful sip of his rum. "I assume you've called me here for a good reason, Donne."

"Zook's dead."

"Yes, yes." Townsend attempted and abandoned a sorrowful expression. "Munroe told me. Such a shame."

"That's two, Mr. Townsend. Two dead young men. And I'd like to make sure it doesn't become three."

Townsend's face went red. "If this is an attempt to extort a larger fee, Mr. Donne—"

"My fee's good enough. All I want is information."

Some of the unhealthy color faded from Townsend's cheeks, and he went from offended to wary. "What sort of information? I've told you everything I know."

"You've told me what you want *me* to know, but lies won't help me catch the killer. I doubt you really care who did in Gage, or Zook for that matter. Tell me what you're really after and I might have a hope of solving this thing."

"I don't know what you mean."

Unlike Abe, Townsend was a poor liar. He probably got through life with a combination of bluster, power, and wealth, not needing much skill at prevarication.

Thomas discovered he'd finished his cigarette so he rolled another. Abe sat with uncharacteristic quiet, his hands folded in his lap like an obedient schoolboy. Looking at that innocent face, nobody would guess the depths of his potential wickedness.

"When you first hired me, I assumed Gage had something on you. Blackmail. Or maybe he'd stolen money from you. But now I think he stole something more important than money, something that's important to someone else too. What did he take?"

"Nothing," Townsend lied. "I simply want justice done."

"I doubt you care one whit about justice. You care about yourself. And that's fair enough—most people do. But I need you to come clean."

Townsend finished his rum and slammed the glass onto the desk. It took him a moment to heave himself out of the chair. "I'm disappointed, Mr. Donne. I'd truly hoped this could evolve into a long-term professional relationship." He started for the coat rack.

"Don't leave yet, Mr. Townsend."

It was Abe who'd spoken, but the accent came from neither Budapest nor New York but instead from London. The voice was higher too, and younger, with none of the melancholy that touched even the jokes Abe made. Hearing it made Thomas's heartbeat turn thready and weak.

Thomas and Townsend both stared at Abe, who remained in his chair. His eyes had turned the color of a summer sky, and his lips curled crookedly, exactly like the lips Thomas had kissed a decade earlier.

"What the devil!" Townsend exclaimed.

Abe stood and walked toward Townsend, but instead of his usual agile grace, his movements were slightly jerky and gangly, like a youth not quite used to newly long limbs. And he glowed. Not visibly —no true light emanated from him—but there was an eerie brightness to him. Thomas was positive that even if the room had been utterly dark, he could have seen Abe.

Townsend leaned back with a look of horror as Abe approached, but he seemed unable to move from where he'd stopped. "Sit down," Abe said.

"Noooo." Townsend's moan was terrible to hear, especially from the throat of a man usually so confident. But he walked to the chair like a puppet badly worked, and he folded into it with a crash and a groan.

Abe danced around the room. He took a moment to gaze out the window—"Pigeons here too," he said with a laugh—before skipping to Thomas's side and bending close. He gave the cheek a light caress, nearly stopping Thomas's breath. "Maturity suits you, Tommy. But your eyes are so cold."

"Birdie...."

"It's not so bad as all that. Dying, that was appalling. But being dead? It's easier than life, really. Fewer worries."

A ragged noise tore from Thomas's throat, but Birdie merely tapped Thomas's nose and stood upright. "Must get on with it. It's quite a strain for poor Avi." He moved nimbly out of Thomas's reach and back to the other side of the desk, where he loomed over Townsend.

"What is this?" Townsend sounded as if he were being pressed to death, and his complexion was pale as whey.

"What was it, Herbert? What did poor Roy Gage take from you?"

"This is not—"

"Herbert." Birdie narrowed his eyes the way he used to before taking aim at a distant target or deciding whether to place a new bet or to fold. Then he flickered—an image so bright Thomas gasped and covered his eyes—before settling back into Abe's familiar form. But now there was a raggedness to his edges that made Thomas's eyes hurt if he looked too closely.

Townsend wailed. He sounded like a mortally wounded animal, and his hands gripped the armrests of the chair so hard that the wood cracked. Eyes wide, his jaw worked up and down soundlessly and his tongue went in and out a few times. Finally a word thin as gossamer came from his mouth. "Aaamuuulet."

"What amulet?" Birdie was implacable.

"Princcccce of Gandhaaaaaara."

"Do you have it back now?"

"Noooooo," Townsend sobbed.

"Do you know who has it?"

"Noooooo. Please. Stop."

Birdie looked at Thomas. For a terrifying moment, Thomas thought he was going to be interrogated similarly, but Birdie only raised his eyebrows. "Enough, Tommy?"

"Enough." Thomas fought back the urge to vomit.

"Go," Birdie said to Townsend. "And you'll honor your promise to pay when he finds the culprit?"

Townsend nodded and then slumped suddenly in his seat, the puppet strings cut. A moment later, he stumbled to his feet and, after clutching the chair for support, lurched his way to the coat rack. He dropped his hat twice before getting it onto his head. Although he was obviously eager to leave, he paused in the doorway and turned around. "Find me the amulet, and keep *that* away from me." He jerked his head toward Birdie. "And I'll pay you fifty thousand." He made his way out of the office on unsteady feet, slamming the door hard.

Thomas wanted to embrace Birdie, but he was unable to stand. He laid his hands on the desk, but they shook so violently that a cigarette or another glass of rum was out of the question.

"Influenza," Birdie said. "A bullet. A blade. Choking on a bite of mutton. Getting run over by a streetcar. It's only death, Tommy, so don't be so angry at it. It's the fairest thing of all." He flickered again, but not so brightly, and for a second or two Birdie's face almost completely obscured Abe's, like one magic lantern slide set atop another.

Then he collapsed bonelessly to the floor.

14

"I need more."

The bottle of Bacardi was empty on the floor, and Abe sat slumped against the wall where Thomas had propped him. The salty iron taste of blood remained on his tongue.

Thomas looked as if he hadn't slept for a week. "That's all I have here."

"Take me to my house."

Thomas nearly had to carry him down the stairs and out onto the sidewalk, and Abe would have fallen if there hadn't been a lamppost to lean on. The taxi driver was unwilling to let Abe into the car until Thomas offered him an extra five dollars. "He pukes or dies, you're cleaning it up, pal."

Abe would have laughed if he'd been able.

He grayed out for the ride to the Richmond District and barely noticed when Thomas dragged him up the front stairs and fumbled in Abe's pocket for the house keys. An endless journey up the stairs, and then Abe was flat on his own mattress, Thomas tugging off his shoes. Abe's overcoat, suit coat, and hat had already disappeared, but he couldn't remember when. "Magic," he rasped.

"You're burning up."

The fever—he hated that part. It hadn't happened when he'd allowed himself to be possessed by a dybbuk; that time he'd been so icy that it took days for him to thaw. An ibbur, though, was all about fire. "Booze. Please."

While Thomas was downstairs fetching liquor, Abe managed to get the rest of his clothing off, although he ripped his shirt in the process. He lay naked and senseless on the mattress until Thomas returned, propped him up, and held a glass to his mouth.

"You ought to go to hospital," Thomas said as he trickled in the slivovitz.

Abe shuddered despite the heat. "No." He wouldn't be able to resist the resident spirits in this condition. Besides, there was nothing doctors could do for him.

Thomas administered more slivovitz and at some point got Abe under the blankets, head supported by pillows. He brought toast, but Abe refused. He couldn't stomach anything but alcohol right now.

Eventually Abe fell into a restless doze. Every time he opened his eyes he expected to be alone, but Thomas was always there, sitting by the window and smoking. When he saw Abe stir, he'd hold the glass for him again. It was a sweet comfort, although Abe knew not to get used to it.

He awoke to find himself wrapped tightly in Thomas's arms. He was going to pretend he still slept, but Thomas huffed at him. "Nightmares."

"Yeah?"

"You were saying things I couldn't understand. Yiddish and Hungarian, I expect. You seemed angry. You got out of bed and fell flat on your face. I had to hold you to keep you here."

"Oh." Abe wasn't prone to episodes like that, but then, he also wasn't accustomed to letting spirits use him to control other people.

They remained quietly wrapped together for a time. Abe could feel Thomas's heartbeat, steady and strong, and the soft fabric of his undershirt and underwear felt nice on Abe's skin. Faint city sounds wafted in through the window: the rattle of streetcars, children calling, a car honking its horn. It was a cloudy day but not foggy, and pale light illuminated the room, making it seem fuzzy and dreamlike.

"I didn't realize it would be that hard on you," Thomas said.

"But it worked."

"Yes."

Two neighbors began arguing loudly in German. Abe could have caught a word here and there if he'd tried, but he let the sound wash over him. "It's not always this bad," he admitted.

"You said Birdie was a good man—a good spirit. You said—"

"He is. It's not his fault. The more time a spirit spends in a living body, the more power it uses, the harder it is for it to leave."

"You could get stuck with it permanently?"

Abe shut his eyes. "Yes. Like that Irish woman." He paused before asking a question. "Would it make you happy if Birdie possessed me for good?"

Thomas answered at once. "No. He's dead. It wouldn't be the same."

"No."

Abe didn't go back to sleep after that. It was pleasant to simply lie in Thomas's arms, drifting. It brought back vague memories of the ship his family had taken to America. They'd been lucky to have a smooth passage, and every night the gentle waves had rocked Abe to sleep.

Then he recalled something he'd long ago put out of mind: there had been a spirit on that ship. A young woman had died on a voyage and spent many years sailing back and forth, unable or unwilling to move on. At age six, Abe already knew not to talk about the spirits; his parents would only tell him he was making up stories. He'd enjoyed the spirit's company, and he wondered what had happened to the ship and whether the spirit had gone ashore or finally disappeared beyond the veil.

Eventually Thomas's stomach grumbled, making Abe realize that he was hungry too. They got dressed and went downstairs for sandwiches and canned soup. Thomas waited until the food was gone before returning to business. "Do you know anything about Townsend's missing amulet?"

"I've never heard of it." Abe rubbed his chin thoughtfully. "I don't know much about amulets at all, actually."

"They're... magic? Real magic, I mean."

"Some people say so. My *bubbe*—my grandmother—kept a hamsa amulet in her kitchen and wore one around her neck, but she was a superstitious woman in general." He smiled as he remembered her putting salt in the corners of rooms and pretending to spit three times after particularly good or bad news. She'd say *kein eina hara* to ward off the evil eye.

Thomas looked troubled, however. "Does real magic exist?"

"Yes," Abe answered with conviction. "I told you before—the world is full of wonders if you look hard enough."

"There are more things in heaven and earth, Horatio, than are dreamt of in your philosophy."

"Ah, there's that public school education showing through." Abe shook his head. "Ghosts. You know what a mess they made for Hamlet." He got up and cleared the dishes, and Thomas joined him at the sink to help wash up.

"Do *you* do real magic?" Thomas dried the soup pot.

"No, I don't have the knack. And anyway, it's far too valuable to waste on entertainments. But I've seen it."

"If we knew the purpose of the missing amulet, we might have a clue about who wanted it so badly. Do you think it was Gage's idea to steal it?"

Abe put the pot into the cupboard. "He didn't know anything about magic. If it looked valuable, though, he might have taken it on that account, hoping to sell it to someone."

"But the killer.... I've known people who'd murder over a few dollars, but I think this was more than that. I have a hunch that the killer knew exactly what the amulet was."

A hunch could be wrong, but this one made sense to Abe. He finished the dishes and wiped his hands on a towel. Thomas was rolling a cigarette, his hands almost steady. He didn't look at all like a man who'd nurse someone through the aftereffects of possession.

"I know someone who might be able to help," Abe offered.

"WHO IS THIS FELLOW?" Thomas asked as the streetcar rattled up California.

"I told you. His name's Emil Magnus and he was my mentor."

"He does stage shows? Séances?"

"He used to." The streetcar stopped and Abe moved closer to Thomas so a group of students could squeeze in. "He was famous back in the nineties, and he made a lot of money. So by the time I moved to San Francisco, I guess you'd say he'd retired."

Thomas fixed his sharp gaze on Abe. "And he took you under his wing out of the kindness of his heart?"

Abe ducked his head. "His heart wasn't the body part that was concerned with me." In the face of Thomas's continued scrutiny, he sighed. "I was in bad shape when I arrived. Losing Ben's friendship, the thing with the dybbuks.... My father had just died; my mother barely spoke to me. I knew very little about how to put on a show, so I mostly survived by cheating at cards. Then I saw Emil at a bar and recognized him from his posters."

"And you persuaded him to teach you."

"I can be very persuasive." Abe grinned. He wasn't ashamed of what he'd done, although some might have called him a whore. Letting Emil fuck him had bothered his conscience far less than what he'd done in New York. With Emil, nobody had been harmed. An aging man got a pupil and some company, and Abe got a valuable education.

Thomas wore a blank expression, so Abe couldn't tell whether he was judging. Didn't matter if he was. There was no way to go back and undo the past, and even if such a thing were possible, Abe would have made the same choices about Emil. Besides, Thomas already knew what kind of man Abe was. Abe had warned him.

Emil lived on Taylor Street, less than two blocks from where Grace Cathedral was under construction. The elegant house was four stories high and two rooms wide, with a fancy entryway, bow windows, and intricate plasterwork. Abe had lived there for a time—until he earned enough money to strike out on his own—but it had always felt more like a museum than a home.

"Magic evidently pays well," Thomas commented as they ascended the steps to the front door.

"I told you he'd done well for himself."

Thomas snorted, apparently unimpressed. But he'd grown up wealthy and then walked away from it. Maybe money wasn't important to him.

Emil's housekeeper, Mrs. Li, answered the door. She hadn't worked for Emil when Abe lived there, but she'd seen him often enough over the years. Usually she welcomed him with a friendly smile, but today she was stone-faced even though Emil must have told her that Abe and Thomas would be coming. She didn't seem to approve of Thomas, but she led them to Emil's parlor, a ground-floor room with high ceilings, an elaborate oversize fireplace, and expensive but old-fashioned furniture. She motioned them to a pair of gold brocade wingback chairs. "Mr. Magnus will be with you in a moment." Then she disappeared through the door to the kitchen.

Thomas sat in his chair, his gaze roaming the room and no doubt taking in the crystal chandeliers, thick carpets, and ornate wallpaper. Silver and crystal ornaments graced several recessed shelves, and the walls held paintings of European cities and landscapes, each one a confection of colored dots and smears. Abe had found it all very impressive when he was younger.

Emil swept into the room a few minutes later. He was as tall as Thomas but much more slender, with a thin, foxy face. His hair had already been white when Abe met him, but it was thick—with an impressive swoop—and matched his equally thick mustache. He wore a custom suit and carried a cane with a gold handle. "Abe, my boy!" He kissed Abe's cheeks in the European manner, even though

Emil was America-born, and then he shook Thomas's hand. "Can I offer you gentlemen a drink?"

They said yes, of course, and Emil opened a wooden cabinet in the corner. He filled three tulip glasses and handed them out. "Cognac," he said to Thomas. "When Abe first came to me, he'd never had it, but I think it won him over."

In fact, Abe would have preferred slivovitz or good whisky, but he didn't say so. Any booze was better than none. It took some effort for him to sip instead of gulp.

"You'll excuse me if we skip the small talk? I have a dinner engagement tonight."

"That's fine," Thomas said. "We just need some information."

"I see. For what purpose?"

"I'm a private eye investigating a case."

Emil's eyebrows lifted. "Really? How interesting! But how are you involved with this, Abe?"

"Thomas is a friend. He didn't have the right connections for the questions he has, so I said I'd help him out."

"A friend. How nice." Emil's piercing gaze said he knew exactly what kind of friendship Abe and Thomas were engaged in, but Abe didn't think he was jealous. He'd never objected to Abe fucking other men, even when Abe lived with him and ended up in his bed periodically, just as Abe had never complained about Emil's other young conquests. They had a business relationship, not a romantic one.

Thomas showed less emotion than a stone statue, the planes of his face solidly set and his eyes opaque.

"Abe says you know about magic."

Emil's laughter rang like church bells. "Yes, you could say that. You most definitely could."

"What can you tell me about an amulet called the Prince of Gandhara?"

There went Emil's eyebrows again, like birds trying to take flight. He swung his head toward Abe. "Don't tell me you're messing around with *that*, my boy."

"I'm not messing around with anything. I'm just helping Mr. Donne."

Emil clicked his tongue the way he used to when Abe was doing poorly at his training. "Those kinds of enchantments are not your forte. We've discussed that more than once. Even the weakest talisman can bring danger to an unskilled user, and the Prince of Gandhara is not weak."

Abe finished his cognac. "I'm not using it or any others, and I don't intend to, so don't worry about it."

"Why is this amulet so dangerous?" Thomas asked.

Emil stood, cradling his glass in one palm, and began to pace. Abe hadn't seen his mentor in full lecture mode for a long time, and it made him feel nostalgic. He used to wonder how many miles Emil walked during a lesson.

"All magical amulets are dangerous," he said in his most schoolmasterly tone. "It's their nature. Magic is a volatile element, and when you place it inside a physical object, it's like stuffing a tiger in a tiny cage. The tiger won't enjoy it much. But of course that tiger is very powerful, which explains why people insist on using amulets in the first place. Employed with great caution, an amulet can grant its handler extraordinary capacities. And it can do so more expediently than incantations, summonings, or other means of invoking the mystical realms."

Thomas had taken only a single sip of his cognac before setting the glass on the small table between the two wingback chairs. Abe was very tempted to grab Thomas's glass and finish it off, especially now that Thomas was leaning slightly forward, his attention fully on Emil. "What capacities?"

"That depends on the amulet. It might be wealth, beauty, intelligence, charm, strength. Military success. Good luck or artistic talent. It might be good health. It might be love, although I have to say that amulets bring a shallow form of affection, one that is never as satisfying as the natural sort."

Abe didn't know whether Emil was speaking from experience. Emil had been married when he was young, to a pretty woman whose portrait still hung over his bed like a sentinel. She and their baby had died in childbirth, but Emil used to speak fondly of her, especially when he grew fatigued.

"What does the Prince of Gandhara do?"

"What the name suggests. It brings authority, the ability to make others eager for your command."

"Ah," said Thomas, as if that explained a great deal. "How does it work? You just wave the thing around?"

"Only if you want to ensure self-destruction. Tiger in a cage, Mr. Donne. The user charms the amulet with the correct recitations and appeases it with appropriate sacrifices. It rewards him with the powers he seeks."

"Sacrifices?" Thomas's face had taken on a grim cast.

"It's old magic and very dark. It will demand blood."

Abe stopped resisting and drank Thomas's cognac. Although Thomas shot him an annoyed glare, he didn't protest. Instead, he stretched his lips thin. "Are you saying that in order to use this amulet, a fellow needs to kill someone?"

"Perhaps."

Thomas sat back in his chair. His fingers didn't so much twitch as dance, as if he were thinking about playing a piano. More likely he was wanting to roll a cigarette. Abe lit one of his own and passed it over, pretending not to notice Emil's scornful reaction.

"All right," Thomas said, exhaling a cloud of smoke. "If the amulet's used properly, somebody's got to die. If it's used improperly—"

"Someone will also die."

"What does it look like?"

"I've read only vague descriptions, so I'm not sure. I believe it's a gold disk with writing in Sanskrit and the image of a lion. Affixed with some small jewels." Emil pulled out his pocket watch and gave a quick shake of the head. "I'm sorry. I must get ready for dinner."

Thomas and Abe both stood. "Thanks for your help," Thomas said.

"I'm delighted to assist." Emil turned to smile at Abe. "Don't be a stranger, my boy. Come pay a longer visit soon."

"Sure."

Emil walked them to the door and ushered them out.

"You fucked *him*?" Thomas demanded as they walked down the hill.

"So?"

"Didn't think that was your type."

Abe blew an amused huff of air. "You mean he's not as manly as you?"

"I mean he used you."

"So? I used him."

Fog began to settle around them as they descended from Nob Hill. They hadn't discussed a destination, but Thomas was leading them down toward Union Square rather than to the nearby streetcar stop. A middle-aged couple walked a tiny dog who barked frantically at Abe as they passed by. Most animals disliked him now that he dabbled with spirits. That was a source of some sadness for him, and he sometimes wished he could have a dog or cat to keep him company.

"Where are we going?" he asked when they got to the next street.

"You're out of booze. We're going to find you some, and then you're going to take it home and drink it."

"But—"

"You look as if you'll collapse any minute. I can't babysit you now."

Abe bit back anger; Thomas was right. Abe wasn't his responsibility, and the notion of collapsing into bed with a bottle of alcohol appealed greatly. Besides, he had two séances scheduled for the next day. "Fine."

They continued toward the Tenderloin, searching for one of the men who sold gin from their coat pockets.

15

After Abe had boarded a streetcar with two bottles of gin in his pockets, Thomas had gone to Bianchi's for meatloaf and potatoes. He'd eaten there alone many times since arriving in the city, yet this time he couldn't get comfortable in his seat. The empty side of the table seemed to mock him.

Over coffee and pie, Thomas read the evening paper, making notes in his book: magicians who advertised shows, spiritualists offering séances. There was Abe France, of course, with séances by appointment only, but there were others too. Any one of them could have been interested in the Prince of Gandhara. Of course it might be someone else entirely, but this was a good place to start.

The problem was in contacting them. He went to his office and tried to ring a few of them, but nobody answered. He didn't much fancy skulking around their shows, and he was certain that knocking on doors would get him nowhere this late at night.

The sensible thing, then, was to go home and get some sleep.

Instead he walked to Twelfth Avenue, where a light shone in the upstairs window. He imagined Abe sitting in bed with his rotgut close at hand, drinking the spirits away. Not getting drunk, because as far as Thomas could tell, Abe never did. Thomas was poised to ring the doorbell, but he let his hand fall to his side. Instead he spent an hour or so sitting on the stoop, a cigarette in his fingers and the sounds of mortar shells faint in his ears.

Eventually he stood and stretched and brushed his overcoat clean. He started toward home but somehow found himself detouring to Calvary Cemetery. It had taken little effort to scale the fence, and now he wandered the gentle hills crowded with grave markers.

Rest in Peace. Wasn't that a joke!

A nearby streetlight cast the gravestone in an eerie glow, and Thomas wondered how many spirits Abe would find in this place. Maybe none, since none of these people had actually died in the cemetery. They'd breathed their last somewhere else, their souls going wherever souls went before their carcasses were put in boxes, dragged here, and buried six feet under. If Abe was right about how spirits operated—and Thomas had no reason to believe otherwise— they'd have little affinity for their rotting flesh and bones. If they chose to reach toward this side of the veil, they'd do it somewhere more meaningful than this. It was a bloody spooky place none-theless, and Thomas didn't know what had drawn him here.

He'd read in the paper that they'd stopped burying people within the city limits nearly thirty years earlier, when he and Birdie had been children in England. Now the people of San Francisco were clamoring to have the graves dug up and moved elsewhere so they could build more houses.

"Progress," Thomas said to a weeping stone angel.

When he returned to Abe's house sometime later, the lights were out.

By late afternoon the next day, Thomas was frustrated and ready to punch someone. Didn't much matter whom. He'd paid visits to every magician he could track down. Some were pleasant, some decidedly not. Some, like Abe, were clearly skilled showmen, while others were hucksters who must have relied on the drunkenness and stupidity of their audiences to get by. As far as Thomas could tell, none of them knew anything about the amulet or the murders.

Of course any of them could be lying. It occurred to him that Abe could allow Birdie to possess him and then use his powers to force true answers from these people. But there would be a cost to that. The experience with Townsend, while it hadn't lasted long, had put Abe out for a good part of the day. Besides, there was the danger that Birdie would get stuck inside of Abe, and Thomas didn't want that.

Did he?

He ran out of tobacco and had to walk two blocks to buy more. When he returned to the hallway outside his office, the phone was ringing. He fumbled the lock open—bloody postwar tremors—and hurried to pick up the receiver. "Donne."

On the other end, Abe muttered something in another language. Then more clearly, in English, "Helen's dead."

"How?"

"In her apartment. I— Come meet me here. Please."

Thomas hung up the phone and raced for the door.

He took a taxi to the Tenderloin, paying the driver extra to go as fast as possible, and leapt out of the car almost before it had stopped. Helen's apartment was on the third floor; Thomas didn't wait for the lift but took the stairs two at a time. Abe was in the hallway, leaning against the wall beside her closed door. He held his hat in one hand.

"She didn't show up for the afternoon séance," he said as Thomas was still walking toward him. "It was Rosie's turn this morning, and that went fine. But then Helen didn't come this afternoon. I did the séance without her." His voice was cool and even, as if he were reporting on the weather, but his expression was drawn.

Thomas waited to enter the room. "Do the police know?"

"Nobody does, except the two of us. I got worried—she's usually reliable. She doesn't have a phone, so I couldn't call her. I came over to check."

"Was her door locked?"

"Yes." Abe didn't need to explain; they both knew that locks posed little obstacle to him.

"What did you do after you found her?"

"I ran down to the corner and called you."

"Why not the police?"

Abe simply shook his head. He remained in the hallway when Thomas went inside.

It was peaceful, as murder scenes went. A young blonde lay on her back on the floor, eyes fixed sightlessly on the ceiling. She was dressed as if for an evening out, in a sparkly dress and shiny beads, but one shoe had fallen off. No blood was visible, and her white neck was unmarred.

Although her flat was a bit messy, Thomas didn't think it had been the killer. He guessed that Helen just hadn't been a particularly neat person. Clothing lay in small rumpled piles, and dirty dishes filled the sink of the kitchenette. A few issues of *Photoplay* occupied a chair. The wall bed had been pushed up and out of the way, but sloppily, with a blanket corner hanging out.

Thomas scanned the room for an idea of what had killed her. It took him a few moments to notice the decorative pillow on the floor beneath a chair. It was small, but big enough to cover her nose and mouth.

Thomas left the apartment and found Abe still leaning against the corridor wall.

"Where are you going?" Abe asked.

"To make a telephone call. Stay here."

"Poor girl," Munroe said, shaking his head as he crouched over the corpse. "How old was she? Twenty?"

Abe answered quietly from the corner. "Twenty-three, I think."

"She have family?"

"They're in Missouri. I don't know exactly where."

Looking displeased, Munroe straightened up. "I'll have the boys look into it." He took a slow drag from his cigarette and exhaled even more slowly. "Three, Donne. That's quite a collection."

"If you're going to arrest me, go ahead and do it."

"I feel like the good citizens of San Francisco would be safer if I did." But Munroe made no effort to approach him. "Why don't you tell me instead what you know about the guy who's doing this. Or the dame, I suppose."

"It's almost certainly a man. This murder and Zook's took a fair degree of physical strength."

"Okay, yeah, I see that. When ladies kill, it's usually with a gun. Or sneaky-like, with poison. What else?"

"I think he knew all three of them."

Munroe nodded. "Right. And you didn't."

"I'd seen Gage and Zook once, the night they were killed, but didn't speak with them. This afternoon is the first time I've seen this woman."

"Hmm." Another long drag, then Munroe swiveled his head to look at Abe. "But you knew all three of them."

If the implied accusation rattled Abe, he didn't show it. "I employed Helen and Roy as assistants. I'd met Zook a few times."

"So maybe I oughtta run you in." He seemed to be seriously considering it.

It was unlikely the police would dig up enough evidence against Abe to make charges stick, but he'd spend weeks or months cooling his heels in jail while they tried. Jails were a nasty experience for anyone, but what would happen if he were stuck in a cell with a couple of unhappy spirits? Dybbuks, maybe. There weren't many righteous men in jail.

Townsend had probably told Munroe some basic details already, so Thomas didn't worry about indiscretion. "Gage stole something from Townsend. Somebody else wanted that something too, and killed Gage to get it. Possibly killed Zook because he was a witness, but I don't know about that part."

Munroe gestured toward the corpse. "And the girl?"

"I don't know what she had to do with it."

"She and Roy were friends," Abe said quietly.

Munroe went to the window, opened it, and flicked out his cigarette butt. Thomas didn't mention littering or creating a fire hazard, but such prudence took quite some effort.

"What did Gage steal?" Munroe asked.

Thomas shook his head.

"That mean you don't know or you won't say?"

"Ask Townsend."

"Right." Munroe huffed. "And who's the someone who wanted the thing you can't or won't tell me about?"

"That's what I'm trying to find out."

"Did he get it?"

Thomas shrugged. He'd been wondering the same thing. He suspected yes, since neither Zook's nor Helen's flat had been tossed, but without knowing more about the circumstances of the murders, he couldn't be sure.

After a long pause, Munroe sighed, fished a cigarette out of a pocket, and lit it. "I did a little background on you, Donne. You had a PI license in Boston before you came here."

"And I've a valid California license now."

"I know. But I got to wondering what led you to migrate west. I hear you made a few enemies in the Mob."

That was true enough. But the real reason why he'd left Boston wasn't the gangsters per se but rather that certain members of Boston's Finest were on the take from the Mob.

Munroe was watching him carefully. "We have plenty of criminals here in San Francisco. I never have to worry about having enough work, that's for sure. But we're not Boston or Chicago or New York. We're not even Los Angeles. The Mob hasn't fully sunk its claws into my city yet, and I'd like to keep it that way."

"We're in agreement on that," Thomas said wryly.

"So this mess... it has nothing to do with anything in Boston?"

"Not that I can tell."

"I guess that'll have to be good enough," Munroe said with a frown. "Okay. You two, scram. And I sincerely hope that this is the last stiff we'll meet over, Mr. Donne."

"Again, we're in agreement."

"I'm worried about Rosie," Abe said when they were out on the street.

"You're running out of assistants."

"These are people! Maybe you don't care about them—maybe hardly anyone does. But they're my—" His voice stumbled and halted.

"Your what?"

Abe's jaw worked. "Almost nobody knows me, right? Some people have heard of Abe France, but *me*, Abraham Ferencz? Not so much. Roy, Helen, Rosie—none of them were perfect, but they talked to me and I could talk to them. They're what I have. What I had."

"What about Magnus?"

"Old news. We see each other a few times a year. But I don't need a mentor anymore, and his tastes run younger than me."

Loneliness was as much a part of Thomas as his arms and legs. He wouldn't have known how to function without it. But looking into Abe's eyes now, he saw a reflection of his own. "I'll find the killer."

Abe smiled. "A mensch."

"Come to my office and—"

"I'll meet you there."

Thomas looked at him quizzically, and Abe shrugged. "I have a little money put away. I'm going to stop by the bank, and then I'm going to Rosie's place. She could use a nice vacation." He winced. "I'm going to have to tell her about Helen."

"Be careful along the way."

Abe's answering smile was warm and sweet.

WHEN ABE SHOWED up at the office ninety minutes later, he looked tired. "A refill for your desk drawer." He set two bottles of Bacardi on the desk.

"How's Rosie?"

"Shaken. But she's always wanted to visit New York City, she says, and now she has a chance to go. I gave her some tips on where to stay. She'll be on a train within the hour."

"And you?"

"I've been to New York."

Thomas grunted. "How are you?"

"My life has never been so interesting. But maybe yours has. What Detective Munroe said about Boston, is it true?"

"For the most part."

"Is that the only reason you moved here?"

"This is about as far as I could get from Boston without leaving the States. Los Angeles is too bloody sunny."

Abe opened his mouth, but before he could rummage further into Thomas's business, the outer door swung open. As Abe froze, Thomas set his Smith & Wesson on the desktop and placed his hand nearby, not quite touching it.

"Hello?" The male voice wasn't familiar.

"In here."

Thomas tagged the fellow for a cop right away. Something about the way he moved with mingled confidence and caution and the way he swept the room with his gaze. It landed on the desktop with the gun and the booze. "Mr. Donne?"

"That's me."

"I'm Ralph Crespo." He reached into his breast pocket, and as Thomas's fingers grasped the pistol, Crespo pulled out a wallet and flashed a badge. "Agent Ralph Crespo," he clarified.

Thomas pointed at the bottles. "You going to run me in?" Apparently that was the theme for the day.

"I'm no revenuer." Crespo stepped further into the office and held out his hand. "Bureau of Trans-Species Affairs, in fact."

"What the hell is that?"

Abe approached the desk, eyes wide. "I've heard of them," he told Thomas. "They have jurisdiction over... over the Hamlet stuff."

"The Hamlet stuff?" Crespo seemed bemused.

"Otherworldly. Monsters."

Now Crespo smiled widely. "There are a lot of monsters. I worry mostly about the non-human ones. And who are you, if I may ask?"

"My name's Abe Ferencz."

"Really?" Crespo looked as if he's just won a prize. "Abe France. Sorry I didn't recognize you offstage. This is great! I've been meaning to meet with you too. What a stroke of luck to find you here!"

"Why *are* you here, Agent Crespo?" Thomas asked pointedly.

Although he hadn't been invited to do so, Crespo sat down opposite Thomas and laid his hat in his lap. Abe took the other chair, which he angled to have a better view of the newcomer. Then they all stared at one another. Crespo was in his late thirties or early forties, with thinning dark hair and narrow eyes that made it appear as if he was squinting. An interesting scar—a trio of long parallel lines— marred one of his cheeks, and although the marks were old and faded, they caused that side of his mouth to droop a bit. His suit was neither cheap nor expensive, and he wore no jewelry.

"I'm feeling a little dry," Crespo said. "Mind if I have a little of that rum?"

Abe ended up pouring, possibly so he could give himself extra. Or possibly so Thomas could keep his hand near the gun. "I didn't realize federal agents could drink on the job," Abe said as he handed Crespo a glass.

"The Bureau gives us more leeway than most."

They all drank; Abe finished first, of course. Crespo smiled pleasantly at them, as if this were a social call. Finally, though, he leaned forward. "I'm going to be frank. I'm not good at small talk anyway, and neither of you seems very chatty."

That was fine with Thomas. Whatever this business was, he'd prefer to get it over with, especially if it wasn't going to end in his or Abe's arrest. "Why are you here?"

"Well, the Bureau... we're fairly new. President Wilson signed us into existence nine years ago, but we're still feeling our way. Our mission is to deal with disruptions related to… well, as Mr. Ferencz said. The otherworldly. Last week, for instance, I helped destroy a jiangshi in Chinatown, and when I leave here, I'm heading to Lake Tahoe, where there've been reports of a dragon."

"A dragon," Thomas repeated doubtfully.

Crespo's smile was wide and white. "Sure. Most of 'em are fine as long as you leave 'em alone, but now and then we get a nasty one. They're kinda like people that way."

Maybe a dragon wasn't any less believable than his dead lover's spirit possessing a living man. If you accepted the existence of one impossible thing, you had to allow that more impossible things might be out there as well.

"Do they really breathe fire?" Abe wanted to know.

"Some species, yeah. But it's the venomous ones you really gotta watch out for."

"I don't know anything about dragons," Thomas said.

"I can recommend a book if you want to learn. But that's not exactly why I'm here. Up until now, the Bureau's been run entirely out of DC, but the West Coast is active and too far away for that to work. We're building a regional headquarters in LA, which is great, but right now our coverage here is pretty thin. Too much territory and not enough agents. We don't even have a regional chief yet—we kind of borrowed someone from DC." Crespo made exactly the same face that Thomas's fellow soldiers had made when complaining about officers. Dissatisfaction with one's superiors was an almost universal condition.

Despite Crespo's easygoing manner and pedestrian discussion, there was something… odd about him. Thomas couldn't put his finger on it. Maybe if he concentrated hard enough it would come to him, like a word he was struggling to remember. Or maybe he was only imagining the oddness.

If Crespo truly was peculiar in some way, Thomas might have expected Abe to comment on it. But Abe remained uncharacteristically quiet, holding his glass with one hand and rubbing his temple with the fingers of the other.

Crespo had paused his speech as if waiting for Thomas to process these thoughts. "So at the moment," he continued, "I'm trying to cover almost all of Northern California with just a little bit of help, which is crazy. This place is crawling with weird shit."

Abe nodded his agreement but remained silent.

"Abe France," Crespo said, shaking his head slowly. "I've seen your show and it was remarkable. You're really, really good. But the séance thing—real or a schtick?"

"You were telling us why you're here," Thomas reminded him.

"Right. Sorry. But like I said, someday soon I hope we can have a talk, Mr. France. Maybe after I get back from Tahoe."

It was his eyes, Thomas decided. It was hard to make out his irises, but they seemed to shift color, briefly flashing to hues not generally seen in humans: canary yellow, magenta, violet, silver. Thomas had no idea what that meant and decided not to remark on it.

"So," Crespo said, winking as if he and Thomas were in on some joke, "why I'm here now. There's a magic thingamabob. An amulet. I think you know about it already. It's bad news, okay? The kind of thing that oughtta be locked away somewhere safe. But everyone wants it, and it's been all around the world. Landed in San Francisco less than two weeks ago aboard the *President Pierce*. Fellow who brought it here turned up dead two days later at a whorehouse in Becket Alley."

Four, Thomas thought. *That makes four*. "Where's the amulet now?"

Crespo spread his arms. "No idea. Look. I know that Townsend is mixed up in this and that he hired you. He's probably offering you a lotta dough for the thing. But the Bureau would really like to see it tucked away somewhere safe. I don't really have time to track it down, and I dunno that I'd have more luck than you at it. So I'm gonna ask you real nice: if you find it, let me know." He took a business card from his pocket and set it on the desk. "Somebody'll answer that number twenty-four hours a day."

Thomas didn't take the card. "Why would I do that?"

"'Cause we're the good guys?" Crespo laughed at his own humor, then his expression became more serious. "I could threaten you, I guess, but I don't think you're the type who reacts well to threats. I hear the last fellows who tried it are sleeping six feet under in Boston now."

Abe snorted as if this amused him, and Crespo gave him a quick glance before returning his attention to Thomas. "How about if I appeal to your better nature?"

"I don't have one."

"Dunno about that. The world will be a safer place if that amulet stays out of Townsend's hands—and out of the hands of every other bastard who wants it. So there's that. Also, we can pay you. Not as much as Townsend probably, but not pennies either. And there's another thing." He leaned forward again. "I think you oughtta consider joining us."

"Joining you?"

"Signing on with the Bureau. Steady pay, interesting work, some travel. Sometimes you get to fight dragons." When he smiled, his teeth looked very sharp.

"I work alone."

Crespo gave Abe a significant look before shrugging. "Like I said, the Bureau gives its agents a lotta leeway. But you can think on it. You too," he said to Abe, who appeared startled. Then Crespo stood and set his empty glass on the desk. "Thanks for wetting my whistle." He clapped his hat on his head and started for the door.

"What if I keep the amulet?" Thomas asked.

Crespo swung around, grinning. "Then I guess I'll come after you next." His eyes went crimson for a split second. Then he was gone.

be reached for the bottle of rum. "That was interesting."

"You know about the Bureau?"

"I've heard a few things."

"From?"

"Magicians. Spiritualists. People like me."

Thomas barked a laugh. "There are no people like you."

Abe wasn't sure how to take that, so he let it go. "Sometimes the Bureau comes nosing around. There was a fellow—he was Konigsmann until the war, and after he became Carlyle the Great. He'd do a hypnosis bit that wasn't bad. But then a couple of the fellows he'd had on stage stole dough from their employers, and they weren't the type to steal."

"Everyone's the type to steal," Thomas scoffed.

"Would you?"

"If I was desperate enough."

"Well"—Abe gulped some rum—"these people weren't desperate. And Carlyle was spending a lot bigger than he should have."

"He was... bewitching them into stealing for him?"

"Maybe. Anyway, from what I hear, the Bureau went around

asking questions—and Carlyle disappeared. Nobody heard from him again."

No great loss, Abe had thought at the time. Carlyle was a mean bastard who'd steal other illusionists' tricks and who liked to cop a feel of his pretty female assistants. But Abe had been intrigued by the idea of the Bureau, as well as slightly wary. Since his scams stayed on the right side of the law, the Bureau never came after him. But Crespo had certainly known who he was, which was a little unsettling.

"Do you think Crespo's the murderer?" Abe asked.

"I don't know why he'd show his face to me if he was. I get a weird feeling from him. But I don't think he's the one I'm looking for."

"Hmm." Abe had also sensed something odd, but although he was usually very good at reading people—he had to be—he couldn't get anything from Crespo. There was an opaqueness to him, as if he were wearing a mask. "Are you going to give him the amulet?"

"Why would I do that?"

"It's what an honorable man would do."

Thomas's lip curled. "I'm not honorable."

"Sure you are. I've seen it myself. Birdie says so too."

"Birdie!" Thomas snarled. "He wasn't all that smart when he was alive. I doubt death has improved him. And why do you keep rubbing your head?"

Abe jerked guiltily. He hadn't realized he was doing it. "Headache. Too involved with Birdie yesterday and with Helen today. And I'm hungry. Let's go have dinner."

"I've wasted too much time socializing already." Thomas pulled out his notebook and stared at the pages, pretending Abe wasn't there.

Thomas was an intriguing man even while sitting motionless. Well, not truly motionless—his hands shook a little. It had grown dark outside, and the office lights cast Thomas's face into stark brightness and deep shadow, like a poorly developed photograph. If Abe tried, he could see Thomas through Birdie's memories: younger, looser, clad in a muddy uniform. Even then, though, Thomas's eyes had been troubled, and he'd trusted almost no one.

But Abe could understand why Birdie had set his eyes on Thomas, then set upon his body. Had eventually fallen in love. Thomas wasn't just a handsome, well-made man, but also the type of man to anchor to, a solid island in the stormy seas of life. Even his hardness was attractive. Abe couldn't abide a soft man.

He wandered to Thomas's side of the desk, and when Thomas still ignored him, knelt beside him and used the arms of the chair, swiveling Thomas to face him. He could smell Thomas now—cigarettes and soap and sweat. Just a few inhalations were enough to make Abe hard.

"Don't—" Thomas began.

Abe was already unfastening Thomas's trousers and reaching in to grab his growing stiffness. Thomas's cock felt heavy and solid in his palm, the pulse rapid, the skin smooth. Maybe Thomas was going to protest again or even push him away, but Abe leaned forward and reverently kissed the crown, and Thomas groaned and spread his legs wide. His fingers threaded through Abe's hair.

Thomas tasted good, and when Abe swallowed him down, the fullness in his throat calmed him. Spirits never bothered him when he had sex. Nothing did. Sucking cock meant he could concentrate on one thing only, the urgency of the moment, the single-mindedness of his objective, the purity of his goals. He was good at it too. Knew how to make a man come fast and fierce or how to draw things out with sweet torture. Knew how to pull sweet blasphemies from a man's mouth or make a man pull at Abe's hair and thrust until Abe's eyes watered and his lungs begged for air.

"Sweet Jesus," Thomas cried and then roughly pushed Abe hard enough that he fell onto his ass.

But Abe was on his feet in a flash, and so was Thomas. And again Thomas was filling Abe's mouth, this time with his tongue. He was just as desperate about it, gripping Abe's shoulders and moaning when he could. It was as if Thomas were starving, as if nobody had ever kissed him before. The ferocity of it made Abe want to swoon.

No time for that, though. Thomas fumbled at Abe's waist until his trousers and underwear, like Thomas's, pooled around his ankles. Then Thomas yanked off Abe's suit coat and grabbed his ass hard.

Abe tried to grasp Thomas's cock, which stood trapped between them. "I want—"

"I know what you want." Growling, Thomas turned Abe and pushed him against the desk, pressing his chest to the wood with one hand splayed across his upper back. He kicked Abe's feet apart as wide as the clothing allowed. "This will hurt."

"Yes."

The sound of spitting. A broad, rough finger intruding into Abe's body. His hips rocking to impale himself more fully. "Yes," he repeated, this time more roughly.

The finger withdrew, making Abe cry out, but then Thomas spat again and pressed the head of his cock against Abe's eager body. *Into Abe's eager body.* Abe rested the side of his face on the desk and remained obediently in place, even as Thomas took his hand off Abe's back and put both of them on Abe's hips.

One of the Bacardi bottles stood inches from Abe's face; beyond that lay Crespo's card, the words unreadable at this angle. He felt the smooth wood, both beneath his cheek and imprisoning his cock against his belly. There wasn't enough friction to get him off, but that didn't matter because Thomas filled him—gloriously, burningly— and the slap of Thomas's balls against his was lovely. Every grunt and gasp from Thomas's throat further fixed Abe to the here and now.

This was life in its simplest, most unadulterated form.

Thomas's thrusts grew harder, and Abe had to clutch the edges of the desk to keep from sliding too far forward. He did his best to meet every plunge with a counter push, to drive Thomas as deeply as he could. The capped bottles shook, then toppled onto their sides, rattling in unison with the creaking of the desk and Thomas's panting. Somewhere far away, a foghorn added to the symphony.

"Abe!" Thomas roared before collapsing on top of him.

That would have been enough—even though Thomas's weight made it hard for Abe to breathe. But then Thomas suddenly stood, flipped Abe onto his back, and swooped in to take Abe's cock into his mouth.

Astonishment and pure pleasure made Abe climax almost immediately.

And when he finally stood straight on shaky legs, Thomas seized his shoulders and kissed him. This time it was slow and tender and Thomas tasted of him, and again Abe wanted to swoon.

It took a few minutes to straighten their appearance, but Abe's hair was a lost cause until he got his hands on some Brilliantine. "Your outer door's unlocked. What if Crespo had returned?"

"Then he would have had a good show." Thomas rolled and lit a cigarette with steady hands.

THEY HAD a good dinner of oysters and steak, although Abe kept shifting uncomfortably in his chair. Every time he did, Thomas shot him a knowing grin. Abe couldn't help but smile back.

"Do you have séances tomorrow?" Thomas asked over a double slice of chocolate cake.

"Canceled. I canceled the whole week, actually. All of my assistants are gone."

"So no income this week and you gave money to Rosie. Will that be a problem?"

It was nice that his had occurred to Thomas, but Abe shook his head. "I can manage for a few weeks."

"After that?"

"Maybe I'll be dead," Abe said lightly. "Then it won't be an issue."

"You joke about dying."

Abe hadn't exactly meant it as a joke. As far as he knew, he would be dead by the time he ran out of money. "Death has always waited just around the corner for me. Sooner or later we'll run into each other."

"Wouldn't you rather it be later?"

The waiter appeared with the bill, saving Abe from the need to respond. He wasn't sure of the answer. If someone had asked him that question a week ago, he might have been indifferent, but now that he'd met Thomas.... Well, if he allowed his thoughts to stray in that direction, they'd end up somewhere impossible.

After Thomas paid the bill, they visited a couple of speakeasies frequented by magicians. Thomas sat quietly as Abe spoke to acquaintances and assessed whether they knew anything about the amulet or the murders. None did.

A late-night rain began to fall—heavy cold drops that soaked Abe and Thomas despite their hats and overcoats. They stood under a shop awning while Thomas smoked. "Come to my house," Abe said.

"You need to sleep."

"I will. I'll sleep better with you there, in fact."

Thomas tossed the butt away, its final glow arcing into the wet darkness. "I should go to my flat."

"Should is a stupid word. Who says you should?" Abe was fully prepared to out-argue him. Thomas might be bigger and stronger, but Abe knew how to talk his way into getting what he wanted, whether it be the admiration of an audience, the belief of a séance guest, or the company of a handsome man.

"You imply I'll keep you safe, but who's to keep me safe from you?"

Abe lifted his chin. "Do you think I'd harm you?"

"I'm positive you will."

But when Thomas flagged down a taxi and Abe got in beside him, he didn't object when Abe gave the driver his own address. Nothing was visible through the rain-streaked windows, and slick streets caused the driver to grip the steering wheel, his knuckles white. Abe had never learned to drive, and he wondered sometimes whether he'd enjoy it. Or whether he might suddenly jerk his arms and send the car head-on into another. He'd once met the spirit of a woman who'd died in an accident during the early days of automobiles and was convinced that motor vehicles were the devil's work. She haunted a busy street corner in New York and exerted a gentle influence to keep careless pedestrians from being struck as they crossed. Abe hadn't even tried to convince her to cross beyond the veil; she was doing too much good on this side.

"I saw a monster once," he said.

Thomas, who'd apparently been lost in thought, turned to look at him. "What?"

"I think it was a vampire."

"I have no idea what you're going on about."

Abe loved it when he mystified Thomas. "Vampire. Like Dracula. This was in New York though. Two nights in a row I saw the same man at a saloon in the Bowery, very pale and creepy, and he was looking around the place like a hunter searching for prey. I mean, a lot of fellows were doing that—it was that sort of place—but he looked more interested in food than fucking. Each night he left with a different man. And each night, the cops found a corpse in the alley nearby. Papers said they were drained of blood."

Thomas gave an impatient huff. "Papers lie. And victims get drained of blood when they're stabbed."

"They also get drained of blood when a vampire gets them."

Abe wasn't alarmed by the idea that vampires existed. It was almost a relief, in fact, to know that the spirits and ghosts that haunted him weren't the only weirdness in the world. There were vampires and dragons and whatever that Chinese thing was that Crespo had mentioned. And there was the Bureau, which tried to keep them orderly.

Had Crespo been serious about that offer to join the Bureau? Maybe he'd only dropped the possibility as a joke, or as part of an enticement to get Thomas to give him the amulet. Surely the Bureau wouldn't want someone like Abe.

It was nice to daydream about it, though. Being a hero, almost.

"What are you laughing about?" Thomas asked.

"Stupidity."

"Mine?"

"Mine."

The taxi stopped in front of Abe's house, and Abe insisted on paying. He and Thomas rushed up the rain-drenched stairs, but Abe froze with the key in his hand.

"We're going to drown," Thomas complained.

But Abe barely heard him over the whisper of Birdie's spirit, battering at the edges of his skull. "Leave! Quickly!" Birdie said.

Jealous bastard.

Abe got the door open and Thomas pushed impatiently past, barreling down the dark hallway toward the stairs.

"Donne!"

Thomas lunged sideways. Gunshots rang out loudly enough to deafen. And a bullet hit Abe with the force of a speeding truck.

17

After a brief pause and a some scrambling sounds, the hallway light switched on. The assailant's brains were splattered over the far wall—a good thing, because it meant Thomas didn't have to verify the bastard was truly dead. Of course there could be someone else in the house, so Thomas kept his gun in hand as he kicked and rolled the slumped corpse so he could see its face.

"Fuck!" He kicked again when he saw who it was. Then he picked up the other gun and slipped it into his pocket. "You've a dead cop in your house, Abe. We need to go."

But when he turned around, Abe was leaning on the frame of the front door, his arm tight against his belly and his complexion gray. "Abe?" Thomas rushed to him.

Abe had a ghastly smile. "I caught the bullet."

Shells were screaming and men were shrieking as the reek of mud nearly smothered Thomas. He struggled to keep his breathing steady. "I'll ring an ambulance. Where's your phone?"

"No hospitals."

"You'll die if you don't—"

"Won't survive a hospital anyway." A trickle of blood appeared at the corner of his mouth. His body slid slowly down, leaving a streak of bright crimson on the door. "Was it Crespo?" he rasped.

"Munroe." Thomas fell to his knees, helpless.

Abe's laugh was a terrible gurgle, and a blood bubble popped on his lips. "Oh. My bank account... if you can... get it to Rosie. My house...." He gasped and shuddered but opened his eyes again. "Yours."

"Don't.... Abe, don't...."

"'S okay." Abe grasped Thomas's arm with his free hand, as if Thomas were the one who needed comforting. But his hand fell away when he shuddered again. The flames in his eyes had dimmed to coals and would soon be nothing but ashes.

"Birdie!" Thomas shouted. He didn't know whether Birdie was there or if he could hear him, but Christ, what else could he do? "Birdie! Help him if you can. Goddamn it, Albert, make yourself useful!"

"Thomas," Abe whispered. He chanted a few broken phrases in what Thomas thought was probably Hebrew.

"Let him in. If he can help you, let him in." And then more loudly. "Let him in!"

"*Igen.*" A third shudder and a gout of wine-red blood came from Abe's mouth. Thomas was sure he was gone, and his own breath caught in his throat, choking him. His tears blurred the view of Abe's face, and—

No. It wasn't tears. For a fraction of a second, Birdie stared back at him. Then it was Abe's face again, although the eyes remained blue.

"Getting shot hurts," Birdie said.

Oh God. Thomas sat on his heels. "Is he— Can you—"

"Give me a minute, old man. I can only work so much magic at once." Color was returning to Abe's skin, and blood stopped issuing from his mouth. He took a few shaky breaths, then deeper ones before holding out his hand. "Could use some help up."

Thomas's legs were incredibly shaky, but he managed to get to his feet and help lift Birdie, who stood hunched, a hand to his belly. He jerked his chin toward the end of the hall. "That's a right mess, innit?"

A horrible thought struck Thomas. "Is his spirit—"

"That bloke's gone. Dunno where, but we're rid of him for good. Get us somewhere safe, Tommy."

Somewhere safe. As far as Thomas knew, no such place existed. He went off in search of the telephone anyway, and when he returned, Birdie had dropped the bloodstained overcoat onto the floor and put on a considerably more expensive one. "Your boy knows how to dress, Tommy," he said as he buttoned it up.

"He's not—"

"Don't. No time for arguments now. Besides, I've been watching you two, haven't I? You need him." Birdie bent to retrieve Abe's hat, which had fallen off at some point, but then he groaned and nearly toppled. Thomas lurched forward and steadied him.

"You should go to hospital," he said, knowing it was useless.

"We'll mend on our own, if nobody shoots us again first. But Avi's wide open now, love. No defenses at all. Put him near loads of spirits and I won't be the only one in here. That would destroy both of us."

Thomas wanted to bandage him up and grab fresh clothes, but there was no telling whether Munroe had friends nearby or if a neighbor might have heard the gunshots and rung the cops. They made their way out of the house with arms around each other, Birdie moaning as they descended the steps. The taxi pulled up just as they arrived at the curb, and the driver gave them a skeptical look. "Taking him to sober up," Thomas explained and handed the driver a five. It was the second time in recent days that he'd needed to bribe a cabbie. And then because he figured there was no point being stingy right now, he said, "St. Francis Hotel."

Four blocks away, several police cars zoomed past in the opposite direction, sirens wailing. The cab driver seemed to think it signaled an opportunity to chat. "You want my opinion, you oughtta stay at the Francis Drake. St. Francis is nice and all, but the Drake's only been open for two weeks, and you ain't gonna find a fancier place nowhere. They got a golf course indoors! And if your pal sobers up and wants more, they got a secret way of delivering booze to your room."

"The St. Francis will do nicely."

"Suit yourself."

Thomas had been in the St. Francis two or three times, mainly out of curiosity. This time, with Birdie hanging on him, he ignored the marble columns, crystal chandeliers, ornate ceilings, and enormous grandfather clock. Instead he settled Birdie in an upholstered chair near the reception desk.

"A room, please." He used his poshest accent.

The clerk cast a doubtful glance in Birdie's direction. "Sir, perhaps—"

"He had a bit too much to eat and drink today. Tourists, you know. Some sleep and he'll be right as rain." A little stack of money stopped any further complaint, and soon the clerk handed him a key to room 812. A minute later the lift operator frowned at Birdie, slumped and looking disreputable.

"Know where he can get some hair of the dog?" Thomas flashed a five to help make his point.

The operator grinned and took the bill. "I'll have something brought to you right away, sir."

The room was suitably opulent, with windows overlooking Union Square. Not that Thomas cared about the view. He helped Birdie to the bed and then efficiently stripped him naked. He had a small round wound in his stomach—already scabbed over, surprisingly— and a larger one on his back, oozing blood. Thomas groaned.

Birdie responded, "Clean us up and fetch some bandages. We'll be all right."

Thomas pushed aside the unsettling plural to concentrate on a problem he'd become well acquainted with during the war. "Infection. Peritonitis."

"I've taken care of it."

It wasn't clear how Birdie had done so, but since Abe was still alive, Thomas had to trust Birdie's capabilities. Still, he hovered uncertainly until Birdie sighed. "Love, I can't stay here much longer."

"Because you'll be stuck if you do."

"Yeah."

Thomas stared at him hopelessly. Anything he asked for would be a betrayal.

Birdie shifted slightly and gave him a sad smile. "You'd lose us both. The result—well, it wouldn't be me and it wouldn't be him. Wouldn't even be entirely human."

A soft knock came at the door. Thomas hastily draped a blanket over Birdie before going to answer. A grinning boy stood there with a large paper bag in hand. "Mr. Dixon? I have your medicine." Thomas snorted and handed the kid a five. He was giving them out like candy.

After closing the door, Thomas threw away the bag and brought the bottle to the bedside. "Want a glass?"

"I'll wait until you get back with the bandages. I don't want to leave Abe alone."

Thomas felt a pang in his heart. Birdie had been the type to worry about stray dogs in a war zone, and now, a decade after his death, he cared about Abe. After a long look at the figure on the bed, Thomas left the room.

He had to hurry several blocks down Market to find a late-night pharmacy, but he was fortunate that it also stocked sundries. Recognizing grimly that the wound in Abe's back needed stitching, he bought a needle and thread in addition to bandages. He also purchased an assortment of basic toiletries—enough for two men— and a small bag to keep them in. He and Abe were going to need clothing as well, but that would have to wait for morning, when the shops were open.

Thomas's rush back to the hotel made passersby stare.

Birdie was exactly where Thomas had left him, smiling from beneath the blankets. "It's too bad we're in no condition to take advantage of this lovely bed," he said.

"You're still interested in fucking?"

"I wasn't, but being inside a body again... maybe. Anyway, Avi is. Not now, but when he's well again."

"Is he.... Can he hear me now?"

"No. It's bad enough to have both of us in here at once, but two minds trying to manage the same sensory information? I think that might drive us insane. I can speak to him if you like."

"Is he all right?"

Birdie gave a small shrug. "No more damaged than when you met him. But he will be if I don't get out of him. Good—"

"Wait!" Thomas had so many things to say to Birdie, but here he stood with the pharmacy bag in his hands and not a single word came out.

"I'm not leaving you, Tommy." Birdie sighed. "Couldn't if I wanted to now—I can't even find the veil. But that's all right. I love you. And Avi's right. You're a mensch."

Before Thomas could ask—again—what that meant, Birdie emitted a long sigh and the blue eyes were replaced by warm brown ones. When Abe gasped, Thomas ran to his side, uncapped the gin that the boy had brought, and held it to Abe's mouth. He gulped it like water.

"Are you in pain?" Thomas set the bottle aside.

Abe's weak reply was touched with humor. "I've been better. But... *a bi gezunt*."

"What's that?"

"'As long as you have your health.' Something my bubbe used to say after someone complained or worried."

Thomas, who wasn't in the mood for a Yiddish lesson, went to the bathroom and dampened several towels. He'd have to ring housekeeping for more, but he had enough for the moment. "How badly are you hurt?" he asked when he returned to the bed. "Birdie said you'd mend and infection wasn't an issue, but—"

"I'll be okay. Thank you for saving my life."

"That was Birdie, not me." Thomas pulled away the blankets and took a moment to assess. He decided to deal with Abe's front side first, since that would be quick. Sitting on the edge of the mattress, he used a towel to dab gingerly at the dried blood on Abe's skin. Abe winced only a bit, so that was good. But cleaning Abe turned out to be.... Erotic wasn't the right word; Thomas wasn't aroused. But he did feel a dizzying mix of emotions, many of them unfamiliar. Tenderness, regret, concern, relief. A visceral connection to a man he'd met only a few days before.

"I'm sorry," Abe said, his eyes fixed on Thomas's face.

"For what?"

"I can't give you Birdie. I would, you know. Let him take over for good. But it doesn't work that way."

Thomas's throat tightened, and he concentrated on a stubborn spot of dried blood near Abe's navel. "Birdie's dead. I accepted that ten years ago."

"I know. But if I could—"

"I wouldn't trade you for him!"

It was unclear which of them was more shocked by Thomas's outburst. Abe blinked, and Thomas felt unaccustomed heat in his cheeks. He ducked his head and returned to cleaning an area that was already clean enough. Then he stuck a self-adhesive bandage over the small wound. Oddly, his hands didn't shake; and although he remembered the times he'd helped medics apply field dressings, those memories weren't intrusive or overwhelmingly distressing.

With Thomas's help and a few whimpers, Abe settled on his stomach with his head turned sideways and cradled on pillows. Under these circumstances, Thomas should not have been reminded of what a very fine arse Abe had, even though the arse in question was beautifully uninjured and temptingly within reach.

"I wasn't with Birdie when he died." This topic was certainly one way to reset his thinking. "I'd been sent to a CCS—a Casualty Clearing Station. Birdie'd reported me to our sergeant and said I had trench foot, but he knew that wasn't the real problem. It was shell shock." He'd never admitted this to anyone. But if you couldn't be honest with a man you'd fucked several times and almost died with, a man who was now patiently withstanding your clumsy doctoring... well, you'd never be honest with anyone.

Abe was gazing at him without condemnation or disgust. "What did they do for you at the CCS?"

"Nothing. I rested for a few days." Lying on a cot, staring at the canvas ceiling, sleeping for hours and hours, hearing nothing that anyone said to him. An impenetrable fog had engulfed him, consumed him. Sometimes he cried without knowing why. Without feeling any sorrow. Sometimes he'd forgotten where he was. The only thing that kept him from sinking into the fog forever was the urge to reunite with Birdie.

"When I returned to the front, Birdie had been evacuated. Influenza. He died alone in a field hospital."

"He died loving you and hoping you hadn't caught the flu too."

This was a gift, really. How many people had lost a loved one without knowing their final thoughts, without having the chance to say how they felt? But Thomas *did* know now, and moreover, he could tell Birdie what was in his heart.

"I loved him," Thomas said.

Abe smiled. "He knows. But I'm sure he doesn't mind hearing you say it."

"Is he here right now?"

"He's always going to be here," Abe said sadly. "He was already fairly solidly on this side of the veil, and now...."

"He said that as well. Is it painful for him?"

"No." Abe patted Thomas's knee comfortingly, which was silly since Abe was the one with the bullet holes. "It's a little frustrating and lonely. But you know what that's like."

Silently, Thomas finished cleaning Abe's back. The exit wound wasn't as ugly as he'd feared, and the bleeding had stopped some time ago, but any movement on Abe's part was likely to reopen it. "I'll need to suture this."

"Okay."

"It'll hurt."

Abe chuckled. "Of course it will." He didn't squirm at all as the needle pierced him, and he didn't utter a sound. Maybe his training gave him excellent control over his body. As the sewing continued, though, his gaze went vague and far away, and finally his eyelids closed. Thomas could only imagine how exhausted he must be. In less than twenty-four hours, Abe had discovered his assistant dead, conversed with a federal agent, had sex with Thomas, gotten shot and nearly died, and been possessed.

"Sleep now," Thomas whispered as he stuck a bandage over the wound. Upon inspecting the bedding, he found only a few small bloodstains, not enough to disturb Abe by putting on fresh sheets. Thomas carefully covered the resting body, gathered the detritus of his doctoring, and shuffled to the bathroom to wash up. He was fairly well done in himself.

The St. Francis Hotel had wonderful showers, with plenty of hot water and a rose-scented cake of soap. Thomas felt infinitely better afterward. He couldn't face putting his soiled clothing back on, so he was nude when he slipped into bed beside Abe, his gun on the nightstand.

"That detective wanted to kill me," Abe said in the dark room.

"Munroe. Yes."

"If you hadn't been with me he would have succeeded."

"He nearly did anyway."

"But he didn't. He's dead now and I'm alive, in bed with you."

Thomas made an affirmative noise. He felt the slight tension in Abe's body even though they weren't touching. "You fancy more gin?"

"Did Townsend send Munroe after me?"

"Undoubtedly."

"Why?"

Thomas wanted to tell him to stop asking questions and go to sleep, but he knew that was pointless. "He's angry over what you and Birdie did to him."

"I don't blame him. But your employer, he's not a good man."

"I know."

"Migulgl zol er vern in a henglayhter, by tog zol er hengen, un bay nakht zol er brenen." Abe chuckled. "Another of my bubbe's sayings. 'He should become a chandelier to hang by day and burn by night.'"

Thomas snorted inelegant laughter. "I like that."

"Nobody expected you to come home with me tonight. Do you think they've figured out you were there?"

"And that I shot Munroe? Maybe. Or maybe they assume you did it. Although based on all the blood near the front door, I'm sure they could tell that Munroe wasn't the only one hurt."

A long sigh. "So at the very least, Townsend and the cops are after me. And possibly after you too."

"Yes."

"We could leave town," Abe said. "I have a little money left."

"You should leave as soon as you can travel. I'm staying here."

Abe was silent for a few moments. "Why stay?"

"I have a job to finish. Five people are dead because of that talisman. You were almost the sixth."

"Almost." Abe shifted on the mattress, moving slightly closer but not touching. He lay on his side facing away from Thomas. "I'm staying with you. If you don't mind."

Thomas scowled at the way Abe's announcement made his heart leap. "Why?"

"There's nowhere else I want to be."

"Okay then. I don't mind." Thomas lightly settled a hand on Abe's hip, feeling his soft skin, greedily absorbing his heat.

"I'm trained in escaping things," Abe said through a yawn. "Maybe we'll wiggle our way out of this cage."

IN THE MORNING LIGHT, Abe was pale and drawn, but he said he was more tired than in pain. His wounds showed no sign of infection, at least, and he ate the eggs and toast that Thomas ordered from room service. He finished up the bottle of gin, gulping it down as easily as Thomas drank orange juice.

"It would be best if we moved somewhere else," Thomas mused. "Are you up for it?"

"Depends how far."

Thomas thought for a moment. "The Palace Hotel."

"Fugitive luxury."

"Better hotels have better security." Which wouldn't keep the cops from getting to them, but it also wouldn't hurt.

"I can make it as far as the Palace, with help. But first I have to piss." Abe groaned as he swung his legs over the side of the bed and started to stand. Thomas rushed over to steady him.

"We can take a taxi."

Abe grinned. "To the bathroom?"

Thomas lightly swatted Abe's bare ass as they shuffled along. Abe whistled at the fancy plumbing fixtures before lightly shoving Thomas back and shutting the door in his face. "Leave a man some dignity, okay?"

"I've had my cock in you more than once. I can manage seeing you use the toilet."

"Well, that makes me feel sensual. Thanks."

Arms crossed, Thomas leaned against the wall beside the door and waited. Abe emerged less than ten minutes later, still naked, with colorful bruises blooming near the bandaged wounds. But he'd tamed his hair and, judging from the scents, washed up and brushed his teeth. "I can walk to the Palace. It's four or five blocks."

He needed help getting into his clothes, though, and he complained about the state of them. "I look like a walking corpse. Might have a slight whiff of one too."

"You can take a bath at the Palace while I find us something to wear."

Abe's sudden smile was bright as the sun. "It's nice having someone take care of me. I can't remember the last time someone did."

It was also nice to be the caretaker, although Thomas didn't say so. He gathered their few belongings and, with Abe leaning on his arm, they made their way to the lift.

THEY TOOK A TAXI AFTER ALL, because by the time they'd walked the length of the St. Francis lobby, Abe was clutching Thomas and trying to stifle moans. He managed to look presentable enough not to scare the cabbie, at least, and he leaned against a pillar in the Palace's long, gleaming lobby while Thomas got them a room. This one was on the fifth floor.

"President Harding died here, you know," Abe informed him as they rode the lift.

"That's promising."

"Everybody has to die somewhere."

And better a posh hotel than an army hospital, Thomas had to admit.

Abe was too exhausted to bathe, so Thomas helped him undress and tucked him into bed. Then Thomas took out his notebook. "Tell me your sizes." Abe grinned and complied.

"I'll likely be gone a while," Thomas said. "But I'll bring you some liquor, and I'll also find us some lunch."

"Okay."

Thomas set Munroe's pistol on the nightstand beside Abe. "You said you know how to use one of these things."

"I do."

"Well, don't unless you have to."

"That's good advice."

Thomas went to the cheap men's goods store he'd frequented in the past, choosing underclothes, socks, and three white shirts for each of them. He also found himself an extra pair of trousers. But Abe needed a whole suit, and this store's wares just wouldn't do. Toting the shopping bags, Thomas went to City of Paris in Union Square, where he found an outfit that was ridiculously expensive but would look great on Abe.

"You're going to burn through your money," he warned himself. But what the hell.

Arms laden, he returned to the Palace and dumped the bags on a chair. Abe gave him a sleepy smile. "What, no lunch?" he joked.

"You're getting spoiled."

"Yeah? I always wondered what that would feel like. It's not bad."

Thomas headed back out, stopping first at a favorite blind pig on Market Street where he bought four bottles of whisky. It was too bad they didn't carry slivovitz; he'd have to ask Abe where he got it.

Finally, Thomas went to States Hof Brau. He could have bought lunch at the Palace, but that tended toward pricy and froufrou, and he wanted something solid. States was a cavernous place packed with tables and echoing with conversations. A short discussion with the maître d', combined with a generous bribe, got Thomas two orders of boiled beef and cabbage with rolls and baked potatoes, a small tureen of goulash, and a couple slices of apple pie. The maître d' handed him everything in a big paper bag and, despite making him promise to return the plates and cutlery, didn't seem assured that Thomas actually would.

Funny, really. A few days earlier he was almost broke, and now money flowed from him like water. But a few days earlier, he had an office and a flat; now he had safe access to neither. And a few days ago, he was alone. Now he had… well, he didn't know what he had.

18

Abe's exhaustion weighed him down like a suit of lead, and he was in more pain than he'd let Thomas know. But he wasn't dead, and that was a surprise. Curled up in a big bed at the Palace Hotel, waiting for Thomas to return, Abe realized he was happy to be alive. Also a mild surprise: he hadn't realized he'd cared much one way or the other.

He considered discussing the matter with Birdie, who was as much an expert on life and death as anyone. But although Birdie was there, hovering just out of awareness, Abe was reluctant to focus on him. Their connection was too strong already, and something inside of Abe was pulling at Birdie, making Birdie the moon to Abe's Earth. He didn't want to destroy both of them by allowing a merger.

But he was so tired, and it was so hard to fight. He massaged his temple and waited impatiently for more booze.

Thomas swept into the room with the smell of rain and good food. "Still hungry?"

"Thirsty." Abe sat up, wincing at the twinge in his gut.

After setting a paper bag on the table, Thomas approached with a bottle of whisky and handed it to Abe. He set three more bottles on the nightstand, near the gun, and then hung his overcoat and hat in the closet.

Abe uncapped the first bottle and swallowed almost half of it in one go. He felt the burn rather distantly and focused on the blessed layer of insulation the alcohol gave him, as if booze created a psychic shell. "Thank you," he said to Thomas and sighed as he set the bottle down.

"Did your stomach do okay with breakfast... and now the drink?"

"As far as I can tell, everything seems to be working okay."

"Jesus. You were seconds away from death yesterday."

"I told you that spirits are powerful. Even more when they connect with the living."

Thomas scrunched the corner of his mouth. "But you get weaker."

"Mostly because I'm resisting... joining with him. If I stopped resisting, the thing we'd become would be very strong indeed."

"Joined." Thomas startled Abe by rapidly approaching and then bending to grasp Abe's bare shoulders. "I don't want that. And I don't want you to be replaced by Birdie either."

"But you love Birdie."

Thomas answered in a fierce growl. "Birdie's dead. You and I, we're still alive."

Abe's throat tightened, and he very much wished he was well enough to make love. Instead he wrapped his arms around Thomas's middle and drew him into an embrace. It was an awkward angle, and Thomas was taking care not to jostle Abe's wounds, but it was powerful and lovely nonetheless.

"Lunch," Thomas said hoarsely after a moment, pulling away. "Shall I serve you in bed, Your Majesty?"

"Yes," Abe replied, hoping he'd captured a regal tone. He'd never had the opportunity to indulge in elaborate sex games. He liked to fuck fast and hard, and he could get that when he wanted. But it was nice to imagine playing a king waited upon by his lord of the bedchamber. And the time after that, perhaps he'd be an innocent farm boy taken captive by a pirate. Or....

"I meant serve food," Thomas said grinning, apparently reading Abe's mind. Which should have been Abe's trick.

"I guess I'll have to be satisfied with that for now."

Thomas poured something from a tureen into two bowls and brought them to the bed, along with spoons. "*Gulyás!*" Abe exclaimed when Thomas handed him a bowl.

Although Thomas didn't reply, he looked pleased with himself as he pulled over a chair so he could eat next to the bed. Abe couldn't remember whether his mother's goulash had tasted better, but this was certainly good. And the company, silent but near, was satisfying as well.

They finished off the stew and then tore into the boiled beef and cabbage. Abe ate a lot, but he didn't keep up with Thomas's prodigious appetite. "The army must have struggled to keep you fed."

"I spent the entire war hungry. Afterward, when I was back in London and... ready to face the world again, I ate so much for weeks that I made myself sick."

"Were you working as a policeman then?"

"I'd been one before, so it was easy enough to get my old position back. Turned out to be hard to keep it though."

"Why?"

Thomas blew a heavy breath. "I was bloody tired of people telling me what to do. I hadn't been all that good at it before the war, and after.... I thought I'd strike out on my own."

"In another country?"

"You're not the only one who's haunted."

Abe nodded knowingly and then finished the rest of the whisky, sip by sip, while watching Thomas eat pie. "I've been thinking about the amulet."

"Oh?" Thomas shot him a wary look.

"Emil said that it requires incantations to be used properly."

Thomas huffed. "Why? Why not just push a button or heat it in a flame? Who makes these bloody rules?"

"I don't know. But magic does have rules, as do spirits and ghosts —and monsters too, I suppose. Extensions of the laws of nature. I had a teacher once who said that before God created the heavens and the earth, there was chaos, and that laws of any kind are what hold that chaos at bay."

"All right," Thomas said with a scowl. "Rules. Pertinent to our situation how?"

"Is Townsend a foolish man?"

"No."

"So when he got his hands on the talisman, he probably looked for someone to help him use it. That someone might have helpful information."

Thomas stood, collected the dishes, and brought them to the table. "Do you know who that someone might be?"

"Maybe. You had me give you a list of magicians, but I think that's the wrong direction. I think we need a scholar. There's a professor in Berkeley who's an expert on these things—I've met her a few times through Emil. I think we should call her."

It took several moments for Thomas to consider this, but eventually he nodded and gestured at the phone.

ALTHOUGH AT FIRST Edith Payne had been reluctant to meet on short notice, Abe bribed her with a promise of dinner at the Garden Court. This was expedient for Abe too, since the famous restaurant was located in the Palace Hotel and he wouldn't have to go far. "It shall have to be an early dinner," she informed him. "I don't want to take the ferry home too late."

"Of course. Six?"

"I'll see you at six, Mr. Ferencz."

When Abe hung up the phone, Thomas was grinning at him. "You are an exceptionally persuasive man, Abraham Ferencz."

"Am I?"

"I tend to get my way through brute intimidation. But you lay on the charm and offer the other person exactly what they think they want."

Abe put on his thickest Hungarian accent. "It is alvays my great pleasure to meet the needs of my acqvaintances, sir." He added a bow, as deep as he could manage with his wounds.

But Thomas's expression had gone thoughtful, his gaze unfocused. "Imagine," he said quietly.

"Yes?"

"What the two of us together could accomplish. If we were partners."

The blood rushed in Abe's ears and he fought to keep his voice calm. "I thought you worked alone."

Thomas lifted his eyebrows and gave a half shrug. "I thought so too." Then he stomped into the bathroom and firmly shut the door.

Abe spent the afternoon alternately dozing and drinking, while Thomas smoked endless cigarettes and stared out the window. His hands were shaking more than usual, but his back remained straight and his jaw steady. The weak sunlight bathed him, smoothing out his rough edges.

At five o'clock Abe got out of bed and made his slow way across the room. Thomas drew a bath and helped him in, then brought whisky so Abe could sip while he soaked. Thomas sat like a guardian on the edge of the tub.

Abe was able to dress on his own, although he exclaimed over the suit Thomas had bought him. "This is expensive."

"I wanted something that fit you properly." The cost had been worth it, just to see Abe smile.

Professor Payne arrived moments after they did. She wore a dress two decades out of style, sturdy black shoes, a strangely shaped black hat, and a colorful scarf worthy of an Asian queen. Abe performed the introductions, explaining that Thomas was an acquaintance interested in the history of magic. She stared at Thomas frankly, without demanding more information. He stared back.

It was fortunate that their table was ready, because Abe couldn't have remained standing for much longer. Professor Payne oohed and aahed over the restaurant, taking in the large and glamorous room, the glass atrium hung with enormous chandeliers, the many pairs of yellow marble columns, and the tasteful gilding—just enough to be elegant but not overdone. "I've always wanted to eat here," she said as she smoothed a napkin over her lap. "But an academic's salary rarely affords such extravagance."

"I'm glad you could join us," Abe said.

"I would have thought you'd invite Emil as well. If we're to discuss your field, I mean."

"I haven't seen much of him lately. He's been busy, I think."

"Of course."

They made awkward small talk for a bit. She and Thomas discussed London, which she'd visited two years earlier. She was a particular fan of the British Museum. She also enthused about the guest lecturer who was coming soon to discuss his work in Egypt. "He was one of the people who excavated King Tutankhamen's tomb, and he's helping Mr. Carter catalog the contents."

"Do you study ancient Egypt as well?" Thomas asked her.

"Not exclusively. My specialty is systems of magic in ancient civilizations, however, so Egypt certainly interests me."

The waiter appeared with the first course. Abe ate his but wished he had alcohol instead. He felt the intrusive buzzing of spirits in his brain, which wasn't something he wanted to explain to Professor Payne. She didn't know of his unique abilities and, unwilling to become the object of study, he'd never mentioned them to her. He was certain Emil never had either, agreeing with Abe that those abilities were best kept secret.

Over the rest of the meal, Thomas asked about some of the professor's work, and she was happy to respond. Abe was mildly curious too. Until now, magical artifacts had never appealed to him as a topic of particular interest.

They were almost finished with the main course before the conversation turned to the Prince of Gandhara. When Abe mentioned it, as if in passing, she made a face. "Oh, that!"

Abe pasted on his most innocent face. "What do you mean?"

"I received a visit recently from a man who claimed to have the amulet in his possession. At first I was quite excited—I'd dearly love to add it to the university's collection. But he wasn't interested in donating it, or even selling it." She made a dismissive *pfft* noise.

"Then why did he contact you?"

"He wanted to use the thing! It requires complicated incantations, you know."

Abe and Thomas exchanged a quick look. "What did you tell him?" Thomas asked. He seemed calm, almost nonchalant, but Abe knew him better by now; Thomas was keenly interested in the reply.

"I told him he was going to have to talk to someone else." She waved a hand regally. Then she gave a mischievous smile, leaned forward, and dropped her voice. "In truth, I possess most of the necessary invocations. They're in Woodedge's *Cantus et maledictus antiquae Asiae*, of which I possess a partial copy. But I didn't tell *him* that. I am interested in the study of magical items, not their actual usage. Or misusage."

The next part had to executed gingerly. Abe smiled at her. "Well, I know you have an excellent collection. So if you don't have the complete incantations, nobody does. So your supplicant, Mr.— What was his name?"

"Townsend. Mr. Herbert Townsend."

"Yes, well, Mr. Townsend is out of luck, I guess."

She set down her fork and took a sip of water. "Oh, he'll find it if he looks hard enough. There's a man in Philadelphia with a remarkable collection of texts, and he doesn't mind using them now and then. You may have heard Emil talk about him. Konstantin Maksimov. He's Russian, you know. He fled his country during the revolution and managed to get all his books here too."

Thomas looked as if he badly wanted to take out his black book and write down the name, so Abe shot him a reassuring look. Abe had a very good memory.

Professor Payne decided to skip dessert, which was just as well because Abe was flagging. He needed bed and booze. They walked her through the hotel lobby and out the doors, helping her into a taxi and waving as the car pulled away.

"Anything helpful?" Abe asked when they'd returned to their room. He collapsed onto the bed with a groan.

Thomas strode over and began unlacing Abe's shoes. "Mostly confirms what we already knew. She seems to think Townsend still has the amulet."

"Which means whoever *does* have it hasn't gotten in touch with her."

"Hmm." Thomas tossed aside Abe's shoes and socks and helped him take off his trousers and undershorts. "Several possibilities. Could be that the fellow who went after it hasn't found it yet—maybe Gage handed it to someone else. Could be the thief has it and doesn't want to use it yet. Or could be he doesn't have the connections to know about your professor friend."

"Or maybe he's in Philadelphia by now."

Thomas seemed disheartened by that thought, but then he shook his head. "You know that bath you took earlier? It looked really nice. I'm going to have one too."

"Want company?"

"No. I'm not sure yet what we're going to do tomorrow, but in any case, you should get as much rest as possible."

Abe sighed. "All right. We wouldn't be able to do anything interesting anyway."

"We're not dead yet. That's interesting."

Thomas walked to the bathroom, loosening his tie as he went and leaving the door slightly ajar.

It took a few minutes for Abe to shed the rest of his clothing. He liked listening to the water run; it was a reminder that he wasn't alone. The sound didn't even bother his pounding head. Walking slowly, he turned off the lights but left the curtains parted. He cracked open a window, then climbed into the big bed and pulled up the covers. Although he wanted more whisky, sitting up and reaching for the bottle felt like too much effort. He'd just close his eyes and rest instead.

19

Thomas couldn't remember the last time he'd soaked in a tub instead of showering. Now he lay back, stretched out as much as he could, and remembered what Abe had looked like in this very tub. Beautiful despite the wounds, his olive skin contrasting with the white porcelain, his hair teased by the moisture into a soft halo of curls.

He knew he shouldn't be distracted like this—visions as if from a fever dream—but he indulged nevertheless. Bathing was unexpectedly relaxing, the quiet sounds of water somehow drowning out bullets and mortars.

And perhaps he'd earned a few minutes of leisure. Soon enough he'd need to come up with a plan, some way to catch the killer without running out of money or getting killed himself. For now, he closed his eyes and thought about Abe's compactly muscled body, the way he moved with strength and grace—when he wasn't recently shot—and the way his tongue worked its own kind of magic.

Thomas wasn't yet sure whether Abe was a good man, but he was certainly interesting and complex, and that was good enough. Besides, Abe's loneliness echoed in Thomas's own heart—a heart he'd long ago assumed had turned to stone.

Now, if only he could—

The bathroom door inched open and Abe appeared.

He was naked, but that wasn't what caught Thomas's attention. Abe was moving with none of his usual agile fluidity. Instead he lurched forward, feet dragging, his back uneven. He bounced off the doorframe but hardly seemed to notice. Then he lifted his right hand from his side and pointed Munroe's gun at Thomas.

Thomas went very still. "Abe. You don't need to do this."

But Abe's lips lifted into a vicious snarl and he pulled the trigger. *Click.*

By the time Abe realized there was no bullet in the chamber, Thomas had surged out of the tub and grabbed him, bearing them both to the floor in a wet heap. Abe bucked and fought beneath Thomas's greater weight like a trapped animal, attempting to gouge out Thomas's eye with one hand while the other bashed him in the head with the pistol. Thomas tried to wrestle the weapon away while also protecting his face and keeping Abe trapped, but everything was slippery and hard to grip.

A swing of the gun connected hard against Thomas's temple, graying his vision. Abe took the opportunity to scramble out from underneath him and dash toward the door.

Fortunately the floor was slick too, and Abe fell face-down. Before he could regain his feet, Thomas threw himself on top, grabbed his wrists, and bent his arms behind his back. Abe still kicked and writhed but couldn't get much traction. Thomas, using his body weight to pin Abe in place, twisted the gun out of Abe's grip and brought it down hard on the back of Abe's skull.

Abe went suddenly still.

"Jesus Christ." Thomas set the gun on the windowsill and dragged Abe's unconscious form to the bed. Then he retrieved handcuffs from his suit coat and manacled Abe to the sturdy headboard.

Water and blood—Thomas wasn't sure whose blood—were everywhere. His face stung, and his head was pounding. He hastily wiped his face with a towel before fetching his Smith & Wesson and his trousers. After getting partially dressed, he pulled a chair near the bed and waited, gun in hand.

It didn't take long. Abe shuddered and groaned, and his eyes fluttered open. He tried to yank his arms free, and when they remained fettered, he growled and spat out words in a foreign language.

"If you want me to understand, you're going to have to tell me you hate me in English."

"Fuck you!"

"Well, good. That I understand." Thomas shifted slightly in his seat and waved the gun. "Where's the amulet?"

Abe said something unintelligible. Little flecks of foam issued from his lips as he spoke.

God, Thomas's head ached! He shook it in hopes of clearing it, but one of his eyes was swelling shut and the movement didn't help. Deep in his heart he'd expected an outcome like this, and yet a foolish part of him had hoped anyway. "Was sex part of the con or did you truly enjoy it?" It wasn't an important question but he wanted to know.

"Sinner!" Abe hissed. And then he laughed mirthlessly.

Which was when Thomas noticed something he should have seen much earlier: although Abe's eyes were brown, right now they held none of their usual clarity and heat. Instead they were as muddy as a trench in Somme.

Thomas shot to his feet. "Get out!" he shouted. "Get the fuck out of him!"

The thing inside Abe gave a ghastly smile. "No. Abe's gone forever. It's only me now. Do you want to fuck me too?" It lifted its hips in a lewd invitation and licked its lips.

"Abe! Damn it all, Abe, you need to fight this. Come back. Birdie! Help me call him."

He didn't see Birdie. And although something might have wavered in the air at his side, it might only have been due to his injured eye. But the dybbuk's lips drew back and its body thrashed and shuddered so violently that the bed frame creaked and the creature nearly disjointed its arms. It was horrible to watch, even worse than seeing someone die, and Thomas could do nothing but stand nearby with the gun in his hand, quietly and rapidly chanting Abe's name.

The dybbuk screeched like a mortar shell in flight, shook once more, and went still.

Abe wasn't breathing.

Thomas shoved the gun into his pocket and shook Abe's shoulders violently. "No. Don't give up, damn it. Don't you dare!"

Abe drew in a noisy whoop of air and opened his eyes, revealing irises a clear amber-brown and warm as an August afternoon. Thomas wrapped him in a greedy embrace. "Abe, Jesus, Abe, Abe." He couldn't seem to find any other words.

Abe was crying. Sobbing in great noisy gusts, burying his face against Thomas's skin, body shaking as if he had a fever. Thomas held him until the tears subsided. Then he went to fetch the key to the handcuffs.

"I could escape from these on my own." Abe's voice was hoarse and weak.

"No need to." After freeing Abe's arms—his wrists bruised and torn—Thomas uncapped a fresh bottle of whisky and handed it over. Abe drained it in one long draught.

Thomas set aside the empty bottle. "I think I need to repair some of your stitches."

"Just kill me." Abe made the bleak plea without theatrics or hesitation, then turned his head away.

"Not bloody likely."

Ignoring for now the mess they'd made, Thomas gathered fresh towels and the items he'd bought at the pharmacy.

Abe remained silent and immobile while Thomas repaired the torn stitches in his back and bandaged his wrists. The wound in his belly appeared unaffected by their struggles, and he didn't resist when Thomas tidied him up, moved him to the clean side of the bed, and tucked him in.

"I'll call for more towels and linens," Thomas said. But first, not wanting to terrify whatever unfortunate hotel employee came to the door, he did a bit of doctoring to his own face. Then he swabbed up the water and blood from the bathroom floor. He drained the tub too, regretful that his bath had been interrupted.

A wide-eyed young woman delivered the bedding and towels, and by the time Thomas remade the bed, he was thoroughly done in. Abe had the same thousand-yard stare that Thomas had seen on so many soldiers' faces. He had once sported it himself, in fact. There had been no easy cure for it, either during the war or after, but the passage of time had helped. As had the occasional comforting word.

Thomas stripped and got into bed beside Abe.

"What if I try to murder you again?" Abe murmured.

"I'll stop you again." To emphasize his point, Thomas wrapped his arms around Abe, who sighed and leaned back against him.

"The gun. Why didn't it work?"

"I removed the bullets."

"Why?"

"Didn't trust you."

Abe laughed. "You shouldn't."

"I don't trust anyone, love, so don't consider yourself special." He kissed Abe's tender nape.

A few moments of silence passed, and Thomas thought how good it was to be alive, even now, under these circumstances. But then Abe said again, as if he'd read Thomas's thoughts, "You need to kill me."

"No."

"You can make it an easy death if you want. Smother me with a pillow like I did to H-Helen." His voice caught on her name. "I won't fight you."

"It wasn't you who killed that girl."

Abe squirmed around in his grasp and pushed at Thomas's chest. "It was these hands, Thomas. The same hands that stabbed Roy and strangled Zook."

"And how many people do you suppose have died at *my* hands? You saw what I did to Munroe. Do you suppose I got that fast and accurate with a gun by tatting doilies?"

"But you were a soldier. A policeman. A detective. You killed because you had to."

"You don't know that."

Abe pushed at him again, but more weakly. "I do. Birdie told me you're an honorable man. A mensch."

Thomas let a chuckle escape. "Has it occurred to you he might be biased? Anyway, if we're trying to deflect blame, let me point out that you were possessed by a bloody dybbuk. Did you even remember what happened with Gage and the others?"

"I still don't," Abe sighed, falling back onto the pillow. "A few vague flashes and that's all. I remember what I did to you, though."

"You pointed an unloaded gun at me."

Abe mumbled something Thomas didn't understand. Then he turned his head to look at Thomas. "What happens when the dybbuk comes back? Next time it possesses me, I won't be able to get rid of it. I'll become a monster."

"We won't let it come back."

"I can't stop it, Thomas! It's strong."

Thomas cupped Abe's cheek. "And so are you. Anyway, tomorrow we go get the bastard who's doing this to you." He'd honestly have preferred to do it tonight, but Abe was in terrible condition and Thomas wasn't at his best either. He'd have to hope that waiting until morning wouldn't be too late.

"I should have figured this out a long time ago."

"Nobody wants to suspect a friend of doing such awful things." And the betrayal would be especially searing for a man who had very few friends to begin with. "I'm the detective. I should have known it was him."

"Emil." Abe spoke quietly. "You don't suppose Professor Payne also—"

"I doubt it. I think she found out about the amulet from Townsend and mentioned it to Magnus. And then Magnus hired Gage— Had they met?"

"Yes."

Thomas nodded, annoyed he hadn't made that connection long

ago. "Magnus hired Gage to steal the bloody thing. Then... I don't know. Maybe Gage got greedy and demanded too much to hand it over. Magnus sent a dybbuk to fetch it."

"In my body."

"Yeah." Thomas petted Abe's shoulder. "Because even on your own you're strong, and Magnus knew Gage would let you get close."

"And I killed Zook because he was a witness. But what about Helen?"

Thomas remained silent, letting Abe work out the painful truth for himself. His expression changed when the realization dawned. "She was in it with Roy."

"Magnus knew her as well?"

"Yes."

Magnus had likely recruited both of them, perhaps not knowing which would have an easier time getting close to Townsend. Tastes varied.

Abe sighed loudly. "Townsend wants me dead because I set Birdie on him. The cops want me because of Munroe. And Emil is just using me as his tool to get what he wants."

That was the sum of it, give or take a few loose ends. It was a grim picture, but not a hopeless one. "You have me on your side," Thomas reminded him.

That made Abe smile broadly. He reached over to stroke Thomas's injured face with a butterfly touch. But then his expression grew more serious. "So where's the amulet? We can't let Emil use it. Even before this—really ever since I met him—I knew he wasn't... he wasn't a good man. I didn't realize how bad, though. People have a lot of shades of gray."

"What happens if he does use it?"

"He'll become a powerful man."

Thomas remembered what Townsend had said: mayor first, then governor, then the White House. It would be bad enough if he succeeded at those goals, and a disaster if Magnus did. It would most certainly mean the end of Abe, which was an idea Thomas couldn't accept.

"I think I know where the amulet is," he announced. "Or at least where it was last night. I don't know if it's still there."

Although it made him wince to do so, Abe propped himself up on an elbow. "Oh? Where?"

"In your house."

20

Despite his physical pain and psychic fatigue, despite the horror of understanding what he'd done and fearing what would likely come next, a strange peace settled over Abe as he spooned, relaxed, in Thomas arms. They might not survive the night, and if they did, tomorrow would bring new risks. Nothing about their future was certain or safe.

But right now they lay in bed together. Thomas hadn't rejected him, not even when he had every right to. Not even when good sense demanded it. Thomas quite literally had Abe's back, and that was a lovely thing. Especially since Thomas didn't seem interested in what Abe could do for him. Thomas hadn't asked for money, the sex had been Abe's idea, and Thomas had nursed him and cared for him as if Abe were someone valuable and dear. Even if this lasted only a few hours, it was worth dying for.

But more importantly, it was worth living for.

~

"Well, you look like shite."

Abe squinted at Thomas, who loomed over the bed. "You're not much better."

"That's true," Thomas sighed. "How's your head?"

"Between the possession and the thunk you gave me? A bullet might have been gentler."

"You think you could eat something?"

Abe assessed the condition of his stomach. "Yes."

"Get dressed if you can. I'll go fetch us something."

Trying not to groan too loudly, Abe sat up. His head hurt, the bullet wound hurt, his muscles were sore from wrestling Thomas, and every inch of his body felt badly used. But, he reminded himself, he wasn't dead and neither was Thomas, which left them both in better condition than some. "Are we going to relocate to a different hotel today?"

"Can Magnus send the dybbuk after you wherever you are?"

"I don't know." Abe had given this some thought. The previous times he'd been possessed, he'd been at home, and Emil certainly knew where that was. Last night it was possible Professor Payne had spoken to Emil and mentioned Abe's location, but Abe had no way of knowing if that was true. "Maybe."

"Then there's not much point in moving. As for Townsend and the police.... I don't know." He chewed his lip pensively. "Let's see if we can find the amulet. We can make decisions after that."

We. It was surprising to hear Thomas use that pronoun, considering he had good reasons not to trust Abe. But it made Abe smile anyway. He'd so rarely been part of a plural—other than one of the parties being a spirit.

"Why don't I join you for breakfast and we can go to my house afterward?"

"Can you manage that?"

"I can try." It was better than sitting around and waiting for something to kill him. "Booze would help."

"We're out. We can get some on the way."

One lovely thing about San Francisco was that you could find a blind pig open even at nine in the morning. If your companion had some money, you could purchase several bottles of bathtub gin and then duck into an alley and drink an entire bottle of the stuff.

"If nothing else kills you, that rot will," Thomas said.

"I wish sometimes I could get drunk. Have you ever tried marijuana?"

"No."

"I have, twice. It intoxicates me, but unfortunately it also makes the spirits easier to sense."

Thomas shifted his feet. "Do you need to drink more?"

"Not right now."

They went to a little restaurant not far from the Palace, where Thomas ate steak and eggs and stewed tomatoes and toast and complained about the bad coffee. Abe was more circumspect, nibbling at some toast until he was sure it would stay down and then ordering a bowl of oatmeal. The waitress gave Abe and Thomas wary looks at first, but she seemed calmer when they ate quietly and the other diners—working-class men recently off shift, from the look of them—paid them no mind.

Abe liked to watch Thomas eat. He was neat about it but single-minded and efficient, as if the goal were to consume as much as possible as quickly as possible but without committing an etiquette faux pas. And Thomas was thrillingly handsome even with the marks on his face, his hands were big and solid and sure, and he didn't seem to mind being stared at.

Glancing around first to make sure nobody was close enough to overhear, Abe leaned forward. "How do we get into my house without getting arrested or shot?"

"You've a back door on the alley?"

"Yes."

"Do you have a key?"

Abe grinned. "I don't need one. But the cops won't be watching the back of the house?"

"They'll have a car or two out front, maybe an officer in the alley. But I have a plan. I'll get us to the house; you get us inside."

"Sounds fair."

They took a crowded Geary streetcar, jostling and rattling up the hill. Abe watched the familiar scenery with a fresh eye and liked what he saw. San Francisco had a brashness, a beauty of mixed artifice and nature, a youthful bravado. It reminded him of the men who put on dresses and lipstick and beads, propositioning specific other men with the confident knowledge that they wouldn't be refused. The city, a mixture of charm and danger, existed on its own terms and according to its own rules.

He didn't want to abandon it.

At Eleventh Avenue they hopped off the streetcar. Mrs. Osinova's grocery was nearby, leading Abe to wonder if he'd ever again taste her stuffed cabbage. But now wasn't the time for food. Thomas walked a half block west along Geary Street and then turned north into the narrow alley.

"It's not going to be this easy, is it?" Abe asked. "Us just marching on up."

"Nothing's ever easy." Thomas stopped and grabbed Abe's arm. "Look. When we get inside, we won't have long. Five, ten minutes at the most. Can you find it that quickly?"

"I don't know." He'd been thinking about where the dybbuk might have hidden the amulet—assuming it was indeed in his house. If the spirit was acting entirely on its own, it might have left the thing anywhere. Under a loose floorboard, perhaps, or at the back of a cupboard. Maybe even up in the spider-infested attic. But Thomas knew where *he* would secrete something small and valuable. If he had only a few minutes to search, that was where he'd look.

"Too bad there aren't any spells to find lost things," Thomas said.

"Oh, there are, but I don't know them. And using them to find a magic item would be unwise."

"We'll have to rely on luck then. Um, any chance you could ask the dybbuk?"

Abe shuddered. "I'm not calling on that thing."

Although Thomas frowned, he nodded. "I understand. And Birdie?"

"He might not know, and I don't want to use him anymore. We've done enough to him already." Birdie had earned his rest, even though Abe didn't know if he'd ever get it.

"We'll have to rely on luck then. And your good sense."

If Abe had good sense, he would have realized long ago what was happening. And he wouldn't be falling in love with Thomas Donne.

They stopped right before Clement Street, still hidden by the shadow of the alley. Abe couldn't quite see his house, but they were very close. He recognized the orange cat watching them from atop a trash bin. Sometimes it would nap on his front porch and let him give its chin a quick rub as he passed. Today he only smiled at it.

"You'll cross the street," Donne ordered. "Then step out of sight in the alley there. Within a minute or so, you should hear a fuss. As soon as you do, run down the alley to the back of your house and get inside. I'll join you when I can."

"Where will you be?"

Thomas grinned. "Making the fuss."

He crossed Clement and entered the alley. Abe could see him jogging down its length toward California Street.

Abe took a deep breath and crossed the street. He wasn't sure how fast he'd be able to move right now, with his head still sore and the stitches pricking at his back. What if he stumbled? What if he couldn't find the amulet? What if the dybbuk—

He had barely gotten settled into the shadows of the alley before shots rang out—three of them, very fast and loud—in the direction Thomas had gone. Glass broke. Something heavy crashed. Well, that sounded like a fuss. He just had to hope Thomas was on the safe end of those bullets.

Abe did a short lope down the alley, heading toward the back of his house. Sirens started up. It sounded as if two police cars might have been parked in front of his house but were now moving away. Nobody accosted him as he reached the back door, and it took him only seconds to manage the lock. The kitchen was as he'd left it, clean and tidy, but blood—his and Munroe's—still marred the floor and walls of the hallway. It smelled like death. Munroe's spirit, however, was nowhere to be seen, which was a considerable relief. Sometimes murder victims didn't rest easy.

Somebody had rummaged through the parlor. Chairs were disarrayed and overturned, the table in the back sat crookedly, and cards, gauze, and bits of paper were scattered everywhere. Several of his slate tablets had been broken and—far worse—the special cabinet he sometimes used for seances lay in chunks and splinters. It had been a beautiful thing, painted in bright colors and equipped with an array of secret drawers and latches. He'd mourn that cabinet later, if he survived.

For now, he rushed to the black curtains hanging along one wall, parted them, and stepped into the small storage space behind. Someone had rummaged through his stash of props, damaging many of them. But... ah, there it was, dented but otherwise intact. The rusty tin box had flowers painted on the side and Cyrillic writing on the hinged top. It had once contained his mother's favorite brand of tea, a drink so beloved that she'd brought a boxful of it in her luggage when the family emigrated. After she emptied it, she gave the box to Abe, who'd filled it with the tiny treasures a young boy found on the streets of the Lower East Side: a penny, a roller skate key, a few buttons, a rubber ball. Abe had later modified the box for some of his very first magic tricks, and later still, had proudly showed the box to his mentor, Emil.

He tucked the box under his arm and was about to leave when someone ran into the room. He peeked around the edge of the curtain and was relieved to see Thomas, panting and red-faced but apparently unharmed. "We have to go," Thomas said urgently. "Did you find it?"

"Maybe." Abe hadn't had time to check.

They rushed to the back door, Abe wondering whether he'd ever see his home again, and then ran north up the alley toward California Street. They'd almost made it when a man in a suit stepped out from between two houses on their left. "Freeze!" he barked, pulling a gun.

Thomas shot him. Just like that, without hesitation, his movements so fast that Abe barely tracked him. The man collapsed with a grunt, clutching his chest. Thomas didn't slow down; he grabbed Abe's arm and pulled him to the opposite side of the alley. "Hurry!"

Abe's wounds hurt, but he did his best to keep up. Thomas led him on a serpentine route between houses and through alleys, finally busting open the flimsy wooden door of a shed and dragging Abe in. He pulled the door closed.

The shed smelled of mouse droppings and rotting wood, and only a little light snuck in through a crack in the roof. The sirens remained distant, and during several minutes of stressful waiting, nobody had barged in on them.

"Did you kill that man?" Abe asked.

"Didn't stop to take his pulse."

Abe wasn't sure what to feel. The victim could have been an honest policeman simply doing his job, or he could have been another of Townsend's men sent to kill him. Well, there was nothing to be done about it now.

"Did you find the amulet?" Thomas demanded.

"Let's find out."

"Do you need more light?"

"No." Abe had managed the box in complete darkness before.

If someone had opened it, they would have found it empty except for the faint odor of tea. But as Abe pressed the inside in exactly the right spots and in the right sequence, hidden springs activated and an entire side swung open, revealing a hidden chamber lined with thick fabric to keep any contents from rattling around. When he was just starting out, it had been the perfect way to con a quarter out of rubes. They'd give him the coin, he'd hide it in the box, and the rube— usually amused enough not to protest—would believe Abe had made it disappear.

And now it was the perfect place to hide... an amulet.

He held the thing up to the light. It wasn't much bigger than a quarter, in fact, although it was heavier. Possibly solid gold, in fact. There were carvings and a few gemstones, but the talisman was filthy, and he couldn't discern details in the poor light.

"Six people have died for that," Thomas said.

"Six that we know of. Objects like this tend to have a bloody history."

"Do you want to keep it?"

Abe looked at him in horror. "No!"

"You could become a ruler."

"I don't want to rule anyone. I'd be horrible at it. I'm not a good man. I'd… I'd never trust myself for something like that."

For some reason, that made Thomas smile warmly. "Right. Then we need to decide what to do with the bloody thing."

The longer Abe held it, the heavier it became. It felt oily in his hand, and warm. "I'd rather you hold onto it while we decide," he said.

Thomas took the amulet, wrapped it in a handkerchief, and tucked it into an inner pocket. "This isn't the best place to decide. Let's get out of here." He crept out of the shed, gesturing with his hand for Abe to wait. Then he disappeared, and for a terrible minute or two, Abe thought he wouldn't come back. He did, though, and this time he waved at Abe to follow.

They spent a good half hour wandering through a maze of alleys, side yards, and shops until Abe, who'd lived in the city for nearly twenty years, hardly knew where they were. He was surprised when, turning a corner, he spotted familiar ground. "We're going to Golden Gate Park?"

"I think we should go see the buffalo."

Abe assumed he was joking, but apparently not. Thomas led them to the paddock, huffed in what might or might not have been approval at the huge animals, and then walked toward a stand of trees. He stopped when they were tucked among the shrubbery.

"A good hiding spot," Abe observed.

"Not all that good. A few months ago I found a client's husband here with a lawyer's cock up his arse."

"What did you do?"

"Told the bloke on the bottom that when his wife asked for a divorce, he'd better say yes."

Abe chuckled. "Did you plan to reenact the event now?"

"Don't think you're in any condition for it, love."

Fair enough. There might have been some parts of Abe that didn't hurt, but he couldn't find them. Besides, the presence of the amulet made him uneasy. He pulled a bottle of gin from his coat and took a long pull, grimacing at the taste. He'd pay a great deal for some slivovitz or good whisky right now. "What do we do next?"

"That's your decision." They had dropped their voices for privacy's sake.

Abe blinked at him. "Mine? Why mine? It's your case."

"And you expect Townsend's going to pay me?"

"I bet he'd pay you plenty if you told him you had the amulet."

Thomas shook his head. "He'd turn around and kill us both. Besides, I don't want him in charge either." Then he surprised Abe by reaching over to stroke his face. "I'm just a private dick, for hire by anyone with a few dollars. Townsend tried to kill you. Magnus used you. That makes this your decision."

"I thought you didn't trust me."

"Don't trust myself either."

Abe considered their options. They could throw the amulet into the ocean and flee the city, but then he'd spend the rest of his life feeling like a hunted rabbit. And he suspected that the right kind of magic could find the amulet, even in the Pacific; objects like this one had a way of not staying lost for long. They could hand it over to Townsend in exchange for a lot of money and a promise to let them be, but he had no confidence that Townsend would honor the promise. Like Thomas, he didn't relish the idea of President Townsend. Then there was Emil... but that was even worse.

"The Bureau," he finally said with a sigh. He didn't know whether that was a safe option either, but it seemed a better bet than the others.

"Right. We'll go find a phone and ring Agent Crespo." Thomas left their hiding place and began striding back toward the buffalo paddock.

It should have been a relief to reach a decision, but before Thomas made it into the open, Abe grabbed his arm. "Wait."

"Yes?" No surprise on Thomas's face. Just... expectation, perhaps.

"Between them, look what Townsend and Emil have done. I have a bullet hole in me and I'm only alive because of Birdie, who's stuck now because of it. As for what Emil did...." He swallowed thickly. "He shoved a dybbuk into me more than once. That's essentially rape, Thomas."

Thomas nodded and gave Abe's lips a quick swipe of his thumb. Such tenderness inside a hard man made Abe want to melt, but there was no time for that now.

"What do you want?" Thomas asked.

"I don't know if the Bureau will do anything to them. I guess they have their own priorities." He licked his lips, tasting the salt of Thomas's skin on his own.

"The government always does."

Abe closed his eyes and thought for a moment, then took a deep breath and looked Thomas in the eyes. "I want to stop both of them. Permanently."

Thomas gave the brightest smile of all.

21

They were in a blind pig deep in the Tenderloin. The place didn't have a name, and although it must have opened after the 1906 earthquake—and probably hadn't been cleaned since—it looked and felt like one of London's most ancient pubs. It was deep and dark, and it served enough booze to meet Abe's needs. Plus the owner was in far enough with the cops that they pretended not to notice the joint's existence, but not so far that he'd inform on Thomas and Abe.

That made it perfect. Thomas and Abe sat at a rickety table in the back, both downing gin and Thomas smoking cigarettes. Abe's face was drawn with pain, but he didn't complain, keeping his back straight and chin up.

"Charming place," he said, lifting a brow at a patron who was passed out drunk and drooling on the table. The man had wet his trousers, but the reek of urine was barely noticeable in the general stink of the place.

"You want to return to the Garden Court?"

"Maybe not." Abe sighed and rubbed his head. "I'd really like to return home, actually."

Thomas didn't miss his own miserable little flat, and it had been years since anywhere had felt like home. But he could understand Abe's feelings nonetheless. "It'd be lovely to fix all this in a way that meant you could go back."

"Do you think that's possible?"

"No. But I've recently learned that loads of impossible things exist."

When Abe grinned back, Thomas's heart beat an obnoxious little pit-a-pat and his cheeks felt hot. No, damn it all, Thomas was not going to fall for this man, no matter how bewitching he was. Despite the fact that he was beautiful. And smart and funny and strong, with a big enough wicked streak to make him irresistible. A man who could be shot and possessed by spirits, could lose his home and be betrayed by his mentor, and yet still sit in a shitty blind pig with a bottle of gin and a genuine smile.

Push it away, Donne. Other problems to solve right now. But he could almost have sworn he heard Birdie laughing the same way he used to whenever Thomas was being stubborn and stupid.

"So, your plan?" Abe asked, his eyes falsely innocent.

"Nothing fancy. We lure them both with the amulet as bait."

"At the same time? That seems risky."

"It's risky any way we turn it, love. But if they're both there, the odds shift, you see. Each of them opposed to the other as well as to us —takes some of the pressure off you and me." He wasn't sure this was true. But in the end, he'd prefer to have all the players in the same spot, where he could see them all.

"Okay." Abe gave a small shrug as if it were as easy as that.

"How did Magnus force that dybbuk into you?"

"I don't know. Emil's not like me—he doesn't usually see spirits. But he knows I do. And he's a scholar. If there's a way to control spirits, he could find it." Abe frowned deeply. "I wonder if he planned to use me all along. God, I wonder if he's used me before." He dug his fingertips into his brow.

"Drink some more." Abe obeyed as Thomas tried to marshal his thoughts. "So we can assume that he'll try again."

"He might be trying right now, for all I can tell."

"Have you any defenses?"

"No. Except now that I know what's happening, maybe I can fight off the intrusion. Or maybe not."

Thomas had assumed as much. It added a layer of danger and uncertainty to an already precarious situation. But he'd never been one to live safely, so no point in trying now. "We'll lure them both at once," he announced. *And hope that the sprits keep their distance.*

SOMEONE HAD BEEN in Thomas's office. The furniture was out of place and the drawers half-open. But there hadn't been anything worth stealing, and the intruder was likely long gone. Thomas opened the windows, and the last of the day's sunlight made bright shapes on the scuffed wooden floor.

Abe started to help him set things to rights, but Thomas growled at him to sit down, and Abe obeyed. It occurred to Thomas—not for the first time—that Abe seemed eager to let him take the lead, both in bed and out. Perhaps if someone spent his life on his own but subject to being taken over by spirits, it was a relief to have a living man in charge. And truth be told, Thomas was enjoying that role far more than he should be, under the circumstances.

Collapsing heavily into the chair behind Thomas's desk, Abe swiveled around to look out the window and spoke without looking at Thomas. "What will we do with them when they get here? Will you shoot them dead?"

"Is that what you want?"

Abe remained silent for a moment, his gaze fixed on the view, and then his shoulders slumped a bit. "No. They both deserve it, but...."

"Could torture them first. Shoot out their knees and make them crawl, carve them up with a blade, scorch them." He took out his lighter and flicked it aflame for emphasis, even though Abe's back was turned.

"Is that what you want?" Abe asked.

"No."

Abe looked over his shoulder and shot Thomas a quick smile. "Good." Then he sighed and swiveled around again. "What do we do? A few stern words and send them on their way? 'No more killing and dark magic, now, *pits'l*.'"

Thomas stroked his chin thoughtfully. "Remember what I said before about using their mutual antagonism to protect us?"

"Of course."

"We can use it as a tool as well."

Cocking his head and leaning forward like an eager student, Abe said, "How?"

"I'll need to ring Crespo."

A WOMAN with a deep voice and disinterested tone answered the number Crespo had given him. Thomas told her the matter was urgent, and she promised to get the message to the agent immediately. After hanging up, Thomas sat on the edge of his desk and mused over how she might do that if Crespo was tromping around Lake Tahoe in search of a dragon. Before he could devise any reasonable scenarios, his phone rang.

"Mr. Donne! I'm very happy to hear from you."

"Will you make an agreement with me?" Thomas had no evidence that Crespo could be trusted, but his gut said yes and he decided to risk it. What was one more gamble among so many?

"I might. Tell me your terms."

Although Abe couldn't hear Crespo's end of the conversation, he was listening closely to Thomas. He reached over to put one hand on Thomas's thigh. Nothing precisely sexual about the gesture; it spoke more of support. Still, Thomas couldn't help but admire those dexterous fingers.

Pay attention to business, Donne.

"We hand you the amulet. In exchange, you make sure something serious and possibly permanent happens to the two blokes behind all of this. Between them, they've murdered and worse."

Crespo took a moment to think about that, during which Abe gave Thomas's leg an approving squeeze.

"Can you provide some evidence of their involvement?" Crespo finally asked. That was reassuring; it meant he wasn't willing to act out of simple expedience. It suggested that the Bureau adhered—at least tenuously—to the rule of law.

"What if I get them to confess in front of you?"

Crespo laughed. "You hand them to me wrapped up in a bow like that, along with the amulet? I can guarantee they will no longer trouble you or anyone else."

"Will Abe and I have trouble from anyone else?"

"Not if I can help it."

That was going to have to be reassurance enough. "Things are getting hot. How soon can you get here?"

"Where's *here*? Your office?"

"Yes."

"Give me an hour."

Thomas frowned. "I thought you were in Lake Tahoe."

Another laugh, this one merry. "Did you know dragons can fly, Mr. Donne?" Then Crespo hung up.

Abe looked at him expectantly. "So?"

"He'll be here in an hour." Thomas held up a hand to forestall more questions. "I don't know. A week ago, I thought the world was a predictable place. Now I have ghosts and magic doodads and bloody dragons, so don't ask me to explain a thing."

Abe withdrew his palm from Thomas's leg and leaned back in the chair. "Do you wish you were as blissfully ignorant as you were a week ago?"

Thomas didn't have to think about his answer. "No. Because then if I'd known of you at all, I'd have thought you were nothing but a handsome conman."

"But I *am* a handsome conman." Abe batted his eyelashes like an ingenue.

"You are. But you're more than that."

Abe's smile became less gaudy and more genuine, lighting up his eyes and bringing color to his cheeks. "Say it, Thomas. Say it if it's true."

"I don't—"

"Either one of us could die at any minute. I know what regrets are like beyond the grave—I've seen the results of them too many times." Abe lifted his chin in a challenge. "Say it if it's true."

Damn. Thomas had faced armies, mobsters, and corrupt cops, not to mention a lover possessed by an evil spirit. But none of those things terrified him as this did. He almost refused. But then he remembered that Abe had let himself be possessed by Birdie, even though it hurt, even though it was bloody dangerous, just so they could get information out of Townsend. Thomas owed him this.

After a sharp nod, Thomas got off the desk and crossed to the outer office, where he checked to ensure the door was locked. He returned to the inner office and closed the windows and curtains before turning off the lights. He didn't want to ring Magnus and Townsend until Crespo arrived, and in the meantime it would be nice if nobody realized he and Abe were here. He had no idea how closely his office was being watched—maybe Townsend and the cops assumed he wouldn't be stupid enough to go there—but it was a good sign that nobody had showed up yet.

Now the room was illuminated by nothing but the last bit of sunlight creeping around the edges of the curtains. Darkness made this easier. Thomas knelt in front of Abe and took his hands. "After Birdie and after the war, I thought I'd never love anyone again. I was too damaged. Damn it, I'm still damaged and always will be—as much as those blokes who lost their limbs or went blind. But it turns out I can still love, and I do. I love you."

There. He'd survived that.

Abe responded with laughter. Thomas was suddenly certain that this had all been an elaborate ruse, and now that Abe had conquered him, Abe would destroy him. But Abe leaned close and whispered, "Birdie says it's about bloody time."

Thomas let out his breath. "Birdie."

"He knows you loved him, Tom. I told you that before. And he also knows you need to move on. It's not healthy for the living to hang on to the dead."

"Tom?" Thomas asked, although that was hardly the important part.

"Yes. Not Birdie's Tommy, and not Detective Thomas Donne, but Tom. My Tom." Abe kissed Thomas's forehead like a benediction.

"Right."

"I love you too, of course," Abe said offhandedly. "I guess some people would say that's not possible since we met only a few days ago. But I know how strong love is. It's enough to keep a spirit from moving beyond the veil, and it's certainly powerful enough to take root in a short period of time. Especially when the soil is fertile."

Thomas might have commented on the awkward metaphor except Abe kissed him again, this time on the lips and with considerable fervor.

"We have some time before our guests arrive, don't we?" Abe asked.

"You've been shot. And possessed."

"So?" Abe got a wicked gleam in his eyes. "Tom."

Enough of that. Thomas stood, strode to his overcoat, and pulled the handcuffs from the pocket, making sure not to jingle them. In the darkness, Abe might not realize what he was fetching. Upon returning to the desk, Thomas quickly yanked Abe's arms behind his back and cuffed his wrists to the chair slats.

"Ah," Abe said, sounding pleased.

"How fast can you escape those?"

Abe gave an experimental tug. "My back and my head hurt, which will slow me down. Five minutes. Six at the most."

Thomas could work with that. He dropped to his knees, unfastened Abe's trousers, and drew out his cock, which was already stiff and eager. "It's a race," he said.

"One I'm going to win no matter what."

Instead of answering, Thomas took Abe into his mouth.

During the war, all Thomas and Birdie could generally manage were a few stolen minutes together without spying eyes. And that was under the best of circumstances. Often all they could do was huddle together under a shared blanket, hands busy at each other's groins, and hope the other soldiers pretended not to notice. Many of them did the same when they could, because regardless of what their preferences might have been, they were young men and any comfort was welcome in the trenches.

The benefit of all of this—although Thomas hadn't seen it at the time—was that he became skilled at giving satisfaction very quickly. He put those lessons to use now, sucking, licking, and stroking for all he was worth. Sometimes he even scraped his teeth along the soft skin, pulling a satisfying moan from Abe's lips.

The handcuffs jingled. Abe arched his back and lifted his hips, and Thomas didn't know whether that was part of his escape efforts or simply an effort to bury himself more deeply in Thomas's throat. It had that effect in any case. Thomas pressed his nose into Abe's soft curls, loving the scent of him—gin and sweat and cotton and salt. Loving the way Abe's pulse beat against his tongue. Loving the weight of Abe's balls in his palm, vulnerable and vital and warm.

"Tom!" Abe choked out seconds before he spilled.

Thomas kissed Abe's cock and tucked it away, then refastened his trousers. He licked his lips before getting to his feet. "I won," he said smugly.

The cuffs fell on the floor with a clatter. "No."

"Five minutes, you said."

"I lied."

Thomas captured him in a brutal kiss, making sure Abe tasted himself on Thomas's tongue, knew this meant that Abe was now his. No amount of slipping out of chains would change that. Judging from Abe's eager response, he understood the message and welcomed it.

Finally, and reluctantly, Thomas pulled away to sit on the desk, leaving Abe panting in the chair. "Strategy," Thomas said.

"Okay."

"You're the one with the gifted tongue—"

"That's not what I'd say after your recent performance."

Thomas tapped his shoe lightly against Abe's leg. "—so this will be your performance."

To his enormous credit, Abe didn't quail. "Give me the story."

"Come up with an excuse for Crespo's presence—one the others won't question. And sweet-talk them into confessing."

"That's a tall order."

"I've seen you work. You can get someone to tell you exactly what you need to know in order to convince them the spirits gave you access to their secrets."

Abe nodded, an indistinct movement in the deepening darkness. "But those are everyday rubes who *want* to be conned. This is Emil Magnus, who taught me half of my tricks, and Townsend, who's no fool himself."

"You'll just have to be more clever than they are, love."

"Call me that again—and mean it."

"Love. My love. Beloved." Thomas huffed. "If you expect me to start reciting love sonnets next, you'll be disappointed." Secretly, though, he thrilled to hear those words from his own mouth, and to know that they were true.

"I'll be as clever as I can be," Abe assured him.

After that, Thomas paced the room and wished he could open the windows and breathe in the fog. Abe remained at the desk, alternately sipping gin and playing with a coin, making it dance between his fingers like a living thing. If Thomas listened very closely, he caught the faintest sound of the Alcatraz foghorn, warning of danger ahead.

But nothing worthwhile was perfectly safe, was it?

He was beginning his hundredth lap of the room when a knock sounded on the outer door. "Crespo," said a voice.

Time for battle.

22

Thomas had said he loved him, and meant it, and that outweighed every lingering pain in Abe's body. Made all his aches and trials worthwhile. If he died tonight, regrets and sorrow wouldn't cement him on this side of the veil—but he hoped he'd get to live.

After turning on the lights, Thomas strode to the door and let Crespo in. His thinning hair was disheveled and his suit crumpled, but a broad smile offset all that. "I'm really glad you called me. Where's our punks?"

"On the way as soon as I ring them," Thomas replied.

"One of them is Townsend?"

"Yes."

"Figured. The other?"

Abe answered. "Emil Magnus."

That made Crespo whistle. "I thought you two were pals."

"You seem to know a lot about me, Agent Crespo."

"The Bureau likes to keep tabs on certain folks. Can't say I pegged Magnus on this one, though. He's never shown signs of being interested in anything more than money and handsome young men."

"Apparently his tastes are more diverse than that," said Thomas.

"Hmm. Okay. Are those two working together?"

"No. The opposite, in fact. Magnus likely hired Gage to steal the amulet from Townsend."

"Hmm." Crespo tended to project an image of careless cheer, but Abe—good at reading people—saw the sharpness of Crespo's eyes. The agent understood more than he let on, and he'd be a formidable foe. But Abe hoped Crespo was on his side. His and Thomas's.

Crespo threw himself into a chair, stretched his long legs in front of him, and rolled his head. "I'm sore. Need something to work the kinks out." Then he appeared to rally. "All right, boys, what's the plan?"

Thomas finished rolling a cigarette and put on his hardest expression, which scared Abe a bit but also made his cock stir. Greedy thing.

"You're going to keep your gob shut and play along with what Abe says." Thomas lit the cigarette, his fingers steady as a rock, and blew a cloud of smoke in Crespo's direction. "Got it?"

Seemingly delighted at this turn of events, Crespo grinned and nodded.

Thomas stared at him, narrow-eyed, for a moment, then turned to Abe. "Ready?"

Abe gave the question serious consideration. This wasn't going to be like one of his shows, where the patter was fully rehearsed. It wouldn't be like a séance either—neither Townsend nor Emil had any interest in conversing with the dead, and Emil knew all of Abe's tricks. He'd taught Abe many of them. The stakes were higher than any Abe had ever faced, and— Wait. He had stood on the planks of a dozen or more stages, the bright lights in his eyes, the audience rapt, and he'd instructed his assistant to point a gun at him and pull the trigger. And every damn time, Abe had caught the bullet. Hell, he'd caught one for real just two days ago—albeit in a very different way— and he'd survived that as well. Sure, the stagecraft relied on certain trickery and his recent survival on the intervention of a spirit. But the risks had been both real and deadly, and he'd lived. This was going to be nothing but another performance. He could do this.

After taking a swig of gin big enough to make Crespo's eyes widen, Abe nodded at Thomas. "Ready. Go ahead and call Townsend. But I'll call Emil."

"Right."

"What do you want me to tell him?"

"That we have the amulet."

The conversation with Townsend was short, Thomas barking his words without emotion or explanation and hanging up the phone with enough force to knock it over. "He's coming," he said as he set it aright.

Now it was Abe's turn. Mrs. Li answered at Emil's house, sounding irritated. She didn't thaw even when he identified himself and asked for Emil, but she did fetch him promptly.

"Abe, my boy! So good to hear from you."

Vicious anger roiled in Abe's gut, but he kept his tone light. "Hello, Emil. I have something here that might interest you."

"Oh?" Was that a catch in Emil's voice? Maybe. "What's that?"

"The Prince of Gandhara."

Emil answered as smooth as oil. "How interesting. But I thought I advised you to stay away from it."

"Which is why I'd like to give it over to you. For safekeeping."

"Of course, of course. Well, bring it on over then. I'll be home for another hour."

It was a weird game, with each of them pretending nothing had changed between them while the truth loomed sharp and glistening. And neither was sure exactly how much the other knew. It was like dancing at the edge of a pit, uncertain whether your partner might push you in.

"I can't come there, Emil. It's not safe. I've already been shot once."

Emil's gasp might have been genuine, considering he wasn't the one who'd sent Munroe. "Shot! Are you all right?"

"I'm fine. But you'll have to come here. I'm at Mr. Donne's office on Montgomery Street. I don't know how long I can stay, though, so you need to get here quickly."

"Of course."

If Abe had held any doubts about Emil's involvement, they disappeared: Emil's agreeableness gave him away. He usually hated having his plans disrupted and wasn't keen on entering unfamiliar spaces. Abe gave him the address and ended the call.

"Were you really shot?" asked Crespo.

"Yes."

"Who did it?"

Thomas answered for him. "Someone Townsend sent. Detective with the San Francisco police."

"And where's the detective now?"

"The morgue," Thomas replied with a death's-head grin.

Crespo whistled and shook his head. "You two have been having adventures."

He looked like he wanted to ask more, but this wasn't the time. Abe looked at Thomas. "You need to play along too, okay?"

"I will."

"You trust me?"

Thomas's mouth stretched into a slow smile. "I don't trust anyone. But I distrust you less than most."

That was plenty to satisfy Abe, who took another long pull of gin.

"Do you do that because of spirits?" Crespo asked, nodding at the bottle.

Although Thomas had placed himself physically between them, as if protecting Abe even from personal questions, Abe simply gave a shrug. "What makes you think that?"

"'Cause I knew an agent at the Bureau who did that. He could drink a whole bathtub's worth of moonshine without getting drunk. He said it kept the chindi away."

Curious despite himself, Abe asked, "Chindi?"

"Evil spirit of the dead. A Navajo word, I think."

Interesting. If Abe survived, he might want to do some research and find out what other cultures thought about the things he called dybbuks. "You used the past tense about this agent."

"Oh, he's still alive. A good man. He mostly does work around

Arizona and New Mexico 'cause that's where he's from. But he doesn't drink anymore. He found some other way to control his problem."

That also intrigued Abe. He'd met only four other people who saw spirits as he did, and none of them knew any solution other than booze—and even that didn't always work. The Irish woman said she'd welcomed the ibbur because it was either that or be overcome eventually by an evil spirit.

Crespo cocked his head. "I can introduce you to him if you want. From what I gather, his skills come in very useful for the Bureau."

Abe acknowledged the offer with a quick nod and shelved that for later too. His head was thudding, and he didn't know whether that was the previous day's possession or that Emil was trying again. Or maybe something else was going on. His father had complained about a headache for months before he started having seizures and losing his vision. He'd died not long after. Abe's mother had never forgiven Abe for the fact that his father went to his grave still disappointed in him. His father hadn't been disappointed enough to come back as a spirit, at least—but Abe couldn't tell his mother that.

Thomas wasn't pacing, but he looked like he wanted to. Crespo sat in his chair with all the easy grace and coiled power of a tiger. Abe drank. Suddenly a prayer came to him, an ancient echo from his youth, and although it had been over two decades since he'd held any belief in religion, he found himself quietly reciting it. "Baruch atah Adonai, Eloheinu melech haolam, asher kid'shanu b'mitzvotav v'tzivanu lirdof tzedek."

"What's that?" Thomas asked. "A spell?"

Abe chuckled. "I guess you could think of it that way. It's a blessing about pursuing justice. Not that I expect it to do any good, but...."

"Don't dismiss it," said Crespo. "If sincerely meant, blessings are words of power."

That struck true in Abe's heart. It wasn't his place to judge whether God existed and, if so, what was God's will. But Abe knew of goodness and evil—he'd seen them himself. Felt them. His own soul had weighed them and chosen between them, and although he hadn't always chosen well, sometimes he had.

He recited again, this time a text that had been among his father's favorites, Psalm 27. Abe said the verses in Hebrew but thought of their meaning in Hungarian, in his father's voice.

When evil-doers came upon me to eat up my flesh, even mine adversaries and my foes, they stumbled and fell. Though a host should encamp against me, my heart shall not fear; though war should rise up against me, even then will I be confident.... For though my father and my mother have forsaken me, the Lord will take me up. Teach me Thy way, O Lord; and lead me in an even path, because of them that lie in wait for me. Deliver me not over unto the will of mine adversaries; for false witnesses are risen up against me, and such as breathe out violence....

"Is that about justice too?" Thomas asked, seeming genuinely curious.

"It's about facing your enemies with your chin up and defeating them."

Thomas responded with his fiercest, most beautiful grin.

Maybe Abe would have ended up leading them all in a full prayer service, but heavy footsteps echoed in the corridor. "Townsend," Thomas hissed a moment before a knock rattled the outer door. Abe gestured at him to let Townsend in.

Although Townsend might have intended to exude confidence as he entered the inner room, there was a definite falter when he saw Abe sitting behind Thomas's desk. Townsend frowned at Crespo, then hung up his hat and overcoat and settled into the chair beside him.

"I take it we will not be having a repeat of our last unpleasantness," Townsend huffed.

Abe and Thomas stared at him until he shifted uncomfortably. He turned his head to look at Crespo instead. "Who's this?"

"One of Mr. Donne's clients, from back East," Abe said.

"Mr. Donne has no clients."

"Until recently. Now it seems he has several, each with deep pockets."

While Crespo managed to look as neutral as a person could, Townsend scowled. "I'm a busy man and I don't have time to play games. Give me the item I hired you to find, Donne, and I'll pay you. Then we're done."

Abe gave him a sweet smile. "How much was it that you offered again? Mr. Donne?"

"Fifty thousand," Thomas said.

"That's right. Fifty," Abe agreed. "A lot of money. Probably even more than it costs to hire a police detective to murder someone."

Townsend didn't say anything, but his mouth pursed and his eyes narrowed.

Abe continued cheerily. "Yes, definitely a lot. But not as much as a hundred thousand, which is what Mr. Nunes has offered." Fausto Nunes, a jolly young man who liked to crack jokes and talk about pretty girls, had been an acquaintance when Abe lived in New York. Crespo resembled him a little, despite being considerably older.

"That's preposterous," Townsend sputtered.

"Is it? So you're saying the Prince is worth killing over but not a hundred grand? How much is a human life worth, Mr. Townsend?"

Townsend's cheeks had gone an unhealthy blotchy red. "I don't know what you're talking about."

"Of course not."

Abe was feeling this, and it was good. Powerful. It was very similar to the little *click* in his mind when he knew he'd sized up a séance guest just right and the guest was now fully under his spell. Thomas and Crespo were proving capable assistants. He planned to play a little more—just for the fun of it—but another knock sounded, making Townsend start.

"Who's that?" he growled.

"Another addition to our party." Abe's headache turned up several notches, nearly driving him to his knees, but he walked over and opened the door. Emil was dressed a little more hastily than usual, his hair escaping the shellac and his tie uneven. He smiled at Abe anyway. "My boy! What kind of trouble have you put yourself into? You look ghastly."

"Hello, Emil. Come join us."

Emil had always had a weirdly long stride, as if he were attempting to touch the floor as few times as possible. It took him only a few steps to cross to the inner office, and then he halted in the doorway. "What's this, Abe?"

"Have a seat."

Although clearly reluctant, Emil took the last remaining guest chair. "I'm afraid I'm at a loss. Will someone kindly provide introductions?"

Abe walked behind the desk, picked up the gin bottle, and used it to point. "Townsend. Nunes. Donne you've met." He waved toward Emil. "This is Magnus."

Donne remained stone-faced, but everyone else in the room had distinctly unhappy expressions. In Crespo's case, it was an act—the sparkle in his eyes said he was having a grand time—but Townsend and Emil were most definitely not happy to meet.

"What is going on?" Townsend growled.

One long swallow finished off the gin. "Another facet to our negotiations. Emil, Townsend offered fifty grand for the Prince of Gandhara. Nunes is willing to pay a hundred. What's your price?"

Emil's face, naturally pale in any case, turned gray. "I told you to stay away from that thing."

"So you did. But words and actions are two different things, aren't they?" Abe turned to Thomas. "Hand it over, please."

After a long look, Donne reached into his pocket and held out the amulet, still wrapped in the handkerchief. Abe took it and let the cloth fall to the floor. The amulet was warm, and he could swear it beat in his palm like a heart, slow and steady and deep. He held it up so everyone could see.

The reaction was interesting. Donne frowned, but his gaze was on Abe and not the bauble. The other three men all leaned forward in their seats. Crespo looked like an eager student in a particularly interesting class, but Emil and Townsend.... Their mouths hung open and they stared with wide pupils, the same way a person stared when he was stupidly, burningly lusting for another.

The amulet's vibration strengthened and traveled down his arm, now matching the pounding in his skull beat for beat.

"Power, right? The ability to command countless others. The person who uses this amulet can bend the country—maybe the world—to his will." He looked at Donne. "Imagine it. In the right hands, this could mean men and women no longer have to hide who they are because others call their love a sin. No more children need to go hungry while the wealthy wallow in gold. No more wars." His voice cracked as he said the last word.

Thomas tightened his jaw. "Abe," he whispered. But he didn't move.

Emil was working his lips soundlessly, and Abe felt it clearly now —the dybbuk clawing at his head, trying to get in. It was cold enough to make him shudder, cold enough to burn him, and it was scratching scratching scratching at his skull. The Prince was also burning him, but with its scorching heat. He staggered back, clutching the edge of the desk to keep his balance, and his stomach twisted and turned.

"My parents turned away from me because I disappointed them so deeply. They said I'd never be anyone worthwhile. None of you know what it's like to be a boy who goes to bed hungry because there's no money for food, who shivers through the winter because he doesn't have warm clothes. And none of you sees me as a person, a man. I'm a barrier or a tool and nothing else. Someone to fuck, not someone to care about."

Rage and hurt made both the dybbuk and the amulet more powerful. Evidently the Prince didn't need incantations to work; the right emotions, properly applied, would do just fine. It would latch onto his wounded, tarnished soul as firmly as a steel lock snapping into place.

"Abe."

At first Abe thought Thomas was speaking to him, but then the voice came again—"Abe, don't"—and the British accent wasn't Thomas's. There was Birdie standing very close to Thomas, invisible to everyone but Abe, who saw him as little more than a shimmer. But he was present, and he sounded sad.

That was enough to give Abe strength to resist a little longer. "Thank you, Birdie," he said, making Thomas startle and everyone else frown in confusion.

Abe took a steadying breath. "One of you sent a policeman to kill me. One of you sent a dybbuk to possess me—to set my hands against two friends and against a stranger for whom I had no ill will. And to set me against Thomas. The question before us, then, is who's responsible? Because right now, even more than money, I value truth. I will give the Prince to an honest man."

When silence sat heavily for several moments, he pinned Townsend with his gaze. "Nothing to admit?"

Townsend lifted his chin. "I'll tell you the truth. That amulet belongs to me. Roy Gage stole it, and that's why I hired Donne—so I could get it back. I have never killed anyone in my life, boy, and I am the rightful owner of the Prince of Gandhara." He huffed. "And I don't know what a dybbuk is and wouldn't have the faintest notion what to do with one. One or both of these other men are the evildoers. Give me my property and I'll make sure the police investigate thoroughly."

"The police do your bidding, Mr. Townsend?"

"I was Assistant Chief until recently. I still hold some sway there."

"With Detective Munroe, for example."

Townsend jutted his chin. "He was an old friend."

"A good enough friend to murder if you asked him to?"

"I wouldn't ask! One of these other men must have paid him off."

Emil made a wounded noise. "My boy, how can you stand there and listen to such baseless accusations? I don't know anyone named Munroe and I most certainly didn't convince him to kill anyone."

"Not me, Emil?" Abe asked. "You didn't want him to kill me?"

"I don't want anyone to kill you! Why on Earth would I? You're my protégé. We've shared so much over the years."

"I willingly shared my body with you, Emil, but I never offered you my soul."

"I don't—"

"You may not know any policemen, but you do know a great deal about spirits. And only you were aware of my particular vulnerabilities."

Emil's eyes had gone hard and opaque, as if he were made of marble, and his cheekbones stood sharper than ever. He attempted to smile nonetheless, and the effect was horrible. "You want truth, my boy? The only reason Roy knew about the amulet to begin with was because Townsend hired him to murder the man who'd brought it to the city. Apparently the fellow wasn't happy enough with whatever amount he'd originally agreed to sell it for, and he was demanding more. *I* convinced Roy that allowing an immoral man such as Townsend to keep the Prince would be extremely dangerous, and I offered to take it from him. Just as I'm offering to take it from you."

This hurt. Abe had never loved Emil, not really, but he'd admired him and considered him a close friend. He'd offered Emil his body and his deepest secrets. And yet Emil was willing to destroy him.

The dybbuk clawed harder. Abe could hear it now, gibbering in a language he didn't understand. He felt its *want*, which was very much like the want Abe felt for Thomas. Only the dybbuk craved devastation, desired to feed off living humans' misery and agony. Abe realized something else as well: thus far Emil had controlled the dybbuk, but it had become much stronger over the past several days. If it crawled into Abe now, Emil would no longer be able to manipulate it, and it would never, ever leave.

"Tell me your truth, Nunes," Abe said quietly.

Crespo shrugged. "I don't know what any of you are talking about. I just want the amulet, and I'll pay good money for it. More than either of these fellows."

"Do you believe these two when they claim they're not responsible for what's happened?"

"Well," Crespo said, "I guess I believe they're guilty about as much as I believe in dragons." He blinked slowly, and for just a flash of time, his irises turned green-gold and the pupils became vertical slits. He blinked again and looked as ordinary as anyone else.

Finally Abe turned to Thomas, who'd been observing all of this closely, an unlit cigarette between his fingers. "And you? Your truth, Mr. Donne?"

Thomas didn't change his impassive expression. He lit his cigarette and tilted his head back to blow smoke toward the ceiling. "I've killed plenty of people, but I wouldn't harm you. I guess that's because I love you."

Not one person in the room looked especially surprised by Thomas's declaration, but the dybbuk momentarily lost its hold on Abe, and Birdie's spirit momentarily shone brighter and more solid.

"Truth is a funny thing," Abe said. "I've spent my whole life telling lies so well that the people I tell them to want to believe them. That's the best con of all—the one where the rube never realizes he's been had. Right, Emil? Took me a long time to work out your con."

Emil was going to say something, but Abe silenced him with a hand. "At least some of you are conning me right now. Maybe you all are. But if that's the case, I'm going to choose the best one. The one I most want to believe."

He walked to Thomas, pulled open his suit coat, and dropped the Prince into the inside pocket. Then he turned to Crespo. "I guess you can arrest them now."

At first nobody did anything—except Thomas, who took another drag of his cigarette.

Then chaos broke loose.

Townsend leapt out of his chair with astonishing speed, and although Abe expected him to go after Thomas, he grabbed Abe instead, pulling him against his chest, an arm around Abe's throat. Before Abe could fight or wiggle free, he felt metal pressing against his temple. A gun. Of course Townsend would be armed.

But he wasn't the only one. Crespo and Donne drew their own weapons and pointed them at Townsend, who didn't ease his grip. "I'll pull the trigger, Donne," Townsend said calmly. "Wouldn't be the first time for me."

"Or me," Thomas growled.

"Oh, I know. But you're as likely to hit him as you are to hit me, and in any case, his brains will be splattered all over your office. I don't think you want that."

Thomas didn't drop his gun, but he didn't fire either.

Then Townsend turned his attention to Crespo. "Arrest me? You're not with the department."

"I'm a Fed. The Bureau of Trans-Species Affairs." Crespo's eyes did that odd fast shift again, and at the same time the skin on his face and hands turned an unnatural gray-green. He twitched his shoulders irritably, but like Thomas, he remained frozen in place.

"I'm fully human," Townsend scoffed. "So were all the people who died. You don't have jurisdiction."

Crespo had a sharp-toothed smile. "Our jurisdiction is very broad, Mr. Townsend."

The arm around Abe's neck was tightening, restricting his breath. But that wasn't his primary concern, nor were the three guns aimed in his direction. What worried him more deeply was Emil, who'd backed to the far side of the room and was frantically chanting something Abe couldn't hear.

Although he didn't have to hear it; he *felt* it as the dybbuk dug at his skull and pushed into him, more painful than any bullet, and more dangerous. He tried to push back, to fight, but he'd been opened to spirits too many times lately and he lacked the strength.

"Shoot me," he gasped, begging any of them, all of them. A swift death would be far preferable to the dybbuk taking him over for good. "God, please, just shoot me."

But nobody did—they glared at one another and brandished their guns, and Emil chanted and chanted, and Abe felt as if he were being flayed from inside. He couldn't even scream because he now lacked the oxygen. His lungs flamed, his heart was a ball of molten metal, and his muscles clenched as if in a death rictus.

"Avi," Birdie said urgently—directly in front of Abe now, his shapeless form fizzing and sparking in the air. "You're a magician, not a fighter."

"Let him go!" Thomas barked, but his voice was faded and far away, like the call of the Alcatraz foghorn.

Birdie's voice was clearer as he said Abe's name. In fact, he looked more distinct too. Sad-faced and very young, with springtime eyes and a muddy green uniform, his blond curls plastered down by fever-sweat. "You know how, Abe. Let me in. I'm a soldier, remember? I know how to fight." A rifle appeared on his shoulder and a pistol in his hand.

"No." If he let Birdie in, the dybbuk would destroy them both.

God, if only he knew how to escape this! But the dybbuk was neither a pair of handcuffs chaining him to a bed nor a cabinet with trick doors. It wasn't a gun pointed at his heart, and he didn't have a bullet tucked away inside his cheek. He'd never been taught this kind of trick.

But.... A thought glimmered at the edge of his fading consciousness. He *had* been taught something that might help. Not a trick at all, but an exercise of faith. An act of compassion. A plea for peace.

"El malei rachamim...." He'd last recited this prayer at his father's grave, with his mother standing silent and pale in her grief. Now he was certain nobody but Birdie heard the Hebrew trickling from his tightened lips, but that was okay. In fact, it was enough to say the words silently because behind him chanted an entire chorus with his father's familiar voice leading them all. Lending Abraham Ferencz—their son, their grandson, their ever more distant descendant—their strength and grace. Their acceptance and love.

Oh God, full of compassion, who lives on high, give infinite rest beneath your divine wings, among the holy and pure who shine like the sky, to this spirit. Protect him forever and tie him with the rope of eternal life. May he rest eternally in peace.

"And let us say, amen," said Birdie.

The dybbuk screeched. No—the sound came from Emil, who'd thrown his head back so far that it seemed his neck must be broken. His mouth was open in an impossibly wide O; his scream was like a siren, piercing and inhuman, enough to shake the curtains and rattle Abe's bones.

Crespo collapsed to his knees, gun still clutched in one hand, and covered his ears with his arms. Townsend released Abe and staggered back a step. Birdie smiled. Thomas surged forward and gathered Abe into his steady arms.

The dybbuk released its hold on Abe and zoomed away, like a suddenly deflated balloon, heading straight to Emil.

Oh, good Lord. Abe suddenly realized that the dybbuk had never been the spirit of a dead person. It was a piece of Emil's living soul.

Emil made a sound no human throat should have formed, and he collapsed bonelessly to the floor. Dark blood trickled from his open mouth, but his eyes remained open and focused on Abe. In his final moments, just before the light in his eyes died for good, he sobbed once and rasped three words: "Forgive me, Abe."

Emil's lungs rattled to a halt.

Crespo rose unsteadily and prodded Emil's corpse with his foot. Abe's attention was focused there too, so he startled when Thomas abruptly let go of him and lunged to the side.

Thomas was too late, however. Townsend's unwavering gun was trained on Thomas, who skidded to a halt. "Give me the Prince," Townsend said.

Thomas snarled. "Shoot me and get it yourself."

"If I do, your Bureau pal will use his gun on me. I'd prefer to avoid that unpleasantness. Give me the amulet and nobody else need die. I might even offer you a job once I'm settled comfortably in Washington."

"I'd never work for you."

They glared at each other, with Crespo adding his own fierce look from near Emil's body. None of them paid any attention to Abe, who was unarmed and expending his last energy in simply remaining upright.

None paid any attention except Birdie, now more visible than ever. He gave Abe an impish grin. "C'mon mate. You know what we need to do."

"I don't—"

"I'm stuck here for good and it's not right. Not comfortable either."

"I'm sorry."

Thomas and Townsend remained in their face-off, both frowning as they heard only Abe's side of the conversation.

"It's not your fault," Birdie said. "But I'd appreciate your help in fixing it."

"How?"

Birdie jerked his chin in Townsend's direction. "Persuade him to let me in. I can't do this without his permission."

Abe shook his head. "How— I can't—"

"Of course you can. You know what to do. Tell him what he wants to hear."

Ah. Moving slowly because his body still felt as if it had been turned inside out twice, Abe shuffled to Thomas's chair and lowered himself into it. All the living men in the room stared, as if afraid he might do something horrible at any moment. Which, in fact, he was going to do. Although it would be the *right* horrible thing.

"Mr. Townsend," Abe said.

"What's wrong with you?"

"Nothing a gallon or so of gin won't fix. But first I have a proposition for you. A solution to the stalemate."

The merest shadow of a smile played at the corners of Thomas's mouth, giving Abe the support he needed. Townsend scowled, but Abe recognized the look in his eyes: he was a fish eyeing the worm that squiggled so interestingly on the hook.

"You want political power, right? That's what the Prince would give you. But what if I can offer you something even better?"

Figuratively, Townsend swam a little closer. "What could you possibly have to offer me, my boy?"

"A much longer life, for one thing. You'll barely age, never get sick, and it will be almost impossible for anything to kill you. But more than that. You will gain several extraordinary talents. Do you remember what I did to you the other day?" Abe smiled brightly.

Townsend shuddered. "I could hardly forget, could I?"

"You'd learn to do that. Your skills wouldn't come to you all at once, but over time—which you'd have plenty of—and you'd be able to do things no living man could even dream of. You wouldn't have political power, but you'd possess a very different kind. Who's stronger, Mr. Townsend? The figurehead in office or the person standing in the shadows, telling the figurehead what to do?"

Thomas was very clearly fighting a full-blown smile by now, so it was fortunate Townsend wasn't looking at him. "How is this possible?" Townsend demanded.

"Ibbur."

Crespo issued a small gasp of recognition, and now he was struggling to keep a serious expression as well.

"I don't know what that is." Without being aware of it, Townsend had lowered the arm holding the gun, which meant Crespo could have shot him; for that matter, so could Thomas. But neither did. They waited for Abe to finish his con.

The best way to fool someone was to tell them as much of the truth as possible, skittering around the details you didn't know or, as in this case, didn't want them to know. It worked with séance guests, who were always happy to know that their deceased mother loved them and wished them well in life. They heard what they wanted to and didn't notice the omissions, such as details that would prove whether the medium was truly in contact with their relative.

"It's possession. The spirit of a righteous man settles within you and grants you his powers."

"Why would you offer this to me when I nearly killed you?"

"Because I'm tired of people dying." And when Abe sighed, his exhaustion and pain were real. "I've fallen in love with Thomas, you see, and I'd like for both of us to remain together—alive. Not hunted like beasts."

Townsend was still swimming back and forth in front of the bait. "Why should I believe you?"

"Because doing so gives you the best outcome. If you harm any of us, the Bureau will be after you. And the Prince won't give you instant absolute authority. Or the ability to dodge a bullet."

While Townsend sucked on his lip, Thomas returned the gun to his pocket and relaxed his stance. Good. He was showing his belief in what Abe was saying, exactly the way Rosie did as a plant in Abe's séance gatherings. Crespo nodded as well, and although he didn't put his gun away, he pointed it at the floor.

"I don't know...." Townsend deliberated.

Abe looked him in the eyes. "This is my truth. Not a single lie amidst it."

"I'll be young again...."

"No. The ibbur won't reverse aging. But it will slow it down to a crawl, and it will restore vitality."

And that was part of a good con too. Don't promise them the moon and the stars because they won't believe it. Show them the limitations of your offer.

"When can you do this?"

"Right now, Mr. Townsend. As soon as you say yes."

And Townsend bit. "Yes," he whispered.

Birdie rushed to Townsend almost as quickly as the dybbuk returned to Emil, but stopped just short of contact. He cast a longing look at Thomas before turning to Abe. "You'll remind him again I loved him?"

"Every day, if you want."

"Nah. Just now and then. And you'll treat him right? Help him learn to bend without breaking?"

"I'll do my very best."

Birdie squared his shoulders, every inch a soldier marching to his fate. "Right, then." He nodded.

Abe... pushed. It was a bit like giving someone a boost over a high wall, or like helping someone lift a heavy load. It was neither of those things really, but it did the trick. Birdie flowed into Townsend like a river flowing into the sea, not disappearing exactly, but mingling, becoming water neither sweet nor fully saline. Townsend's eyes went very wide and the gun tumbled from his hands, luckily not going off in the process.

"Oh!" he exclaimed, and then he fell to the floor with a thud.

Abe collapsed right after.

23

"It's a scheme." Thomas stood by the open window, blowing smoke down toward Union Square.

Abe groaned a second time, louder and more theatrically than the first. "What is?"

Thomas turned slowly, just for the pleasure of seeing Abe alive and bare-chested, blinking groggily from the rumpled bed. "You're trying to get me to take you to every posh hotel in the city."

Blinking slowly, Abe looked around the room. "Which one is this?"

"Sir Francis Drake."

"Ah. Nice."

Thomas snorted. "Should be, considering what they charge." Three dollars and fifty cents a night, which was outright robbery. But the bed was like heaven itself, the view was nice, and the staff delivered food—and liquor—via a clever panel in the door.

Abe groaned a third time. "I need to piss."

"I'd imagine so."

"Don't think I can make it by myself." Abe lifted a hand a few inches and let it drop back to the mattress with a little thud.

Thomas stubbed out his cigarette in a glass ashtray and strode toward the bed, where he tugged the covers off of Abe.

"I'm naked," Abe said.

"Made it easier to care for you. Can you walk with help or shall I carry you?"

"Walk."

In fact, Thomas ended up nearly dragging him to the bathroom and seating him on the toilet. Abe protested weakly about the indignity of it all, but even he had to admit that standing and aiming was beyond his current capabilities. Thomas leaned in the doorway, far enough away to give him a speck of privacy but close enough to dart forward and catch him if he collapsed.

"Wow," Abe said finally. "That was a full bladder."

"You've been in bed for thirty-six hours."

Abe gaped. "I slept that long?"

"You stirred a few times, but yes. Now, what next? Food? Booze? Sleep?"

"That's... a really nice bathtub."

"You want to bathe? Now?" Thomas was incredulous. "You're barely conscious."

"I feel— What Emil did to me— Yes. Now."

Thomas could have bullied him into waiting, or he simply could have carried him back to bed, but Abe had spent enough time being controlled by others. So Thomas turned on the taps and adjusted the water temperature. "Will you be all right alone for a minute?"

"Of course." Slumped on the toilet, Abe smiled, despite the bruised and tender-looking skin around his bullet wound.

Thirty minutes later he lolled in the bath like a pharaoh, nibbling on the fruit and biscuits Thomas was hand-feeding him, bit by bit. On the side of the tub sat a bottle of slivovitz—thanks to Thomas's very substantial tip for the bellboy—but Abe had drunk only a little. After plenty of fresh-squeezed orange juice and an egg and toast, he was looking stronger.

And beautiful. Good Lord, such a sinfully beautiful man.

Abe grinned at Thomas's expression. "You're not thinking of shooting me, are you?"

"After all the work and money I've invested in you? I should say not."

The splash Abe aimed at him was too half-hearted to reach its target.

"This floor is bloody uncomfortable." Thomas shifted his position on the ceramic tile. "Are you ready for dry land yet, Your Majesty?"

"I sup-pose." Abe drew out the word lazily.

Thomas helped him up and toweled him dry—a hardship, with all that tempting skin right under his hands—but Abe made it back to bed with only a little assistance, and he even managed to adjust the pillows himself. "There's a wireless on that table!"

"Every room has one, I'm told. We can listen when your head stops hurting."

"I didn't even notice the headache." Abe chuckled. "Too many other aches clamoring for attention."

"Get some rest, then."

Abe gave him a close look. "You too. Have you slept at all for the past couple of days?"

In truth, Thomas hadn't done more than doze, even though Abe hadn't needed much direct care. But Thomas had carried an irrational fear that if he slipped too deeply into slumber, he'd awake to find Abe gone. Not run away, but simply disappeared, like a coin in a magic trick. Now he shrugged and reached for his tobacco.

"Don't," Abe said. "Take off your clothes and get into bed with me."

"You can't possibly—"

"Tom."

The name did it. He'd been Thomas or Donne to nearly everyone, and Tommy to Birdie, but he was Tom to Abe alone. A special enchantment, probably, wrapped up in those three little letters. He didn't mind.

Efficiently but not hastily, he undressed until he was as bare as Abe and then slid in beside him. He tried to leave some space between them, but Abe scooted over at once and half draped himself over Thomas with a contented sigh. This was something new, something he'd never had the opportunity to enjoy with Birdie, nor any interest in pursuing with someone else. This was true intimacy, and Thomas may have sighed. He rested a hand on Abe's warm shoulder.

"How did you get me here?" Abe asked.

"Crespo helped. He rang some other agents to take care of the mess in my office. I've no idea where they came from or how they arrived so quickly. Then he helped me carry you to a taxi, bribed the hotel staff to pretend they didn't notice you were unconscious, and helped me get you up here. I undressed you without his assistance, however."

Abe's chuckle tickled Thomas's skin. "He's a good man. Or... whatever he is."

Thomas had been wondering about that last bit himself but had decided Crespo's identity was nobody's business but his own. "He gave me all the money in Townsend's wallet. It's plenty to keep us comfortable for some time." Nearly a thousand dollars, actually. Why he'd been carrying so much was a mystery—but not one Thomas would bother to solve.

"Townsend." Abe tensed against him. "Is he...."

"He was breathing when I left. The Bureau has him now."

"It's not him any longer. Not Birdie either."

"I know." Thomas had grieved Birdie a decade earlier and had no more room for it in his heart. "He was a hero, wasn't he? Even after death."

"He was."

Thomas held Abe slightly tighter and dropped a kiss on his messy curls. "So were you."

"I almost let that fucking amulet convince me—"

"But you didn't. Anyone can be brave when there's nothing to fear, and anyone can resist when there's no temptation. A hero makes the right decision in the worst circumstances. You're a mensch, Abraham Ferencz."

Abe's laughter gently shook them both. Then he sighed, his

breath ghosting across Thomas's chest. "What did you do with the Prince?"

"Gave it to Crespo."

"Do you trust him with it? Trust the Bureau?"

Thomas stroked Abe's warm back, loving the smoothness of his skin and the hardness of the muscles beneath. He loved the contradictions of this man, the complexity, the stubbornness. Loved the way that, when he was with Abe, he could let his defenses down a little, because Abe could see through to his real self anyway. And he loved that Abe could hold his own.

"I've told you before that I trust nobody. But I suppose I distrust Crespo less than the average. And you, Abe. I have faith in you."

Making love was out of the question, but the tender kiss Abe gave him was just as good.

24

Abe stood with his hands on his hips and surveyed the room. "It looks strange."

Thomas flashed his now-familiar grin. "You used to have this room stuffed full of glowing gauze and trick cabinets and black curtains and decks of marked cards and Lord knows what else. *That* was strange."

"Not for a séance room."

Now it was a very ordinary parlor with modern furniture and bright draperies and two framed advertising posters from Abe's magic shows. There was a third framed print as well, one that Thomas had chosen, showing hundreds of ghostly soldiers walking across a poppy-strewn field toward a war memorial. Entitled *Menin Gate at Midnight*, the original had been painted two years earlier by an artist named William Longstaff. Sometimes Thomas stared at the print for a long time, and afterward his hands would shake so badly that Abe had to roll his cigarettes. Those nights, he usually woke up screaming. But he insisted on keeping it in the parlor anyway, and Abe figured that every person was entitled to their own form of prayer.

Thomas stepped close and ran a broad thumb over Abe's lip,

making Abe shiver with want. "Are you missing the séances and the shows?"

"No," Abe answered honestly. "I liked being Abe France, but I like it even better being Agent Ferencz. Especially when I have the best partner in the Bureau."

As soon as the mess in Abe's house had been cleaned up, he'd returned home and Thomas had come with him. The past year had gone by fast enough to make Abe dizzy. They had both joined the Bureau, which was delighted to have them, and went through an accelerated training. They could have been assigned anywhere, but when they'd asked to stay in San Francisco, the Bureau had obliged. Now they split their time between dealing with an astonishing array of creatures and creating a home that suited them both. And making love. They spent a lot of time on that as well.

"You have that look in your eyes," Thomas said, his voice huskier than usual.

"Have I? Do you want to chain me to our bed?"

"I always want that."

Thomas moved behind Abe and wrapped his arms tightly around him, drawing their hard bodies flush. He gnawed gently at his neck and squeezed Abe's cock through the fabric of his trousers, making Abe moan. Thomas slipped his other hand under Abe's shirt and gave his right nipple a hard pinch. Oh, God. He could make Abe climax just like this, fast and dirty, and then Abe would spend a long, long time sucking Thomas's cock, teasing him until Thomas begged, and— Thomas let go and stepped back. "We've a meeting to get to."

"You're cruel."

"Only when you want me to be."

Dragging his feet more than necessary, Abe went to fetch his hat and coat.

A spate of unseasonably warm and bright days had finally passed, leaving the city clothed in its more usual cool fog, like a grande dame in a chinchilla coat. The air smelled of the sea, and when Abe and Thomas boarded the streetcar, it clanked along the familiar streets. In speakeasies and restaurants and stores, people were talking about the stock market crash and wondering uneasily what the effect would be and when the market would recover. But here on the streetcar, people were simply going about their days—off to work or shopping—and all seemed normal enough.

Sometimes Abe and Thomas speculated what might happen if the public knew about the strange creatures that lived undetected among them. "They'd call them monsters and want them all dead," Thomas insisted. And maybe he was right, but the worst monsters Abe had met had been fully human.

They disembarked the streetcar and walked to Montgomery Street, where Crespo waited for them outside a massive Neo-Gothic building with three towers, the highest of which made it the tallest building in the city. Abe had never been inside.

"Why here?" he asked Crespo as soon as he and Thomas were close enough.

Crespo rolled his eyes. "Long story, pal. The Bureau was considering moving West Coast HQ here from LA, so they rented some office space as soon as this heap was finished." He hooked a thumb toward the building. "But now that we're getting a new regional chief, well, it's best to stick to LA."

"Why?"

"You'll see soon enough." Crespo scowled, which wasn't very promising.

Thomas scowled back—more impressively, Abe thought; but then again, he was biased. Thomas had certainly had more practice than Crespo. "And he wants to meet with us why?"

"I don't know."

"Who is this fellow?" demanded Abe, irritated that Crespo was clearly holding back information.

"You need to see for yourself. Just, um, stay calm, okay?"

That was reassuring.

They traipsed through the lobby, footsteps echoing on marble, got into the elevator, and rode to the thirtieth floor. Two stories short of the top, but still higher than Abe had ever been. Because the building was almost new, he was surprised to sense a ghost as soon as they exited the elevator. It seemed content enough, however, pacing silently up the corridor with a spectral nod at Abe as it passed.

Unaware of the ghost, Crespo led Abe and Thomas to an unmarked set of double doors. He opened one to reveal a reception office bare of everything except a coat rack and a small table containing a yellowing edition of the *Chronicle*. Four interior doors were closed, but the fifth was ajar, allowing a little natural light into the windowless reception room. Dust motes eddied slowly through the air.

"We're here," Crespo called. Nobody answered, but he continued onward and pushed the door fully open.

Thomas stepped through after Crespo but before Abe—and had his gun drawn before Abe was fully inside.

Herbert Townsend stood silhouetted in a large, uncurtained window, a cigarette and shot glass in one hand. Apart from him, the room was bare.

"Boys," he said evenly.

"What trick is this?" Thomas spat viciously at Crespo.

Before Crespo could answer, Abe pushed forward. "Look at him, Tom. That's not Townsend. Not really."

The expensive suit barely contained his bulk, and his face was the same. The only surface difference, really, was the lack of rings on his fingers. But if you looked closely, really *stared* at his eyes, you'd notice the change. The flat sureness and easy malevolence were gone, replaced by something deeper and much more complicated. Something inhuman, but not cruel.

"*You're* the new Chief?" Abe asked.

"I was the perfect choice." His voice was different too, although Abe couldn't have said exactly how. It carried more emotion, perhaps, and also more power. "Townsend had experience in law enforcement administration and talent at influencing people. Albert Dixon had courage and integrity and a capacity for doing real good."

With obvious reluctance, Thomas holstered his gun. "What do you want?"

"I'm meeting all my agents. And perhaps recruiting more. The

Bureau needs a special kind of man, you see. He can't be soft, and he can't be too traditional in his notions of good and evil. He must be able to understand that the entire world is as gray and opaque as the thickest fog." He gestured toward the windows with the hand holding the glass.

Abe took a step closer. "Are Tom and I like that?"

"You are, my boy, you are. You understand that the line between a moral decision and an immoral one is often whisper-thin, and that what makes a monster isn't who someone is, but what he does."

"And a man who loves another man?" Abe took a step closer to Thomas, who moved in to wrap his arm around Abe's waist.

"Such a man has seen firsthand how starkly the world can judge."

Townsend drained his drink—whiskey, Abe guessed—and placed the glass on the windowsill. Then he took a last drag before crushing out his cigarette in a ceramic ashtray. "There are lines. Good and evil. Alive and dead. Friend and enemy. And we think of them as these very solid things, these impassable walls. But you know as well as I, Abe, that those lines are flimsy and porous. People pass through them all the time."

Thomas stiffened. "I didn't ask for a lesson in philosophy."

"It's not philosophy," Townsend countered. "They're cold, hard facts. The most important facts of all. And it's the central mission of the Bureau. We could talk about repentance if we liked, because it's important too. But it's only a stepping stone, a means to an end. The Bureau is in it for the long game and so am I." He smiled. "So it's fortunate I won't die anytime soon."

"What is the long game?" Abe asked. He *almost* knew, like a word on the tip of his tongue, but he couldn't quite grasp it.

"You push in the right directions. Those lines? You twist them slowly, very slowly so they won't break, but with a gentle nudge here and there, so that, in the end, they're in the right place."

Abe shook his head. "Are you talking about salvation? Because I don't—"

"Not in the come-to-Jesus sense, no, not at all. I mean redemption in a broader sense. The protection of everything that's valuable in people—and not just in *human* people. That is my long game, and the Bureau's. It's a hard one, boys. But is it your game too?"

Abe still didn't fully understand, and judging by Thomas's frown, neither did he. Yet something about what Townsend was saying rang true. Maybe it was a con: Townsend saying what Abe wanted to hear. But he hoped it wasn't.

"Tom?" Abe said quietly.

Thomas let go of Abe's waist and tugged at his shoulder so they faced each other. Thomas's eyes were the same gray as the fog outside, but a light shone deep within them just as the sun blazed behind the fog. And after a moment, Thomas's mouth stretched into a broad, fierce smile. "Yes."

Abe lifted his chin at Townsend. "Our game too."

"Very *good*, my boys. Difficult times are coming—times to test us all."

Abe and Thomas exchanged glances and shrugged in unison. They'd faced difficult times before, and yet here they were.

Townsend rubbed his hands together. "I have a new assignment for you. We've been getting reports of something nasty in the California Delta. It's been destroying levees and has drowned a few children. Or so the stories say. I'm sending one of my boys up from LA to work with you on this. Interesting fellow named Grimes."

Thomas took Abe's hand and started walking to the door. "Right. He can brief us when he gets here."

Abe grinned as they hurried to the elevator. The monsters could wait. But as for the comfortable bed with the sturdy headboard waiting at home—along with the handcuffs he could escape but never wanted to? They were calling him right now.

ABOUT THE AUTHOR

Kim Fielding is very pleased every time someone calls her eclectic. A Lambda Award finalist and two-time Foreword INDIE finalist, she has migrated back and forth across the western two-thirds of the United States and currently lives in California, where she long ago ran out of bookshelf space. She's a university professor who dreams of being able to travel and write full time. She also dreams of having two daughters who fully appreciate her, a husband who isn't obsessed with football, and a house that cleans itself. Some dreams are more easily obtained than others.

Kim can be found on her blog: http://kfieldingwrites.com/
    Facebook: https://www.facebook.com/KFieldingWrites
    and Twitter: @KFieldingWrites
    Her e-mail is kim@kfieldingwrites.com

THE BUREAU OF TRANS-SPECIES AFFAIRS

For many years the United States government has been aware that *Homo sapiens* is not the only sentient species inhabiting the country. Some other species were native to the continent, while others immigrated along with humans. Early on, these nonhuman species (NHS) were largely ignored when they lived peacefully within human communities. At other times they were deemed a threat and local efforts were made to eradicate them. The federal government was not involved in these early efforts.

During the Civil War, both the Union and Confederate armies recruited members of the NHS, with varying degrees of success.

By the early 20th century, some local law enforcement agencies expressed frustration with their inability to deal effectively with the special needs of NHS. Localized incidents of mass violence occurred in several locations, most notably the Omaha Zombie Epidemic of 1908, the Manchester (New Hampshire) Melusine Drownings of 1911, and the Eugene (Oregon) Sasquatch Riots of 1915.

In response to these incidents, as well as a heightened desire for increased federal control, President Wilson created a new federal agency in 1919 called the Bureau of Trans-Species Affairs. The mission of this agency was to communicate with NHS, to control them, to investigate reported dangerous actions committed by them, and to bring them to justice or eliminate them when necessary. Since then, the Bureau has been quietly active throughout the United States. Its jurisdiction has expanded to include humans who engage in magical or paranormal activities.

Over the decades, a great many dramas have unfolded among the people who work for the Bureau. The **Bureau stories** are a collection of these tales. Each involves different protagonists and is set in a different era, yet all focus on the adventures and struggles of the Bureau's agents. These novellas can be read in any order.

The Bureau of Trans-Species Affairs: Strength, Intelligence, Honor

More about the books in this series.

- **Book One: Corruption**
- **Book Two: Clay White**
- **Book Three: Creature**
- **Volume One (Compilation of Books One through Three)**
- **Book Four: Chained**
- **Book Five: Conviction**
- **Volume Two (Compilation of Books Four and Five)**
- **Book Six: Conned**

9 781952 724107